Holly Lane

J. B. Morgan

Holly Lane
First Edition

Published by J.B. Morgan

The characters, places, and events portrayed in this book are fictitious. Any similarity to real persons, living or dead, is coincidental and not intended by the author.

ISBN 13 9780692336595
ISBN 10 0692336591

Acknowledgements

Cover Design by: Wolf Cover Designs
Blog: http://wolfcoverdesign.blogspot.com/
Facebook: https://www.facebook.com/wolfcoverdesign

Photography: CanStockPhoto
Scenery & Couple
Website: http://www.canstockphoto.com

Edited by: Missed Periods Editing for Indies
Facebook: https://www.facebook.com/missedperiodediting

Formatter: Champagne Formats
Website: http://thewineyreader.com/champagneformats/
Facebook: https://www.facebook.com/ChampagneFormats

Research provided by: My brother, J. & long time friend, Hope.

Dedication

To everyone who helped me make this dream a reality. No matter how small, or big of a part in the process you played in, I appreciate every bit of time, effort and support. Thank you for your encouraging words as well as your help in getting this book out there, and for cheering me on.

Thank you for holding my hand through the process as I achieved something new.

Prologue

3.5 years ago

THIS IS IT. *The big moment.* All of the excitement and anticipation that has been building for months for this one day has finally arrived.

Ava Walsh, Jenifer Gustafson, and I were finally leaving high school in the dust of our rearview mirrors and traveling towards our futures, with the exception of a pit stop for a bit of fun in the sun first.

We've been the best of friends from kindergarten clear through high school, and now we have finally graduated together. Funny, crazy, and klutzy would sum us up in a nutshell.

Graduation took place last week, and this week is our final nod to high school and the last time we will all be together for a long time. Ava and Jenifer have ambitions to get out of this jolly town of ours and hit some bigger cities. They want to travel and live it up before heading to college, getting as far away from the busy-bodies of Holly Grove as possible. Then there's me, good old Hollie Reed, staying behind to attend a local community college and work at my parent's pharmacy. Overall, I was okay with where my life was headed. I loved Holly Grove, and saw no point in changing who I was or moving far

1

away to live out a dream. *I was happy, end of story.*

But today . . . now today was something to be excited for. Today we were boarding a plane for the very first time in our 18 years of life. It feels as though there is a battle raging deep in the pit of my stomach, and my heart wants to jump right out of my chest. My brain wants to push its way into the fray, screaming at me, *Why did you pick a flight that's over seven hours long to be your first flying experience?* I know it wasn't my brightest idea ever. But it is what it is, and it's too late to chicken out now.

The girls and I move up in the boarding line. It formed along the large glass window that allowed you to look out and see the giant airplane that will hold hundreds of people, flying over water for hours, and the vast majority of the flight. *Who wouldn't be scared?*

This is where the *crazy* comes into the group, because that's what we are. Or at least I am. *Why didn't I start off small, selecting somewhere closer to home and over dry land?* We inch our way along the window for a few minutes more until it's finally our turn to hand over our boarding passes to the lady at the gate. She takes Ava's ticket, then Jenifer's, and finally mine, where she scans the bar-codes, electronically doing a roll call for all of the passengers. *So why does handing over my boarding pass feel like I'm handing over my life?*

Passing the gate agent, we head down the ramp towards the plane in a slow-moving line, listening to excited voices and crying babies. *I really hope I'm able to sleep through most of this flight.* Not just because of the babies, but for my own sanity and nerves as well. Yes, my nerves were on pins and needles, and I hadn't even set foot onto the plane yet. *Will they go into hyper drive when I finally sit down?* I may need a horse tranquilizer by the time this trip is all said and done with.

It's a miracle when we get through the line to finally step over the threshold of the airplane's entrance. Ava, Jenifer, and I follow the other passengers like a bunch of lost sheep being herded into the cabin, and slowly make our way down the aisle to our seats. It's a relief to see that we have a small row to ourselves on the right side of the plane, as opposed to a large one in the middle. There are way too many seats next to each other over there, with little to no real legroom. There's no way I could last for seven-plus hours sitting next to some stranger, the side of my body pressed up against him. *Then again, who wants to sit next to a nervous, freaked out 18-year-old on her first plane trip?* I think that list would be two names long, consisting of my best friends.

We find our seats, and thankfully Ava and Jenifer let me slide into the row first, firmly planting my rear in the seat next to the window. On the bright side, I can lean my head up against the side of the plane and rest. Granted, the window shade needs to be drawn. *No way will I be looking out that window anytime soon.* The last thing I want to think about is plummeting to my death and . . . *Oh, great now that's what I'll be obsessing over next.* Letting out a sigh, I grab my seat belt and buckle up. I lean my head back against the seat's headrest, close my eyes, and grab the armrest, not even realizing at first that I'm white-knuckling it until Ava taps my left hand.

"You know we won't actually take off for awhile, right? We were some of the first to board, and there's a ton of people left who still need to enter the plane and find their seats," Ava helpfully points-out, like I didn't know this information already. I look over at her and give her a tight-lipped smile before turning my face to look out the window. Okay, I take it back; I can at least look out the window *now,* as we haven't actually left the ground yet.

"I know. I'm just preparing myself now," I tell both her and the window. "If I'm lucky, I'll be relaxed enough to pass out before we take off," I can only hope, while silently sending up a prayer to the heavens that this will come true.

"The more you tense up, the harder it will be to relax. You know that, so why don't you take one of the Valium's that Dr. Peters gave you?" Jenifer reminds me, seeing as how I had forgotten I even had any with me. "You'll definitely be sleeping, long before we even leave the ground."

I don't necessarily know whether Jenifer's statement is true or not, so I give a non-committal shrug, telling both of them, "We'll see," before returning to facing forward. I know they won't push me and will back off, giving me the space I need while they chat about the things they want to do and what to see during our week-long vacation.

Other students that we know board the flight, saying hi to us as they pass. Eventually the airline attendants give their spiel over the loud speaker, then execute a quick safety check of the cabin doors, luggage compartments, and lastly, check our lap belts before heading to their own seats to secure themselves for take-off.

The pilot comes on over the intercom and gives us an estimated time for our arrival to the destination, then gives additional instructions to the flight attendants. Next thing I know, our plane is moving, and I'm holding on steadfastly to the seat's arm rests. I've never been one for roller coasters or big, scary, heart-stopping, stomach-dropping rides, so being on a plane worries me. I pray I won't get sick, and that I'll have a lovely nap that will last for the rest of the flight.

It's our turn to leave the runway now, and it's finally hitting me completely, like a ton of bricks. *There's no turning back now.* I'm stuck right here, in my seat on this plane, with hundreds of people for the next seven or so hours. This isn't a dream anymore; it's definitely real. I can't believe I'm about to fly over an ocean, leaving Holly Grove behind me for a week. This will be the longest and furthest trip away from home for me, and hopefully also a memorable one that will last a lifetime.

Here we go. Our plane is starting to pick up speed as it heads down the tarmac, preparing for take-off. Everything feels surreal at this very moment, and I know that my adventure is just beginning.

Hawaii, ready or not, here we come.

Chapter One

IT'S THAT WONDERFUL, magical time of year, where anything can happen, and children's dreams come true. It also happens to be my most favorite time of the year, but maybe I'm a little biased, since I was born only a day before my favorite holiday, Christmas.

Since I had the day off from work, I decided to take a stroll down Holly Lane, the main street in Holly Grove, before I met with my friends. The air is cool and crisp; people are trying their best to stay warm, bundled up in sweaters, scarves, hats, and gloves. The sidewalks and streets are covered in snow, while the sun hangs low in the sky this late morning. Everywhere you look, you can see Christmas decorations in the window fronts of the town's shops, and in the middle of the town square, there's a very large, decorated Christmas tree, ready and waiting for the annual tree lighting ceremony to take place.

Holly Grove is a small town with a slower pace of life, not in a hurry to catch up with the rest of the world. My love for this town has grown over the years. While the rest of my classmates and friends were eager to get out of this town and explore the world, I was content to stay here. I've never felt that strong need to leave, so here I am. This is where I'll stay.

I continue my walk towards *Noelle's Café*, where I plan to have brunch with my two best friends, Ava and Jenifer. They both came home this year for the holidays, and I can't wait to catch up with them. It's been nine months since we've seen each other last. They're so busy with their own lives that communication has become like an art form these days. Both girls are still in college, have boyfriends, and work odd jobs in the summer.

As for me, I'm currently single, and mostly content with life, living in my own apartment, and still working at my family's pharmacy. Sure, I'd love to have someone special of my own to be with. I miss the hand holding, shy smiles, the kisses, and just being around the one you truly love. It's been a year since my last relationship, and my heart still hasn't picked up the pieces of its shattered self. I know it's going to be a long time before I'm ready to find someone again, so I just take every day one step at a time. Eventually the pain will lessen, and I'll finally get to the point where I can actually move on. It doesn't mean that it will hurt any less than it does now, but I know that I can't dwell on the sorrow of my loss forever. It's best that I get off this topic, or I'll be in a melancholy mood for the rest of the day, and who wants that when I have a brunch date with my two best friends to get to?

Pushing my thoughts to the side, I enter the café where the girls and I are meeting. This month it's decorated with a Christmas theme. Noelle, the owner of the café, has hung decorative ornament balls in the front window, with white lights lining the outside of the window, which will be turned on later in the evening. There's also an elaborate-looking holly wreath hanging on the door, with a giant red bow at the top in the center, with little berries, ribbons, and gold jingle bells intertwined throughout the wreath.

Inside the café, there's a small Christmas tree sitting in the corner. Every year, Noelle puts the tree up and adds name tags to the branches. This tree represents the giving tree. Everyone is encouraged to draw a name tag and buy a present for the unknowing recipient who is in need of some help during the holiday season. Usually the names are of children whose parents can't afford much, or the elderly in our town who have little to no family around to give them something to put smiles on their faces. I can hear faint Christmas music playing through the speakers in the ceiling as I survey the tables, where Mason jars are filled with colorful candy canes sitting joyfully in the center. The jars all have garland bunched up around the bottoms, with little red bows attached in a few places.

I immediately recognize Ava and Jenifer, and make my way further into the café toward them. They both have big smiles on their faces, and quickly get out of their seats for a round of hugs. It's so good to see their beautiful, happy faces, and to hear their voices again.

"Hey! It's good to see you ladies. I was beginning to think I was Casper the Friendly Ghost these days," I joke.

"Yeah, sorry about that. I've been so busy with school this term, then finals, and finally meeting Jay's family. Life has been such a whirlwind lately," Jenifer says with a dreamy look. Just seeing her face brings a slow smile to my own. She's happy, content with what she's doing, and more in love than ever.

"Well, it looks as if this relationship just got more serious if you've already met Jay's family. Does that love struck look on your face and all of the stars in the universe shining from your eyes mean that you got the stamp of approval from his parents?" I tease her.

"Yes! They were great, and we had a wonderful visit. I can't wait to go back up to their home and spend some more time with everyone. I feel like I really fit into his family. Jay will be here in a couple of days to meet my family next. Since we did Thanksgiving at his house, we decided he would come here for Christmas. My parents are eager to finally meet him, and I feel like it will go smoothly. You know how laid back my family is," she gushes at us. *I think someone is on cloud nine, and the high she's on isn't just sugar, but bona fide love.*

"Well, this is good news, then. Maybe we can have a get-together with all three families before you leave. I think maybe we should have a birthday bash for Hollie. Let's keep up with the Christmas Eve birthday party tradition, but invite all of our families to come." Ava says, overly excited. I want to join her in that feeling, but I don't know if I'm happy about it. *Celebrating just isn't the same anymore, not ever since—*

"Oh, that's a great idea, Ava!" Jenifer exclaims, jolting me out of my thoughts. Turning toward me now, she continues, "We can coordinate with your mom."

Sighing, I say, "Yeah, sounds like a plan. Just tell me when and where, and I'll be there."

Yeah, right.

Hmm, it looks like it's time to turn the spotlight toward someone else.

"And what about you, lady?" I eye Ava with a quirked eyebrow. "What's your lame excuse for the lack of communication? Other than you leaving a voicemail telling me that you two crazies were coming home for Christmas."

"Well," she says slowly, with a grin, "I've got some important news I wanted to share, and I knew if I called you, I wouldn't be able to tell both of you at once."

"You're pregnant! I knew it. Of all of us, it had to be you." I throw out at her with a grin on my face.

"What? No!" she feigns exasperation, but laughs right along with Jenifer and I, knowing it's the furthest thing from the truth. "And keep it down. We don't want the town gossipmongers out spreading that to my parents before I even leave the café. *Yeesh!* Can you imagine?" she laughs, and sadly, we can all imagine. This is a great town that we love dearly, but there really are some incredible gossipers around here.

"You're getting married. Are you trying to beat me to the altar?" Jenifer punches Ava in the shoulder.

"Okay, Miss Violence. And no, it's not that—well, at least not yet. I do have my suspicions that Sean is planning something before the year is out." *I just hope she isn't getting her hopes up too high if it's not what she's expecting from him.*

"Anyway, what I was trying to say when you two chatty Cathy's couldn't put a cork in it, was that I have some exciting news. I wanted to tell you both in person. Sean got a job offer from *Mentor Graphics!*" she excitedly shares with us. "And guess what?" she asks without waiting for our reply. "It's here, in Oregon. Isn't that exciting?" She beams at us.

She's extremely happy, but I don't know why she couldn't share that with us over the phone or individually.

"Okay. And what does that mean exactly?" Jenifer asks.

"It means that Sean has asked me to move back to Oregon with him, and I'll be semi–closer to home. I've already checked out the schools where he'll be located, and I can transfer all of my credits to one of them. He made a trip out to meet the team of people he will work with, and has already found us a nice apartment close to his job. Isn't that exciting?" *Okay, maybe the girl does know what she's talking about, and Sean will be proposing sometime soon.*

"Wow. That's just—wow. What do your parents think about it all?" I ask her.

"Well, they weren't happy at first. It will be a big change, as well as a pain to move and get all of my paperwork for school done and things fixed and all of that jazz. But, they are slowly accepting it now. I don't see how they can't be happy, though. I'll be closer to home, after all."

"Don't you think you're a bit young for such a big step? Why not stay at school where you are and finish out the year? Give yourself time to prepare. That would give Sean a chance to settle in, make friends, and get to know the area before you go out there to meet them." Jenifer, the sensible one of our trio, rationalizes. Or at least tries to, with Ava.

"Sean and I have been together for 12 months now. We are happy, and we know what we want. We are both on track, with his career and my education. This is an awesome opportunity, and Sean wants to share it with me. Why wouldn't he? And why wouldn't I want to go? I don't want to be separated for another half of the year," she says with a frown. "Don't you think we've been separated long enough?" she asks before she automatically realizes her slip. "Oh, I'm so sorry, Holls! That was very insensitive of me."

"Its okay, Ava. You didn't mean anything by it. No need to worry." I assure her. "And we are excited and happy for you and Sean. We just want to make sure it's the right decision for you. But if you feel this is a good thing, and you're positive, we will do our best to support your choice," I say, reaching over and squeezing both of her hands with my left hand, while giving her my best smile. "It just means we will see you even less than we do now, and will probably hear less from you, too." I add with a little pout. "You know how much we love and adore Sean. Please don't think we meant anything negative about him."

Just then the waitress comes over with waters, a plate of Noelle's homemade pumpkin bread, and our menus. We set about slathering the warm bread with butter and watch it melt quickly. My mouth is watering, and all of a sudden, I'm starving.

"Good morning, ladies. It's great to see you three. It's been awhile since you've all been in here together. Do you need a minute to look over the menu or do you already know what you want?" Jinger asks us enthusiastically.

"No menus for us. I'm pretty sure we will all want our usual order." Jenifer eyes Ava and I, to which we both nod, and she turns back to Jinger. "We'll have three mugs of pumpkin spice hot chocolate with whipped cream, and three orders of pumpkin chocolate chip pancakes. Along with three sides each of sourdough toast, bacon, and the cheese and onion scrambled egg mix." Jenifer tells her.

I hand Jinger back the menus, and thank her with a polite smile, before returning my attention back to my friends.

"Okay, if I wasn't hungry earlier, or after my walk here, just listening to that order is making my mouth water," I tell the girls as Jinger walks away with our ticket.

We hear a *ding,* then Jinger shouts, "Order up, Jerry!" *Here's hoping Jerry isn't a slow poke, and we'll see our food sometime this year.*

And just like that, we fall back into our old habits and catch up with each other, laughing and joking while I update the girls on the recent gossip that's been spreading around town. That always gives us a good laugh or a few tears, depending on the news.

Jinger comes back over after about 20 minutes to deliver our scrumptious-smelling food, and we all dig in. *Who cares who's here watching, this is too good to not tuck into right away.* A little while later, one of the girls decides to be the brave one and bring up *him* in a roundabout way. Well, Ava did semi bring up the subject a bit ago, but I should have known I wouldn't get out of this café without a little interrogation on the status of my own love life.

"What's going on in the fabulous and exciting life of Hollie Reed?" nosey old Ava asks.

"You already know all there is to tell. We just sat here for the past 45 minutes, hashing it all out. What's left to discuss? Zip, really." I try to change the subject, but before I can think of a topic to start in on, Jenifer jumps into the conversation.

"Really? Nothing? No good looking new guy in your life?" she asks, like she knows something I don't.

"Umm, honestly? I have no idea what you're getting at with this line of questioning."

"Oh." Ava says, shooting a furrowed look at Jen.

"Oh?" I ask her curiously. *Is there some new rumor in town going around that even I hadn't heard about yet?* "What's this about? Have you heard something that I haven't?"

"Oh, no, it's nothing like that. We just thought for sure that you would have met someone by now," Jen says, peeking over at Ava again before continuing. "We just think that it's time you start to move on and find your own happiness. That's all. We didn't mean anything else by it Holls, really. We love you, and we're just trying to be here for you and look out for you." She reassures me with a smile, but I can see the unveiled sympathy in her eyes.

"Thanks, I appreciate it. I know I need to jump back into the dating world. It's just hard after—after—" I let out a deflating breath. "I'm sorry. I still have a hard time talking about it."

"We know. But it's been a year since you last heard from him. You don't know where he is, or what's happened to him. He hasn't even tried to contact you that we know of. I hate to be the bearer of bad or unwanted advice, but you have to let him go," Ava says as she wraps an arm around my shoulders for a one-armed side hug.

"Well, I really should go see if my parents need extra help today." I say as cheerfully as possible. "Thank you for meeting me for brunch and catching up. I've missed you both so much! It was so good to actually see you and talk with you. It's been way too long. Keep me posted on the birthday party, and when Jay gets to town." I tell the girls then swoop in to give them each another hug. I really do miss them. They're like sisters to me.

"Okay. We'll give you a shout when we know what our plans are for the rest of the holiday vacation, and so on," Jenifer promises.

"I better be off, too. I need to check in with Sean before he heads out to his family's house and we miss each other. See you ladies later." Ava waves to us before heading out into the semi-warm day.

"I guess I'd better go, too. I need to check with Jay and see exactly what time his flight arrives and then get the guest room set up. I'll keep you posted about Christmas Eve, and Hollie?" she turns to me with a warm look on her face.

"Yes, Jen?"

"Ava and I, we both love you." She hugs me then walks away and continues right out the door, leaving me standing by our table, alone. *How did that happen?* I was trying to escape them first, not the other way around. *They know me too well,* I think to myself, before walking down Holly Lane to *Reed's Pharmacy.*

The sun is a tad higher in the sky now. The weather is still pretty cool, and the sun is trying to warm the town up as best as it can this time of year. I take in my surroundings again, noticing for the first time today that all of the light poles have garlands wrapped all the way around from top to base, with red ribbon mixed in. I make a further assessment of the Linden Trail and notice all of the white, twinkling lights interspersed throughout the trees.

Linden Trail is a nickname that the town has for a cobblestone walkway that is lined with linden trees that were planted really close together. The trees form an archway-like covering over the path that leads down to the town square, on the other side of Holly Lane. I had forgotten how beautiful the trees could be in winter, when the leaves turned all white before they started to fall off. It's a gorgeous sight, and one that I often take for granted, even though its beauty greets me each new day.

And with that hope, I believe I can find it in me to pick up the pieces of my heart and start to mend them back together again. I'm excited to see what the New Year brings my way. Until then, I'll allow myself a little more time to mourn the one that got away.

Chapter Two

June, 2013

"JEN," I TUG on her shirt, trying to get her attention while she's yapping away with Ava about wanting to get to the beach as soon as possible. "Look behind me, without being overly obvious about it, and tell me if you recognize anyone." I say with a slight, tilted backward nod, trying to be nonchalant about getting her to follow my directions, without appearing obvious myself.

"Oh my gosh," she breathes, bugging her eyes out at me.

"You see them too, right?" I ask. *Because I really want her to verify I'm not seeing things.*

"Who? Who are you two talking about?" Ava butts into the conversation, way too loudly. I give her a big *knock it off*, wide-eyed glare, but she's either clueless or doesn't see what I'm trying to do as she keeps trying to look around us on her tippy toes.

"Knock it off, Ava." Jen scolds her. "I believe I see Mr. and Mrs. Frost straight in front of us, behind Hollie's back. But, why are they here and how come no one mentioned they would be here at the same time as us?" Jenifer wonders aloud.

"They're probably here on vacation, like the rest of us. So, what's the big deal? It's a free country. Come on," Ava pulls on Jen's left arm. "Let's go say hi to them. Maybe they want to have lunch or dinner with us one day while we're here."

I bug my eyes out at her, like she just said 'The aliens have landed, the aliens have landed!' "Are you crazy? We can't just march up to the president of *Frost Bank* and say, 'excuse us. We would love to share a bit of food with you.' That's just nuts. He probably has better things to do than hang out with some teenagers. Plus, he's here with his wife. Maybe they're having a cozy, romantic getaway from all their nosey neighbors in Holly Grove?"

"Oh, don't be so dramatic. The Frosts are actually pretty nice, mellow, and down to earth people. You know that. They wouldn't turn their noses up at us. Stop being silly, and let's go." Ava says with an air of authority to her voice. *Who does she think she is, my mother?*

"Are you taking over the role as my mother while you're here?" I ask her, echoing my thoughts.

Rolling her eyes and sighing heavily, she asks, "Seriously Holls, did your fun gene take a vacation, too?" This cracks her and Jen up, and they start making their way over to the Frosts, leaving me to trail after them alone.

"Hi Mr. and Mrs. Frost!" Ava enthusiastically calls to them with a wave. "What a pleasant surprise, running into you all the way over here. What are the chances?" she says, holding out her hand while going in for a handshake with Mr. Frost.

"Well, it's sure lovely to see you three wonderful ladies. It surely is a pleasant surprise to see you here as well. We didn't realize this was the week of the graduation trip," Mr. Frost replies.

Yeah, I don't know how, since this is a big deal, and it has been talked about all over town.

"Oh dear, I hope you all don't think we're here to keep tabs on you for your parents, do you?" Mrs. Frost frets, earning her a shoulder pat from Mr. Frost.

"Nonsense, don't be silly, dear. They know better than that, right ladies?"

"Yes sir." Jenifer replies, showing off her good manners.

We shake hands with the Frosts and exchange a few more pleasantries before Jenifer says, "We would love to have lunch with you while we are all here. If you would like to, that is."

"That sounds like a grand idea, dear." Mrs. Frost replies with a warm smile that brightens up her whole face. *I think we just made her day.* Maybe when we return, I'll go around to their place once in awhile to say hi.

We exchange cell phone numbers, and decide on a day to meet before parting ways. Once we are alone again, Ava says, "See? I told you so. You were worried for nothing. I'm actually excited to see them. We may get homesick, and by the time we meet up again, we'll be put at ease seeing two adult faces we know. It's good to have them here. You never know if we'll need some 'parental' help."

"Okay, now let's forget you just said that, because I'm thinking someone just sucked some fun cells out of *your* brain. Let's get our luggage and skedaddle out of here before we get left behind," I remind them as we head over to the baggage claim area.

"Who even says *skedaddle,* anyway?" Ava asks.

"Me, that's who. Now shut it, and march like a good soldier over to our bags." I command as I head over to the carousels.

"Well, someone just took over the role of being 'mother hen' for this trip," Jen giggles, earning her an eye roll from me.

"No thanks. I'm here to have fun, not play mommy dearest to you two." I tell her over my shoulder while trying to locate our bags. We find them a few minutes later, and head out to find our group so we can all take the same mode of transportation to the hotel, and so no one gets separated, or lost. We eventually find our school friends shortly after exiting the airport, and we're automatically slammed with the warm humidity of the day.

"I'm all for changing into our swimsuits and hitting the beach as soon as possible." Ava says as she fans her shirt in and out to cool herself down.

"I second that," Jen says.

"And I third it."

Jude, a boy from our graduating class, walks over to us and addresses the group. "Hey guys. The airport is going to shuttle us all over to our hotel with some big, ten passenger vans, so we'll take two over there, and then maybe we can come up with a game plan. Let's all have a fun but safe trip while we're here."

Now, why isn't Jen dating Jude? He would be perfect for her! *It's like Papa Jude and Mama Jenifer have taken all of their kids on vacation.* But I don't say that out loud; I just nudge Ava in the arm and she secretly shares a smile with me, knowing we are on the same wavelength, as always.

"Sounds good, Jude. Thanks for doing that for us," Jen smiles over at him. He smiles back at her before turning away and making his way to where all of the luggage sits. He and some other guys start to load everything into the vans.

Ava and I give Jenifer a look, and she just shakes her head and walks off in a huff at us, causing us to crack up. Yep, she totally knew what we were thinking about, which makes me laugh even more before heading her way to climb into one of the vans. I can't wait to get into my swimsuit and jump into the ocean. I've seen picture after picture of the green-blue, almost clear water. *It's beautiful.*

After we checked into the hotel, met with everyone in the lobby, and made a safety plan, we went to our rooms and prepared for the beach. That's where we find ourselves now, enjoying the sun on the beach and relaxing. I'm thinking about nothing while enjoying the cool sand between my toes as I keep digging them in and out repeatedly. Ava and Jen have gone down to the water with some of the guys from class, while I hung back with a few of the other girls. I know them, but we aren't that close, and I don't mind the nice, quiet solitude we have going on here.

I've been people watching for the last 30 minutes, and it's starting to get a little scary with some of the clothes, or lack thereof, I'm seeing here. If my eyes aren't deceiving me at the moment, there's a woman walking towards the water with no top on. *Say what? Is that even allowed?* I don't know, and I certainly don't want to find out anything else, so I quickly avert my eyes as a shiver runs down my spine. I'm glad she's down a bit further on the beach, as that was a scary sight to behold. I think it's time to get off of this towel and head towards the water myself. *Just not in the same direction.*

I walk a path in-between beach goer after beach goer, as I find my way down to the ocean and start to wade in, taking my time to adjust to the temperature. Finally, I'm warm and brave enough to venture further out. I eventually spot my friends quite a ways out, playing in the waves. They're trying to jump up before the wave hits them, but each time one builds up higher, then crashes down on them, making them all laugh as they get carried away or pulled under by the waves. It looks fun, so I make my way out there, not realizing that there are sandbars between their location and me.

After a few jaunts of walking on sandbars and dropping off into the ocean for a quick swim, I make it over to the group.

"Hey! You finally made it out here. We were placing bets on how long it would take until you were bored to death by people watching. Do you want to know who won?" Jen asks sourly.

I think she's trying to throw me off with that look. "Let me guess—" I pretend to look like I'm thinking really hard. "You," I finally say.

"Nope, not this time," she frowns over at the boys. "It was actually Jude, if you can believe it." She says under her breath, so no one but she and I can hear. *That is a shocker.* Jen is normally the best at this game, and Jude's not one to make bets. *I wonder why he did that.*

"Really? That is a surprise. How much do you owe him?" I laugh at her pouty face.

"I don't owe him anything," she says, which confuses me. "I have to take him out to dinner," she mumbles.

Okay, what? Does Jude like her after all? What the world is going on here? I'll find out later, but as for now, I want to see how far I can tease her before she cracks.

"What's that? I don't think I quite heard you right. Can you speak up a little louder? With all of these waves, it's making me a bit hard of hearing." I lay on the innocent act. I want her to have to say it louder, and watch as her face blushes a brighter shade of red. Sometimes I think she has a secret crush on him, but refuses to admit it.

"Oh, you heard me, big ears! I'm not repeating it." She huffs and puffs, and I think she's about to tackle me. However, she decides to splash water in my face instead, and it gets in my eyes and mouth.

"Hey, it's on, now!" I shout before diving towards her, causing her to scream and laugh while trying to escape me, but she can't swim away fast enough. I manage to get to her and push her head underwater, then swim a bit away from her. She comes up for air, sputtering out water while trying to wipe her eyes. She looks around, and spots me before diving my way, causing me to freak out because she's good at payback and no way do I want to be near the ocean when she gets her revenge. The boys are egging her on while laughing at both of us. I swim to the nearest sandbar and get out on it as fast as I can. Pretty soon, the boys and Ava have joined us as I try to run away from Jen, looking like a crazy lady while cracking up. I'm laughing so hard that I end up tripping as I step wrong and go down for the count.

Next thing I know, it looks like we've started our own Wrestle-Mania match before someone shouts, "Let's play chicken!" If that doesn't get the boys' full attention, then maybe that topless lady down the beach will do the trick. *Seriously, did you have to go there?* I scold my brain, causing my arms to form involuntary goose bumps. *I'll have a nightmare about her tonight, that's for sure.*

By the time we crawl out of the ocean, flopping onto the sand like beached whales, our waterlogged bodies are exhausted. The skin on my face feels hot and tight from the sun, and my limbs are all like limp noodles. My brain has given into fatigue, and no one dares to move from our spots. But eventually we do get up and make our way back to the hotel. I'm not sure how we even managed to get back to our rooms without dropping dead on the way up, though.

I'm lying on the bed, when suddenly a pillow smacks me in the face, eliciting much laughter from two people at my expense. "Oh, so mature," I laugh with them, because I'm too tired to care or do anything else. "Let's just stay in tonight, rent a movie, and order in our dinner." I say, right before Ava pegs Jen on the side of her head, which makes me laugh so hard. But I'm so tired that I can't move to join in on the fun.

"Hey, watch it, woman! I have a sunburn, and geez, that hurts." She laughs then quickly winces when she feels the stinging of the sunburn hitting her at full force. I'm not sure why, but right now this makes me laugh like a hyena. *I can't help it. I'm so exhausted that everything is funny, I suppose.*

"Are you high?" Ava eyes me suspiciously.

"Are you even playing right now?" I ask her, cracking up. "Oh my gosh. Why would you even ask a stupid question like that?"

"I don't know. I figured you must have gotten a contact high after being in the elevator with all of the potheads from the floor above us. Can't you smell it?" she asks, rolling her eyes at me.

"How do you even know what that smells like? I know nothing

about it, and plan to keep far from it. So there's your answer. I'm not high," I state as I roll onto my side so I can pull myself up to a sitting position. "So, what's the plan for dinner?"

"I know we're tired, so maybe we can rest for an hour then head out and find food after?" Jen hopefully asks both Ava and I.

"Sure. A nap would be nice. How about we all take turns in the hot shower to rid ourselves of this saltiness, and then nap off our drunken, sun-induced state before heading out. Sound like a plan, Stan?"

"Why do you always look at me when you say 'Stan?'" I ask her.

"I don't always look at you," she says as she heads to the bathroom to shower first.

"Whatever. Just go shower, Joe Schmo, so we can all get this nasty salt off. I'm closing my eyes for a bit until you're both done." I say as I flop back down onto the mattress and relax.

The next thing I know, I'm waking up with salt on my body, sunburnt skin, and a roaring headache. I look over and see that no one else is in the room with me. I feel slightly dazed and just plain rotten. I take a glance towards the sliding glass door and see that it's visibly later in the day, so I climb out of bed and head to the bathroom. I'm sure the girls are off visiting others from our school. I decide to hop in the shower and get ready before they get back so we can eat soon. I'm starving, and my next meal is as far as my brain can really let me think about.

About 45 minutes later, I'm ready, and I hear people at the door. I pop my head out of the bathroom, where I was adding the last touches of makeup, to find that the girls are back, along with some guests. I eye them with brows raised, doing my best to give them the 'mom look,' while crossing my arms over my ample chest.

"We have company," Ava cheerfully states the obvious, a bit too late.

"I can see that, smart-aleck." *Oh my gosh, I just sounded like my mom right then.*

"So, this is our friend, Hollie." Jen says, trying to dispel the embarrassing moment.

"It's nice to meet you, Hollie. I'm Jason, and these guys are my friends, Chase and Evan." Jason says with a slight nod toward his friends.

"We're actually your upstairs neighbors. Our room is directly above yours," Evan states.

"And how did you all meet, exactly?" I look to Jen for the truthful answer.

"Oh, see, earlier while you were sleeping, the guys were goofing off and dropped a shoe over the edge of their balcony, and it landed on our patio. So, we threw it back up to them. Then we got to talking, and they invited us up to hang out until you woke up." Ava explains, instead of Jen.

"The guys were just talking about ordering a pizza and hanging out here. They were tired of being around all the smoke on their floor," Jen fills me in.

"And once again, how do you know about this drug?" I wonder aloud, for the second time today.

"We've never tried it, as you should know, but we've heard about it around school. You live in a bubble sometimes, and you don't always realize what's right under your nose," Ava chides me a bit.

"Mom? Did I remember asking you to come on this trip with me?" I say to her, reminding her to check her *mom-a-tude* at the door.

"So—anyway, what do you ladies say to pizza?" Jason asks hopefully, while giving Jen his best charming smile.

"I think it sounds good. Though, we should get out of this hotel and find a place to eat at. I know I could eat a whole pie on my own. I'm *that* hungry right now." I embarrassingly blurt out. *Oh well. It's not like we'll see these guys again after this week is over.*

"Awesome. There's a *Round Table Pizza* right across the street," Evan shares with us. We all end up easily agreeing to it, as it sounds to me like the best possible plan at the moment.

"Follow us, boys," Ava says in her best flirty voice. I roll my eyes over at Jen, then go to grab my purse and hotel key before heading out the door.

Once outside of the hotel, we make our way across the street, enjoying the late afternoon weather. I'm glad I put on shorts and sandals, as it doesn't seem like it will cool off any time soon. *This weather is nothing like Holly Grove, that's for sure.* One could get spoiled by this weather every day. *It's perfect.*

Over pizza, the girls flirt to their hearts' content, and the guys eat it up like it's ice cream. They just can't get enough. They joke around and tease us, and in the end we all have a really good time. Even if I was a grump at first, and didn't feel so great, I'm really enjoying my-self now. These guys are pretty funny, and have turned out to be a lot of fun to be around.

After our late lunch or early dinner—because I honestly can't decide what that just was—we get up from the table and head out of the chilly restaurant and into the pleasantly warm air. I sigh with relief upon exiting the doors. My body went from freezing to warming up instantly.

"So, the guys and I were talking earlier today about renting mo-peds. Would you want to come with us?" Jason asks, giving Jen a hopeful look. "It's supposed to be a lot of fun. We may even be able to double up."

"Sweet, that sounds like fun. Let's totally do it." Ava excitedly says to me and Jen.

"Sure, why not? We did say we wanted to do all that we could while we are here. I'm down for it." Jen says, which makes Jason seem happier.

Jason *is* a good-looking guy with his dark hair, amber colored eyes and tall, toned form. But I still think Jen and Jude would be the perfect match. They would make cute babies together, all with blond hair and blue eyes and creamy pale skin. I feel an elbow in my ribs be-fore I realize I've been caught daydreaming about my much too young friend and Jude making cute babies.

I blush with embarrassment, even though they have no clue what I was thinking. "Umm, sure that sounds like fun. I'm in." I manage to get out.

The guys are happy, and Evan shares a smile with us. "Awesome. Okay, let's go rent some mopeds and explore while there's still day-light."

I sure hope we know what we're getting ourselves into. We don't even know these guys, and here we are being extremely trusting. But as we make our way towards the moped rental place, we see other kids from our school headed in the same direction.

And oh look, there's Jude. "Hey Jude!" I call out, just because I can. For some reason, I want to giggle. Jen gives me a sharp look. *Oh boy.* Someone doesn't want me to rain on her happy little parade with Jason.

"What are you doing?" Jen hisses quietly at me.

"What?" I ask with my best innocent look. Ava and I crack up quietly, so the boys don't know what in the world we're up to as they walk slightly ahead of us, yammering on about sports.

"You know what. I don't have a secret crush on Jude. He's cute, nice, and just not my type," she says in an annoyed tone.

"Sure, whatever you say." I laugh then pick up my walking speed to catch up with Jude and the gang.

"Hey Hollie, what's up?" he asks as soon as I make it a few feet over in his direction.

"We're on our way to the moped rental shop. What are you guys up to?"

"We were actually headed that way, too. Cool. We can all ride together."

"Perfect! I'll tell the others, and you can meet our new friends." I smile over at Jen and Ava as they catch up to us. "Guess what?" I say to them, fighting a smile.

"I don't know. What?" Ava plays along.

"Jude and the guys are headed the same way we are, and said they would love to ride with us. Isn't that great?" I make my voice sound overly excited.

"Yes, great it is, indeed." Jen says coolly. I know that later, she will exact revenge on me.

"Good. Let's introduce all of the guys together, and get this party started!" Ava shouts.

Jason, Chase and Evan make their way over to us and I make the introductions. Then we set off to *Honolulu Moped Rentals.* It's about a mile-long walk from our hotel, and it feels good to walk off the greasy pizza we just ate. It's also a good way for the guys to get acquainted, and to enjoy the sunshine in a leisurely way. One thing I can say about Jason and his crew is that they are efficient with information and directions. They told us at the restaurant that they had mapped out everything that there was to do here that morning. They wanted to try as much as possible, and didn't want the hassle of being lost or taking excessively long routes around the island. They scouted the area out, and asked a lot of questions at the front desk. They also have a map of the area, highlighted and scribbled on. They would make great boy scouts, which makes me wonder if they ever were.

We had a blast riding on the mopeds, and bringing Jude along was a great idea. We drove all around the area, making sure we didn't end up on the highway to the North Shore. After all, we did have a time frame to have the mopeds back by.

After walking us to our hotel room, the guys say goodnight to us, then head down the hall. However, we notice that they stop in the middle of the hall and put their heads together, talking quietly for a few moments. Then they look back at us with grins on their faces and make their way back over. Jason nudges Chase in the ribs.

Clearing his throat, Chase says, "Tomorrow, the guys and I are planning to take a trip to see *Diamond Head* and the *Polynesian Cultural Center.* Do you ladies want to join us for the day?"

"Oh, that sounds like a lot of fun!" an enthusiastic Jen exclaims. "I want to get out, see the sites, and learn more about the island we're on."

"Well, you just said the magical words," Ava laughs out loud. "Jenifer loves history, and here's her chance to explore. And hey, it helps to tag along with three good-looking guys." She winks at the three guys. "We're not sure what we're doing tomorrow. How about we talk about it, and then give you an answer? We'll just yell up to you from our balcony, so leave your sliding door open."

"Sounds like a plan. Talk to you ladies later, and hopefully we will see you tomorrow, as well." Jason says before they turn back to the elevators and climb to the next floor for the night.

We walk into our own room, and I throw myself onto the bed, while Ava shuts the door. Jen flops down next to me. Shortly after that, Ava claims the other bed. It's been a long day, and we are all definitely worn out.

"So? Do we want to tour with the guys tomorrow?" I ask, but already know the answer. "I know you want to go, Jen, so why didn't you just say you would?" I question her.

"We *do* want to go, but we can't just jump at every invitation they throw at us. I like them a lot, and had a great day hanging out. However, we don't want to seem too eager," Ava says.

But it's Jen who points out, "We should figure out what else we want to do and make sure we have back up plans. We should also bring our own ideas to the table, too. We can't just rely on them to come up with everything. There could be a day we don't want to do what they have planned. I just know that it's good to do some things on our own and make memories with just the three of us before we split and go our own ways after the summer."

"Okay, mood killer. *Yeesh,* we don't need to get all serious up in here." Ava tries to lighten the mood. "I want to have fun memories, and we can make those no matter if we have extras with us or not. But, I know what we can do. How about this? We tell them we'll hang out with them tomorrow, and then invite them to go snorkeling with us on another day?"

"That's a great idea. That way it doesn't look like we just want to mooch off of their ideas. Great plan. I like it," I say. "Jen, since Jason seems to like you so much, I nominate you to share the wealth of news with the boys upstairs. You can act out a scene like you're Juliet and he's Romeo." I crack myself up, which only earns me a pillow to the face, causing Ava to join in, and soon we're in an all out pillow fight. That is, until we hear a thumping at the sliding glass door, which makes us all scream and jump over the side of the bed, freaked out. Ava, who seems to be the brave one of the group, sticks her head up and starts laughing before jumping up and running towards the door.

"Are you crazy? What are you doing? It could be some peeping tom. What if he has a knife, and he wants to do us harm?" Jen shouts after her.

"Seriously, Jen? Why would she laugh and run for the door if a killer was on the other side?" I say before jumping up myself. "Oh look, it's Romeo on the other side."

That has Jen up quicker than if I said her favorite singer was here.

Ava unlocks the door then slides it open before Jason walks through.

"Are you crazy? I can't believe you climbed down to our balcony. What if you had gotten hurt?" Jen fusses over Jason. *Wow, that's not a case of instant like, nope, not at all.* I grin like a big loon over at her.

"The guys and I heard some yelling and banging noises, so I was selected to come check it out. The quickest route was going over the edge. So, here I am. What were you all doing in here, anyway?" Jason looks at us curiously.

"Oh no! Sorry we were being so loud and crazy in here. I was getting ready to yell up to you, before we got sidetracked." Jen says with an embarrassed expression on her face that soon gives way to a grin.

"Oh, and just what were you doing?" he asks her, giving her his own charming grin.

"We were having a pillow fight," she laughs.

"Oh dang, and you didn't invite us? You break my heart!" he feigns being hurt, while putting his hand up to his chest.

I roll my eyes at Mr. Cheese and toss a pillow at his head. He totally didn't see it coming, and it gets in a good *whap,* causing us all to laugh.

"So, what's the verdict about tomorrow, now that I know you're all safe and I couldn't be the white knight to save the day?"

"Yes, we would love to come out with you guys tomorrow." Jen tells him.

"Great!" Jason says excitedly as he fist pumps the air before a faint red hue washes over his cheeks. He gives us a sheepish smile then heads back to the sliding door and steps through it. Once outside, he yells up towards the sky, "She said yes!"

We hear some whooping and hollering before he comes back through the door and pulls it mostly closed.

"Well, as you can hear, the guys are excited about tomorrow," he laughs. "We have to be up early, as it's a long trip and takes up most of the day. Are you okay with that?" he now sounds like he thinks we may change our minds, knowing that we have to wake up before the sun. Or at least I assume before the sun.

"I guess if we're getting an early start, then that means you, my dear Romeo, must bid Juliet and her ladies farewell so we can get our beauty rest," Ava teases the poor guy. He looks a little embarrassed, but we all know that he's clearly infatuated with Jenifer.

"Yeah, you're right. Okay then. So, I'll see you all tomorrow? We'll swing by your place at 7:30 tomorrow morning, then head down to the shuttle bus together." Jason says, making sure that we know the game plan and when to be ready as he starts heading back to the balcony.

"Uh, I'm not sure that's the best way to exit the premises safely. Why don't you try using the door like real live boys do, and not fake boys, like Spiderman or some super hero like that?" Ava says, pointing out the obvious escape route.

"Oh, yeah, right. Good idea. Well, goodnight, ladies. Sleep tight and we will see you bright and early in the morning." Then he makes his safer escape, leaving us erupting into a fit of giggles over his embarrassment.

"He sure is cute when he's all flustered and embarrassed," Jen says.

"Someone's got it bad. Or should I say two someones'?" Ava giggles, and this time I take a pillow off the bed and whap her with it before she tackles me, causing us to fall on the bed, laughing. All of our noise causes a great big thump on the ceiling that makes us laugh even harder.

Jen closes the sliding door and locks it, drawing the curtains closed while she's at it. Then we get ready for bed, and turn in for the night.

Chapter Three

Day 2

THE NEXT MORNING, I wake up to this loud annoying noise. In my sleepy haze, it takes me a few moments before I figure out that it's the alarm on Jen's phone. I take my pillow and chuck it at her. "Turn off that awful noise, woman!" I yell at her over the strange, irritating buzzing sound she set it to. "Ugh. I don't feel good. Like death warmed over. Turn it off! I need more sleep." I say, flopping back down on the bed while pulling the covers back over my head. *I do feel nasty sick.* My stomach hurts, my head is pounding, and my eyes burn and I feel like I haven't slept in days. Let's not forget that I'm also slightly sunburned, and it feels like I'm burning up with fever and freezing with the chills at the same time. My skin feels tight, too. Basically, I feel like a hot mess.

Finally, Jen shuts off the alarm as I hear Ava groan, "Whose bright idea was this, again?"

"Juliet's, if my memory serves me well." I mutter. "What time is it, anyway?"

"It's six freaking thirty in the morning! Why oh why did we say yes to the cute boys?" Ava whines from under her pillow.

"Get up, you lazy bags of bones. If I'm going, then so are you." Jen says as she flips the light switch on, bathing the whole room in its bright, cheery artificial light. *I'm so not ready to be alive for the day yet.*

"Get to stepping, people! Times-a-ticking." Jen singsongs as she perks up all of a sudden.

While Jen heads to the shower, Ava groans one more time before dragging herself up from the bed. I watch her as she makes her way to the TV and flips it on.

"Uh, hello?" I call over to her. "Still sleeping over here!" I say, as I feel like I have to remind her.

"Hey, if you don't want to come with us, you can sleep when we're gone. I need to wake myself up, and music does the trick. If I can find MTV, then I'm flipping it on." She cranks at me.

"Whoa, crab apple, you are one cranky woman in the morning. I hope the boys know what they're getting into with you." I laugh, but then stop just as fast as I started. My body is hurting, and laughing is not helping. I burrow a little more into the covers, stealing Jen's pillow. We've decided since there are only two beds in our room, every night we would take turns for who slept where. Last night, Ava and I shared a bed. Tonight, I'm thinking they will kick me to my own bed and share one so they don't get sick. *They'll get no complaints from me.*

"If I didn't feel so sick right now, I would definitely go with everyone. But I'm worn out and exhausted. It must be a combination of last night's food, jetlag and too much fun in the sun," I fill her in on my condition as I try to get in a better, more comfortable position in the bed.

While I'm trying to rest, Ava ends her channel surfing by landing on MTV, and to our amazement there's an actual music video playing this morning. Lorde's *Royals* is on.

Wow, just what I wanted. If there was ever a song that would annoy you in the morning, this would be the one. Now it's my turn to groan. I turn my head over Ava's way, and she's singing away while she goes through her suitcase to grab all of her items to get ready with. She's bopping her head up and down, causing her long, strawberry blonde ponytail to swing all over the place. She's truly a sight to behold. Then she starts getting a little crazier and makes me laugh while she shakes her butt. This chick is nutty, and I just want to go back to bed.

Jen finally walks out of the bathroom with a towel wrapped around her head, and she's wearing really cute linen shorts, paired with a coral short-sleeved blouse.

"Hey good lookin,' whatcha got cookin'?" I wiggle my eyebrows at her a few times while Ava whistles at her.

"Glad to see you two Scrooges are in better spirits." She says as she flips her head down, pulling off the towel and shaking out her blonde hair.

"The guys will be here in a little while. Why aren't you getting ready?" Jen asks as she starts to comb her hair out.

"Oh, Hollie isn't feeling well. She's staying behind. Something to do with the sun, jetlag and food? I don't know, but I need to shower before everyone arrives." Ava replies before she closes the bathroom door.

Just as she shuts it, there's a knock at our other door. Jen creases her brows, looking at me.

"I'm just as clueless as you are. Why don't you go find out?" I point out.

She walks over to the door, opening to finding empty air. No one's there. "That was strange," she says. Then we hear the knock again. Jen makes her way to the sliding door, and there's Evan with a big, fat smile on his face, like he's just won a big prize when he see's Jen. She opens the blinds, then unlocks and opens the door.

"What in the world are you doing out there? You boys are determined to plunge to your deaths, aren't you?" she asks in a bewildered state.

"I just thought I would pop by to give you a wakeup call. So, consider this it. Good morning." He smiles as he takes us all in. "Where's Ava? And how come you're still in bed?" he asks me.

"Ava's getting ready, and Hollie isn't feeling well. And you're late for a wakeup call, but way too early for us to leave. What's your angle?" Jen wants to know.

"Oh, I thought I would chill here until you're ready." He smiles over at us. *Uh-huh.* Some boys are just clueless, especially when they're 18 years old. "Plus, the guys went down to grab breakfast for everyone from *McDonalds.* I hope that's okay?" *Is he really asking or just telling us?* Either way, it's a belated inquiry, but definitely wins them some brownie points.

"That was thoughtful, thanks." I say and hope that I can even stomach anything at this moment, let alone stand the smell of anything in the way of food.

Jen goes back to getting ready, and I tell Evan to get comfortable then watch as he goes to sit in one of the chairs by the table and kicks his legs out in front of him while he sinks into the chair, finding a comfortable position. Not long after, we're all watching MTV and making wisecracks, just as Jason and Chase come into the room with yummy-smelling food. They picked up a breakfast sandwich and hash browns for everyone.

As they wait on the girls to get finished up, they sit on the bed and chairs while they polish off their food, shooting the breeze with me. Finally, the girls are ready, and I'm disappointed that I'm not feeling well enough to go, as much as I really want to. However, there is no way that my body feels like taking a hike up the *Diamond Head Trail,* and then suffering through an hour or so drive to the *Polynesian Cultural Center,* in my condition. I'm still seriously bummed that I'll miss out on something spectacular, though.

"Well kids," I begin, "be good while you're gone. Drink plenty of water, and use lots of sunblock. Don't talk to strangers, and make sure you take lots of pictures for me."

This statement earns me a round of chuckles from the group before a few of them say, "Yes mom." They bid me goodbye, and tell me that they hope I feel better soon, and to get plenty of sleep and be safe. Then they head out the door, and I'm alone.

I get up and lock everything back up, drawing the curtains again. I take a quick bathroom break then brush my teeth. I decide that since I'm already up, I might as well take a quick shower before passing out again.

When I finally wake up again, I look over at the clock and see that I've slept until 2:30 in the afternoon. My stomach is growling fiercely at me. Apparently, I needed that nap. I really believe that jetlag and the sun yesterday wore me down, and even though I'm feeling better, I don't want to push my luck trying the hotel's room service just yet.

Realizing what time it is, and that I really should eat something, I decide that leaving the hotel could be a good way to get out of this stuffy room and catch some fresh air. So, I climb out of bed, throw on some denim shorts, flip-flops, and a sloppy peach colored t-shirt, then twist my hair up in a messy bun before making my way to the door, stopping long enough to grab my wallet and room key, which I slip into my back pocket.

I make it down the smoky hallway and take the elevator to the hotel lobby. I know I need some food, but I don't want a lot of greasy goodness again, so I ask the lady at the front desk where the closest convenience store is. She points me in the direction of an *ABC Store,* telling me it's about an eight to ten minute walk from here. Or, if I didn't want to walk, I could wait for a hotel shuttle. I could use the walk to stretch my legs, so I thank her, and say that there's no need for a cab. I move toward the lobby's exit, and out into the late afternoon sun.

I take my time getting to the store, looking at my surroundings, and checking people out. Eventually, I make my way to the corner where I need to take a left, when I suddenly slam into a solid brick wall, or so it feels.

"What the—" I start to say, as I look up at a good-looking guy, who's also currently looking down at me. As soon as we catch each other's eye, he starts to let his mouth turn from a frown into a nice, lazy half-smile.

"I'm so sorry!" I continue. "I wasn't looking where I was going. Well, obviously, I was paying attention to other things and I didn't see you and—"

He boldly puts his finger up to my lips to hush me. All while he's still smiling down at me with a sweet, relaxed look on his face.

"It's okay. It was an accident. Sometimes people do run into each other around corners. It happens," he teases.

I groan inwardly, feeling like a big dork. And, *oh my gosh,* I look like a total slob. Great, this older, good-looking guy is teasing me, smiling at me, and I look like death's sloppy cousin. I had figured I didn't need to doll up or throw on makeup just to get food.

You know, this incident makes me remember what my mom always tells me, *"If you're going to leave the house, make sure your hair is always fixed, and your makeup is always on, even if you are wearing sweats."* I used to tell her that I didn't really care, and too bad if someone saw me looking junky for a few moments. *Who knew that my flippancy would come back to haunt me?*

He steps back a tad, giving us some personal space—at least I *hope* it's for that and not because of my appearance. He's still staring at me and with a small smile on lips. *What's he waiting for?*

"So, I guess I'll just be moving out of your way now and finish my walk to the store." I say as I start to make my way around him. But as I do, he steps to the side and places himself in my path, again.

I look up with raised brows, wondering what on earth he's doing. But no need to wonder further, because he's opening his mouth to speak, and I'm just standing here, staring at his mouth. While I know words are coming out, my brain isn't working properly, and I hear nothing he says. He waves a hand in front of my face, causing me to blink a few times. He raises his brows at me.

Clearing my throat I ask, "Can you repeat that?" Then things start to go downhill. "Sorry, I'm a little out of it. I wasn't feeling good this morning, and I was just on my way to the store and—" but once again, he puts his finger to my lips to shush me. *What's wrong with me?* I'm turning into a rambling fool.

"No need to apologize, or explain anything. I was just saying that my name is Layne, and this is my friend, Miller," he says while hooking his thumb over his shoulder toward another body, one that I didn't even notice was standing there. *I want to face palm myself so hard right now.*

"Oh, right." I say, displaying my brilliant conversational skills. "I really should be going. My friends are probably back at our hotel, wondering where I am, and I need to grab something from the store, and I really haven't been feeling well, so I'll probably need some medicine, too, and—" I stop abruptly, trying to shut my lips. I really want to lock them up and toss the key. I'm so embarrassed, and he's just chuckling, while his friend is looking at me like I have issues, but still gives me a polite smile.

"Okay well, I really should be off now. So, umm—I'll see you later?" For some reason unknown to me, my brain decides to throw that out there. I need to nip this awkwardness in the bud, like *now,* so I tell them bye with a lame wave and hurriedly walk away, disappearing inside the store. I finally do smack my face with my palm then I shake my head, thinking about how lame I just was, and how I can't believe that I actually ran away from a cute guy and his friend. *They probably think I'm nuts.*

"Did that really just happen?" I say out loud, to no one and everyone.

"Did what just happen, dear?" I hear the response off to my right, and look over to see a kind, elderly native woman staring at me. I give her a smile and shake my head.

"Oh sorry, it was nothing. I didn't realize anyone was standing here, or that I just said that out loud. I'm just being my crazy, silly self. No worries." Then I head off in the direction of where I might find food, which is preferably a sandwich and 7-Up.

I find what I'm looking for, and throw in some sunblock and chocolate, then head up to the register to find the same cute little older woman at the checkout counter. She looks up when I approach, and asks if I found everything okay, and did I need anything else. I start to tell her no, but then I think about that guy named Layne and his friend, and how I don't want to run into them again. Well, that's not entirely true, but definitely not right away, and I ask if she can call me a cab. Then I proceed to hide out until the cab shows up.

After I made it back to the hotel and was safely behind the door to our room, I flip the TV back on and start to chow down. I'm really hungry at this point, so I gobble my purchases up while watching MTV and playing on my phone. I had just pulled Ava's name up on my text messaging app when *Royals* makes another appearance on the screen. Okay, that's twice today. *Weird.* I turn it up louder with the TV's remote, and type a message out to Ava. '*Royals*' is all it says. Then I toss my phone back onto the bed, giggling to myself.

It's about 3:30 in the afternoon now, and I'm just about bored to tears, so I decide to fix myself up a little bit more this time, and head out to the beach. I type out a text to Jen stating where I'll be, then leave our room and walk over to the elevator. While I'm waiting, I see a few people sitting on the floor by their door, looking pretty dazed. *Hopefully it's their room,* I think to myself. Looks like the rumor is true—they are definitely on something. Shaking my head, I hit the button one more time, mentally willing it to come faster, when it suddenly dings and the doors slide open. I hurry onto the elevator and push the *close door* button, then hit lobby. Once I reach the ground floor, I make my way back through the lobby doors and out to the crosswalk. When the illuminated person turns green, signaling that I can walk, I cross the street, thinking about how lucky we are to have found a hotel so close to the beach. It's across the street, down a couple of blocks or so. The weather has been awesome since we've been here, and I can't wait to go relax in the cool sand again until everyone gets back from their own adventures.

Once I get to the sand, I kick my shoes off and place them into my beach bag as I walk down the shore in search of a good spot to lay out. I don't want to be too close to others, but I don't want to be isolated, either. I'm trying to play it safe while having a good time, too. But as life would have it, or I should say, *as Hollie would have it,* I manage to trip over something hard and face-plant into the sand. I decide to just lay here for a few moments, because this is seriously embarrassing, and I'm too afraid to see who has noticed my blunder. As I do so, I think about how—as usual—I was too busy paying attention to my surroundings and not where my feet were going. If my feet had eyes, then I could avoid all of these coordination issues.

"Well, if it isn't the one and only, Bruiser." I hear a deep voice say behind me.

As I'm turning my head to locate the unfamiliar voice, I feel someone's arms go around my waist and haul me back up to a standing position, steadying me before they let go. Turning around again, I look up to see who owns the arms that were just around me.

Oh no. *This can't be happening again.* "How is this possible? Two times in one day?" I ask the familiar and very cute face I literally ran into earlier today.

Just then, a middle aged couple jogs over to us, stopping at my side.

"Are you okay?" the woman asks out of wariness, placing her hand on my shoulder. "We saw you trip and fall," she says, as she and the man eye Layne and his friend.

I don't know the two guys, at all, but I don't feel as if I'm in immediate danger around them. However, I don't get a chance to say anything to the woman as the man starts to speak now.

"Sorry, my wife worries too easily, and she hates seeing people get hurt. She had to know that you were okay." The man looks back and forth between Layne and I. It seems he has come to some conclusion though, and he looks back over at Layne, before finally smiling down at his wife.

"But, as you can see dear," he says to her, "everything seems to be just fine. We'll just be heading off now. Sorry to interrupt." He gives us a knowing smile before starting to turn to walk away.

What the heck just happened? How can he tell that from a conversation that has amounted to about one minute long, maybe two minutes, tops? I'm confused, as I look back to Layne.

"Thank you for checking on my wife," Layne has the audacity to tell the kind couple.

My mouth drops open, and I decide right then that he needs to be set straight. But he doesn't let me get a word out as my mouth continues to open and shut like a fish.

"We appreciate your kindness," he continues as he wraps his hand around my elbow, drawing me closer to him. "I believe she's going to be just fine. I've been learning that she's a bit clumsy," he winks at them before turning his grin back to me, like I'm going to corroborate his story or something.

"And she's not good about looking where she's going. She totally missed her own husband on the beach. Though, I guess it would be like playing *Where's Waldo,* out here amongst everyone." Layne's friend laughs causing the others to chuckle, too.

And once again I'm shushed by someone else's words, as I frown over at the friend.

"We're newlyweds, you see, and we haven't known each other that long, but it was love at first sight. How could I *not* want to marry someone like my sunshine? Her clumsiness adds to her charm." He tells them as he wraps his arms around me, hugging me to him, trying to hide my face into his chest so they can't see my reaction.

However, I win this battle, as I look over to see that the couple is completely eating up his bologna sandwich of a story.

If I didn't feel like stomping on his toes or something before, I definitely do now. Though, I know I need to just wait until this couple leaves.

"That's so sweet. I believe in fate, too," the woman tells us, as she lays her head on her husband's shoulder. "We'll be on our way, now that I know everything is fine, and that these gentlemen aren't strangers after all."

"She's a worrier, but sometimes you just have to let fate play out, and if it's meant to be, then you just can't fight it," the man confirms.

I decide it's best to just keep my mouth shut, since it's not like I'm going to see the couple again. Or, even Layne, for that matter. But as for Layne, I'll deal with him later.

The husband salutes the guys before he and his wife bid us a good day and a happy marriage. As they start walking away, I pray that they head in the direction away from the beach, permanently.

We stand there for a moment, making sure they're out of earshot, before I pull out of Layne's arms, standing back at a safe distance.

"Really?" I eye Layne and his friend, who is shining his bright smile on me as he shakes his head once and turns to look at Layne.

"Well, this is an interesting turn of events. That was quite the story you conjured up," he laughs.

"What? I think fate is trying to tell us something here. What about you, sunshine?" Layne asks me, totally eating this up with that same big grin on his face.

"I think its fate warning you to steer clear of me, because obviously I can't walk on my own two feet. Every time I walk near you, one of us gets hurt. And one of us still might get hurt after that story," I huff.

"I don't know about that." Turning to his friend, he says, "You know what, Miller? I think you're right. Bruiser fits her." Smiling at his friend before looking back at me, I don't miss the subtle examination he just gave my body.

"So," Layne starts, "I thought you weren't feeling well?" *Of course he would remember that part of my ramble from earlier.*

"I wasn't, but I've taken a turn for the better," I tell them, promptly making my face flame red with embarrassment from the state they saw me in. "Funny how the world seems so small. Who knew I would run into you twice in one day, after I told you I would see you later." As I remember what I said earlier, I produce a small smile. "Anyway, I was just about to lay on the beach for a while as I wait for my friends to get back, so I'll just be on my way now—"

"If you're alone," Layne cuts in, "then I think we should stay with you. We wouldn't want you tripping over any other men. You never know who they could be. And, you know, it's just until your friends show up, that is." He looks around the beach, then back at me. "And, I don't like that you'll be out here all alone."

"Why? So you can carry on with your 'husbandly' duties? You don't have to stay and babysit me. I *am* old enough to care for myself, you know." Is that the best thing I can come up with? *Oh my gosh, why do I say the stupidest things sometimes?* I take a deep breath in and out, trying to clear my idiotic brain.

Layne and his friend laugh, yet again. *Why am I always making them laugh?* I've only run into them two times yet, I seem to be a source of good entertainment for these guys.

"Oh, we didn't believe for a second you weren't old enough, sunshine." He's grinning at me yet, I see a hint of seriousness in his handsome features.

"Since you brought up the taboo subject, you now have to tell us how old you actually are," is his friend's ever so clever response. "You know, we don't even know Bruiser's name yet. Why don't you start there, sweetheart?" Miller, I believe is his name, says to me.

"You know, my mom once told me that I should never talk to or go anywhere with strangers. That whole, 'stranger danger' thing," I say with mock seriousness.

Laughing, Layne says, "That's exactly why we need to stick around. So we can kick any dangerous strangers to the curb and get to know you better. What do you say?" Oh he's completely serious now. I have a feeling I won't be getting rid of them any time soon.

Even with that stunt he pulled, how could I not want to hang out with Layne? He's funny, a clever story teller, and he's good looking.

Well, at least we're in public, *right?* If they aren't going anywhere, then hanging out in public is my safest option.

"Why do I suddenly feel like a small, helpless chick in a movie with a creepy villain and his sidekick?" I laugh, knowing that I'm not really going to say no to them. I'm having a great time with these two jokesters, even if I'm a little nervous not having Ava and Jenifer around. "You're not going to give up, are you?"

"Now, what kind of question is that, sunshine?" Layne replies.

"Well, looks like this just became a party of three." I say as I turn around and start heading for what looks to be a good spot, wondering how the girls will find me later. I turn my head to make sure the guys are coming. They pick up their towels and follow after me. A few paces further down the beach, I find a great spot where there are fewer people around, and place my beach bag in the sand before laying my towel out. The guys set their towels down close to mine before taking a seat, joining me.

I glance at both of them, feeling a bit shy at first, but decide to suck it up and take off my cover-up, revealing a black and white tankini. Avoiding eye contact, I sit down on my towel and reach into the beach bag for my new bottle of sunblock. I open the top and squeeze the lotion into my hand, slathering my legs first, while still feeling a little bit awkward. Here I am, sitting between two attractive and well-toned men. Who wouldn't feel a bit awkward or nervous? *Or maybe it's just me.*

"Alright, sunshine, you never did give us your name," Layne points out.

"We could just call you Bruiser. I have no problems with that," Miller teases me. "Or, we can get the introductions out of the way now, so I can make some waves."

"Hollie," I tell them, holding my hand out to Miller.

While shaking my hand, Miller says, "Nice to officially meet you, Hollie. As you may not remember, I'm Miller. But somehow, I don't doubt that you remembered my friend, Layne, over here," Miller says, hooking a thumb over at Layne, who's openly grinning at me. *Yeah, somehow I think he's right about that one.*

"Relax, Bruiser. Enjoy the sun, and Layne. I'm going to leave you two alone for a bit and hit the ocean." Miller informs us as he picks up his boogie board, which I just now noticed was laying off to the side.

Huh. I wonder if I tripped over his board or if it really was one of the guys? Though I doubt I'll ask, as that's just too embarrassing to relive.

"Well, sunshine—what do you want to do?" Layne asks, as he brings my attention back from pondering how I keep hurting and embarrassing myself around him.

"Personally, I vote to playing out in the ocean." He winks at me while his lips slowly curve up into a lopsided grin.

"Personally, I vote that we get to know each other first." I say, as I make myself comfortable on my towel. I look over at him expectantly, waiting for him to start digging into my life or his.

"Okay, we'll play it your way, for now. But make no bones about it. You will be in the ocean with me later. So, why don't you start us off, Hollie, by telling me a little bit about you?"

"To be honest, my life isn't all that fascinating, but if you really want to know, then I'll tell you my short story," I warn him, as I settle more comfortably on my towel by laying on my side with my head propped up by my hand. I'm feeling uncharacteristically bold with this move.

Where is this new Hollie coming from all of a sudden? Considering the stunt he pulled a little bit ago, maybe my move isn't as big of a deal as I think it is. But there's no time to dwell on it as I have a story to tell.

"I'm from a very small town in California, where my parents raised our family on a farm. My parents are produce farmers, so you can imagine that we never had time to take many trips, if any at all. This is my first major trip, anywhere. I'm 18 years old, and I'm the oldest of eight children." I pause, raising my eyebrows at him, wondering if I should continue on, or if he's thinking about hightailing it out of there. When he makes no move to say anything, or leave, I continue. "I've just graduated high school, on the farm where my parents homeschooled all of us. I'm on this trip with my two best friends, and when we go back home, they'll be headed to college. I'll pick up more work around the farm, helping my parents out. My dad plans to groom me to take over the farm one day, seeing as I'm the oldest, and it's a generation farm." I deadpan, all the while staring at his face, waiting for a reaction to what I just imparted on him.

However, Layne just sits there, staring at me. He's probably a little dumbfounded by what he's just discovered about me. I'm not sure if he's freaked out, wants to run for the hills, or thinks I'm pulling his leg.

"What about you? Do you live here? Or are you on vacation, too?" I ask, not giving him time to flip out over my life story.

"Sunshine, you are not what I was expecting," he says with a crease between his brows. "That's for sure," I quietly hear him admit.

"Is that a bad thing?" I question.

"No, sunshine, it's not. And that's a good thing." He gives me a half smile. "I suppose it's my turn to answer your questions. It's only fair, after all. I actually live here. Miller and I are in the Army together. We're stationed at Schofield Barracks. Though, we are a bit from home."

"How far is the base?"

"About 45 minutes to the—"

"Whoa," I cut him off. "What brought you all the way out here? That's a bit of a drive just to scope out the honey's."

Layne starts laughing, shaking his head. "*Honey's?* Really?" he winks.

"Well, what other reason could you have for being up here?"

"There's more to me than meets the eye, sweetheart. I'm not out for playing around. I'm getting too old for that. I want to meet a girl worth my while." He quirks his left brow at me. "Do you know anyone who could apply?"

Blushing, I duck my head. I'm in a little over my head, here. I peek back at him as I realize that he hinted a little bit about his age to me before. "So, soldier, just how old *are* you?"

"That little bit of knowledge depends on if you're applying for the job." He shoots right back at me.

"Oh, I didn't know I was at an interview, or I would have dressed more for the part."

"I think you came to the interview in the perfect attire. Don't you?" he's full on smiling at me now. "And, I don't see anyone else on this beach worth my time, do you?"

"Let's get back to how old you are before we revisit the *honey's* part."

That cracks Layne up. "Alright, Bruiser, I'm 23. And I really didn't come down here for the *honey's,* as you put it. It's just nice to get a break from the guys and the base. Miller and I like to get away and have a change of scenery once in awhile. We love to come out here and surf or body board. We don't have to worry about many people recognizing us."

"The girls, you mean."

"Yes, the girls. Partying isn't our scene, and the guys back at Castle Grayskull can keep the tag chasers. We've had enough messing around to last us a lifetime. Now it's time to enjoy life in another way." He says, clearly reflecting back on his life while he stares out at the ocean.

"Tell me more about you and your family. Family is important to me." I say, bringing him out of his reverie.

"I have two siblings, a brother and a sister. My sister is a senior in high school. My brother attends the University of Oregon. I originally grew up in Eugene, and that's where my family still resides."

"Funny how the world is a little bit smaller than you can ever know. We don't even live that far from each other. Well, we do, but we don't. Anyway, tell me about your parents."

Oops. I just realized that my bright idea to fool Layne about my life may have backfired a bit. I guess I'll have to see if he caught that or not. If he didn't I'll be shocked, as he seems like one to pay close attention to details.

"Growing up, my mom was a stay-at-home mother. My father was in the military, hence the reason why I joined the Army. The military tradition runs in our family and goes back many generations. Now that my father has retired, he teaches ROTC at the University of Oregon. ROTC stands for, The Reserve Officers' Training Corps, in case you were wondering. I guess I should also explain what a 'tag chaser' is too, right?" he asks. "I forget that you're probably not familiar with military lingo. Sorry," he says with a frown.

Perhaps I'm off the hook? *Hopefully.* I'll tell him my real story if I get to know him better. For now, I feel like playing the role of the mysterious vacationer.

"It's okay," I touch his arm, letting him know it really *is* okay. "And I'm going out on a limb here, thinking that a 'tag chaser' is a woman who chases after military men?" I answer.

"Yes, or men chasing military women, both of whom basically only want to be with or marry a service member," he replies.

"What is your job?"

"Now that's classified information, ma'am. If I tell you, I may have to kiss you."

"Shouldn't that be, 'I'd have to kill you?'"

"No, it's definitely kiss you," he says seriously. "I think I would know." And by the look on his face, I know he really does want to kiss me. So I decide to steer our conversation into a safety zone, instead.

"How long have you known Miller?"

"We started out in basic training together when we were eighteen. Eventually, we both ended up at the same duty station here in Hawaii, and that's been about three years now," he tells me. "I think you've asked a lot of questions, and now I believe it's my turn to ask one."

Crud, is he going to bust me?

"Oh, that's all? Just one?" I nervously tease him. "You're not bursting to know more about my exciting life, are you?"

"It's the only one that matters to me at the moment, so yes, just one for now. Don't worry, though. I plan to make it my mission to get to know you throughout the rest of this week. Do you have any objections to that, sunshine?" he asks.

"I can't say that I have any objections, counselor. So, what do you want to know?" I feel like I'm ready to sweat bullets. *Why, am I freaking out?* It's so dumb really. But for some reason, I'm not ready for Layne to know my real story yet.

"Do you have your own 'Hollie Chaser' back home?" he asks with a small grin on his face. But his question serves to make me laugh, and he's done a good job at it.

"No, sorry to bust your bubble, but there's no chasers back home for me," I wink. *Okay, I think I just stepped further into the flirtation zone.* I don't think I've ever winked at a guy before, at least not in a flirtatious way.

"That's where you're wrong, Hollie. You *would have* burst my bubble if you had said there was a guy back home, pining over you."

I'm about to reply to that little gem when I hear someone yelling my name. Layne and I turn our heads and see my friends waving at us like a bunch of crazy people in their attempt to flag me down. I lift my arm and wave back, then turn my head back to look at Layne.

"Well, looks like the gang's all here!" I say cheerily, though a part of me is disappointed that I won't have more alone time with Layne.

Jen came down to the beach with Jason, Ava, Evan, and Chase after their long day at the *Polynesian Cultural Center* and the *Diamond Head* hike. They decided to join me, to cool down in the ocean while soaking up the last of the sun's blaring heat for the day, thinking I was alone. Needless to say, the girls were a little shocked that I would make a friend on my own, let alone a *male* friend, without them. I definitely got a couple of eyebrow raises and wide-eyed looks. Based on their reactions, I knew there would be a promise of being ambushed with questions later in our hotel room.

By this point, the group had set up camp around us then headed out to the ocean for a little while. But now they're back, as is Miller. The last couple of hours or so, I've been sneaking looks at Layne every chance I could get. And not to my surprise, I would find him checking me out as well, causing little butterflies to float around in my stomach. I, of course, couldn't help the small smiles that would play around the corners of my lips, especially when he would give me secret little smiles too. Really, he hasn't gone too far from my side this afternoon, and at times even plays with my hair or my fingers.

Now, everyone's relaxing and chatting. It's nice sitting here with a big group like this, getting to know our newfound friends and exchanging funny stories of our pasts. Of course, the guys try to outdo each other, but I know us girls could come up with a few good ones, if we felt like embarrassing our own selves. So I'm crossing my fingers that Ava and Jen keep their mouths shut.

Though, I should have known better.

"Once, Jen had this major crush on a baseball star at our high school," Ava begins. "He was sitting on the bench on this long walkway that you have to take to get to the cafeteria. I believe it was right before 6th period, after the last lunch. She's walking down this walkway, and he's sitting on the bench with a bunch of his friends. It's a really nice day, and she's wearing shorts, and he calls out to her, 'Hey! Are you wearing nylons?' But she wasn't, and she tells them so. Connor, her crush, says to her, 'You're not? Wow. Your legs are really white. They're nearly blinding me!' Then he and his buddies crack up at Jen's expense."

"I'll never forget that, as it took me two more years before I dared to show my legs at school again," Jen states.

"I remember that. You were so crushed. But what was awesome was, the next year he ended up in your science class and tried to cheat off of you, but you refused to help him. Served him right for teasing you like that," I laugh.

"I see nothing wrong with your beautiful legs," Jason reassures Jen, as he wraps his arms around her, hugging her to his side as she rests her head on his shoulder.

"What about the time in history class when Ava split her pants?"

Jen asks me, cracking up. That sets me off, too, causing me to snort indelicately. That makes Layne laugh, along with the rest of the guys.

"What? It's funny enough to snort over. Trust me. You had to be there. She was wearing her favorite pair of cord pants that day. She obviously wore them too much that year. The washer had to have weakened the material by the time she had her accident," I laugh.

"So, here's Ava, walking up to the front of the class to turn in her test, when someone in the front row drops their pencil. Being nice, she bends over to pick it up—"

"And let's remind them that it was pretty silent in the room," I say, cutting Jen off.

Everyone looks over at Ava, who's not even trying to hide her embarrassment, though she is shaking with silent laughter, trying to hold it in, when Jen continues on with the story.

"And the next thing you hear is this loud, ripping noise, and Ava never does come back up. She's just stuck, in front of the whole class, with her butt sticking up in the air, frozen. At this point, all eyes are now on her, and I remember her looking up at us—"

"As her whole face is drained of color and the biggest eyes I've ever seen on her face." I say, laughing openly. Now everyone else can't hold it back either. "I remember rushing up to the front of the classroom and tying my sweatshirt around her waist while gaining permission from the teacher to go to the office. Ava wouldn't turn around, either. Even if it meant still facing everyone as they laughed. We made it out the door, then hightailed it to the office to call her parents."

"Too bad it was my brother who was home. He was so mad that I woke his lazy butt up to pick me up. At first, he told me to walk home or find a ride. At that time though, the three of us didn't have a car. Finally, the office assistant talked him into coming down to the school. Honestly, he was a real butthead back then. Anyway, he refused to go through my drawers for a new pair of pants, so he had to just bring me home," Ava adds to the story.

"Yeah, but didn't he make you wait for like an hour before he showed up?" Jen laughs, as I nod my head in confirmation.

"Wait a second," Layne says, turning to me. "I thought you said you were homeschooled?" he frowns. He looks at my friends who are looking at me with confused faces.

"Why do you think she was homeschooled?" Jen asks as I just bite my lips, trying not to giggle.

"And here I was just thinking that it's too bad that you had to miss out on all the fun parts of school, but it would seem as if someone was pulling the wool over my eyes." Layne says, with a sly grin on his face. *Uh oh.* I don't have a good feeling about this.

"Maybe we should clear a few things up before I enjoy a little punishment." He eyes me before turning back to my friends, and I decide it's best to get up and start edging my way back towards the hotel so I can make a run for it.

"Where do you think you're going, Bruiser?" Miller asks, causing me to jump. I glance up at him, as he's smiling down at me with a mischievous look on his face. *Crud and double crud.*

"What are you, a ninja? How did you sneak up on me like that?"

"Infantry, baby," is his response. *Well, I guess that answers the question of what Miller does.*

"Didn't I promise that you would end up in the water with me at some point today?" Layne reminds me with his question.

"Oh, no you don't!" I shout-laugh. "It's time to clean up and go to dinner, right?" I ask my friends, looking around the group, but they all look useless, even Romeo's gang. *Great.*

"You know what, Miller? I think Bruiser just bought herself an all-day date with us tomorrow. Don't you agree?" he asks his friend.

"Just think of the fun we'll have, too." Miller teases me.

"You have five seconds before I catch you, Hollie. You better start running."

And boy, do I. The race is on, especially as Miller is now in hot pursuit of me, too.

I don't even make it near the vicinity of where I was going. Instead, they've got me headed towards the ocean, right where Layne wants me.

"Don't do it, soldier boy!" I yell over my shoulder as I try to veer off to the left to dodge them, and then circle back around.

"Sorry Bruiser, we're well aware of evade and escape tactics. Just a tip, we help plan secret maneuvers, like the one I'm in the middle of right now." He taunts me.

Just as I'm about to make a comeback, I feel two bands of muscled arms wrap around my waist, causing me to squeal. "Looks like

Miller is good at distracting the enemy. Don't you think, Sunshine?" he laughs in my ear, then tosses me over his shoulder as he runs us out into the ocean. "Hold on tight, Bruiser, looks like we're going down," he says, just as he throws us deeper into the depths of the ocean.

I barely come back up for air, finding Layne already waiting with open arms for me. I decide to splash his face instead as I huff my way back toward the shore. Too bad I don't get far, as I'm once again caught back in his arms of steel. "Not so fast, sweetheart," he breathes into the crook of my neck, causing a tingling sensation to run down my arms as butterflies take up residence in my stomach. I wrap my arms around his that are still keeping me caged against his body.

"I want to ask two things of you." He says as his chest rises and falls against my back.

"Before I go there though, I want to know why you tried to dupe me earlier." He continues to hold me against his chest, as I look out further into the ocean, while his back is to the shore and our friends.

Well, if that's not embarrassing enough. I'm glad the sun isn't beating down on us, and that I'm not facing him, so he can't see the pink cheeks I'm sure I'm sporting.

"Honestly? I wanted to mess with you a little bit after that whole husband and wife story you made up," I quietly admit.

"Though, in reality, my true intention was to see what it would feel like to be someone else. No one knows me here, outside of my school friends, and I felt like being anonymous for a little while. Back home, everyone knows me, but here, I can be whomever I want. Honestly, I meant no harm with my fib."

"All right, sunshine, that's good enough for me, for the moment. Now, the first thing I want is to spend more time with you."

I can only nod my head, feeling a bit overwhelmed by the nearness of his body and his breath on my skin, along with the route of this conversation, and where it's leading.

"Not only do I want to spend time with you, but I want to see you every day this week," he says as he skims his nose up my neck to my jaw. "And Hollie," he pauses for a moment, "I want you to make me a promise, too." He slowly spins me in an about-face so he can look into my light blue-grey eyes.

"I want you to live for *you*. Like nothing and no one else matters for the rest of the time you're here, with me. I want you to let go of all your inhibitions, and be free. I've noticed that you only truly let go sometimes. But, I can see that there is more to you than meets the eye. And that, Hollie – that is what I want to shine through this week. You just told me you wanted to be someone else, so here's your chance to do it in a way that isn't a lie."

He draws me closer to him. "Are we on the same page, sunshine? Do you get what I'm saying to you?" he asks as he searches my face for the answers he wants.

I stare at his handsome face for a few moments, first studying his hazel eyes then roaming his facial features, trying to commit every little detail to memory. There's something about Layne that has me gravitating towards him. We've been in each other's company for only a day, and already I'm loathing having to leave it. I mean, who wouldn't want to be around an attractive, fit soldier. *But what I don't know is, why is he so interested in me?*

"Don't you think we're going at warp speed? I just met you, as in, *today.* You don't even know me, so how is it you can read me so well?" I question him.

"Hollie, it's what I do for a living. I need to be on guard at all times when I'm in other countries. It's important to be able to read people's faces and their actions, so I can keep my team and myself safe. But this is a conversation for another time." I can tell he's serious about this, so I let that topic go.

"Okay, what about the other question?"

"Sunshine, sometimes you just have to take a leap of faith and go with your first instinct. That's what I'm doing right now. I see something I want, and it feels right and good, so I'm going for it. Think about it, Hollie. There are no guarantees in life, or of what the next tomorrow will bring us. What I do know is that I have this opportunity to get to know an amazing woman, and I'm going to hang on to this chance with all that I have, and see what comes of it." He stares intently into my eyes.

"Promise me you'll let yourself be carefree and just live for you. That's how I want to spend my time with you, Hollie. No matter what we do, be here in the moment, and live it to the fullest."

So I do something I wouldn't typically ever do, *especially* not on our first day together.

I step closer into his arms, reaching up on the balls of my feet, and press my lips to his cheek.

As I pull away, he whispers into my ear, "*The second thing I want, Hollie, is to kiss you. I've been wanting to kiss you since the moment I laid eyes on you.*" And before I even have the chance to agree or not, his lips are pressed against mine. They're warm and firm, but start to soften with his unyielding kiss. Too soon, he's pulling slightly away, as he holds me gently in his arms, looking into my eyes before he imparts the sweetest smile on me.

"By the way, sweetheart, I didn't forget that you still owe me the real story of who Hollie is. I'll be collecting on that promise soon enough. We have all week to get to know each other better." He informs me as he pulls me to his side, walking us out of the ocean and up to the group, now staring at us, wondering what just took place.

"Let's get some grub!" Miller says as he rubs his stomach.

Everyone picks up their belongings, and we all start walking towards the hotel so we can clean up and change. Once we've made it back, the guys stop by the parking garage and grab workout bags from the truck that belongs to one of them, then head to Jason's room so they can change too, before we all go in search of something to eat.

Ever since we left the water, I haven't stopped thinking about that kiss. It has caused a perma-smile to take shape on my full lips, and my mind to think a million miles a minute about the promise I made to him. I'm scared and excited all at once about what this week has to bring. This is definitely out of my comfort zone, but Layne is right; I'm not living my life to the fullest yet, but that's what I want from this trip. I want to feel what it's like to dare to be whoever I want to be. Funny how he doesn't know me, yet he already gets me after such a short time together. Maybe I'm being naïve, but I can start to feel a real connection forming between us, and it's both thrilling and a little insane.

To new beginnings, I think to myself as the elevator climbs to our floor and Layne holds my hand, skimming his fingers across the back of mine. And just like that, I've found my happy place.

Chapter Four

Day 3

THUD. THUD. THUD.

This is the sound that woke us up this morning. The lover boys from upstairs decided that dropping in on us, literally, via the balcony, was a clever way to get us up. Luckily they waited until the later morning to make their noisy approach. *Heck, they should be glad we were even here.* They could have been locked out there for a long time. *It probably would have served them right.*

The night before, the girls and I had agreed that waking up early today was not on the agenda. We were all exhausted when we arrived back to our room around 11:00 that night. Upon entering the room, Jen went to wash her face, I went in search of pajamas, and Ava turned on MTV. *Why she keeps going there, I don't know.* And shockingly enough, *Royals* was actually playing, yet again. We were wiped out from the day's events, so all that song accomplished for me was to help prolong a pounding headache beating against my skull. Honestly, we had to be three of the most deflated people on the planet by the time we got ready for sleep and fell into our beds.

Yet somehow, Jen and Ava still managed to question me about

Layne and what was happening between us. Even with a blasting headache and being exhausted, I couldn't help my goofy grin when they brought the subject up.

"What's going on with you?" Jen asks as I hear her moving around, trying to get comfortable in the bed she's sharing, this time, with Ava.

I can't see them, as it's pretty dang dark in here but I can feel their eyes trained in my direction once all of the rustling of sheets quiets down.

"As in?" I prompt her.

"For starters, what's the deal with you and Layne?" Ava questions me instead. "You two seem pretty serious, and you just met this guy!" she semi-exclaims. "As in, you just met him today. Or did you forget that part? What's going on in that thick head of yours?"

"You must be thinking of your skull, not mine." I tease, trying to evade the questions. I've not had a lot of time to process any of this myself. How do I properly convey my feelings, and the craziness of the situation, to my two best friends?

"You two were really cozy down in the water at the beach this evening. Don't you think you're going a bit fast?" Jen asks, a mix of concern and confusion evident in her tone of voice.

"I know," a way too interested Ava says. "Let's start at the beginning, as that is the most logical place to begin," she continues, a bit of amusement in her voice. I can tell she loves that the attention is on me and Layne. I know she's secretly going crazy on the inside, wanting to hear all of the details.

"*Okay,*" I slowly drag out the word, as I too, find a warm, comfortable spot in my bed, before I launch into the story of how I met Layne and Miller earlier in the day. After the store incident, I share with them that, by weird chance later that day, we ran into each other on the beach.

"So, does that mean you just happened to cross paths? Or did you literally *run* into him?" Jen tries to ask me in a serious manner before losing the battle with laughter.

"That sounds more like the truth right there," Ava laughs.

"*Fine.* You know me too well. I actually tripped over him. Better?" I stick my tongue at her, forgetting that she can't see me in the dark.

"Put your tongue back in your mouth, woman." Ava laughs harder. "Just because I can't see you, doesn't mean I don't know you. You just said it yourself."

"Busted," I admit.

"I know," she says smugly.

"Back to story–time. I'm tired, but I can't sleep until we know more details. So, spill it, lady." Jen throws the conversational ball back in my court.

"I know this all seems fast. It really is, and I do freely admit that. I know I'm young, and he's older, and in a dangerous line of business. But, there's just something about him that draws me in, like a moth to a flame." I share with them a bit nervously, as I'm worried about their reactions.

"Because that's not a bad analogy at all. Nope, no sir!" An amused Ava says on a grin, I'm sure.

"I don't have a better analogy," I admit. "I'm still trying to process all of this, too." I finish sharing with them. "When, and if a better analogy comes my way, I'll be sure to post it on Facebook." I try to joke. It's also a tactic to try and stall this conversation.

What am I supposed to tell them?

"At least get to the good parts." Ava urges me, like the entire worlds answers hinge on what I'm about to say next.

"Right, like the part where you two looked like swim-suit models basking in the waves during the sunset." Jen teases me and causing Ava to lose it more then she already has been.

Okay, *that,* I can do. It's the easier part of this interrogation.

"Pipe it down you two. This is serious. I've essentially known Layne for all of a day now. I have this crazy pull towards him and I know he feels it too. I don't even know what's going to happen when I leave this place or what he's playing at." I say on a sigh.

The room is quieter now that the two hecklers have calmed down.

"What happened in the water?" a serious but curious, Jen, asks.

"He asked a couple of things from me."

"And?" Ava prompts.

"He wants to spend the rest of this week with me, like every waking chance he can get, basically. The other part is him wanting me to be free."

"What's that supposed to mean?" a confused Jen wants to know.

"Basically, he thinks I'm holding myself back. He thinks I should live life and just have fun. What he wants is for me to throw caution to the wind and be who ever I want to be while I'm here." I say.

"So, does that include you being open and doing whatever comes natural, even in the way of feelings, when it comes to Layne?" Jen questions me.

"That's it, in a nut-shell." I confirm.

The room is dead silent.

"And that big show you two put on before you joined the group on shore?" asks, Ava.

"That was Layne letting me know that he was done waiting to kiss me." I state.

"That was clearly obvious all evening." Jen shares her thoughts with us.

"I'm surprised he held out as long as he did." Ava chimes in.

"Well, it was somewhat of a surprise to me. I thought he would wait until he knew me for another couple of days."

"Hollie, you're not that naïve. Come on. It was written all over his face. He couldn't take his eyes off you. Jen and I knew he was going to kiss you before the night was over. That was a given." she continues.

"I knew he wanted to kiss me, sure, but I didn't think he would really do it. That's what surprised me." I clarify for them.

"In the mean time, just be careful in whatever happens. The last thing you need is to go home, pine over some guy who lives in another state, with a traveling job, and nothing comes of it." Jen cautions me.

"I don't know what will happen, remember I admitted that? Who's to say it works out when I leave? I can only go off what he said earlier. He told me his party days are over and he's looking for more. It could be me, it might not. For this week it is. So, I'm going with it, even if it scares me to no end. This is all new for me. His job scares me. I'm still trying to figure out my own life but here, for the next few days or so, I can be and do whatever I want. So, it's probably crazy or dumb or whatever you want to call it, but I'm going to try it Layne's way." I tell them.

One of them loudly sighs.

"I just hope you know what you're doing and you don't wind up on misery lane when it's all said and done." Jen says.

"I might. I might not. We can't predict everything in our lives. That's okay. I want to have fun and live a little before I go back to my job at the pharmacy, and you two go off to college. I'm ready for more excitement in my life and that's what Layne is gifting me this week."

"I say we cut the girl some slack. She's her own person. She can make her own choices and she can live with the fall out, if it happens. Besides, who are we to rain on her parade? We do have Jason and Sean, do we not? We would be hypocrites if we continue saying otherwise." Ava makes a good point.

"You're right." Jen concedes.

"We know you're beyond smitten over Jason and you're in the same boat as me. You barely know him too." I remind her.

"Yes, but we aren't on a collision course. There's a difference." she reminds me back.

"Oh, is that the Driving Miss Daisy course?" say through a laugh.

"There's nothing wrong with taking things slow. Not everyone is in a rush to get to the altar." She tries to scold me.

"Ha! Who said anything about marriage? I might be crazy and taking things at warp speed, but not that crazy. Give me some credit. *Yeesh!*" I exclaim. "I would throw a pillow at your head, but I don't want to give up mine."

"If you two are done now, I would like some sleep. Who knows what tomorrow brings and it could rain lover boys on our balcony bright and early if Romeo has anything to do with it. Or it could wash up some military men at our front door. So both of you put a zipper on your lips and go to sleep, or I'll be knocking some heads!" exclaims Ava.

Sleep didn't come that easy for me as I wrestled with my own thoughts and feelings and how quick things were progressing in one day. But I had made a promise and now a choice to do something bold for me, and I plan to stick to it.

Funny how I had forgotten all about my headache talking about Layne. Eventually I find a comfortable position on this hotel mattress, curling up in my warm blanket as Mr. Sandman finds me. I can only hope that good dreams, hopefully of Layne, come my way.

So when the guys decided to drop in, literally, and wake us up, I was ready to wreak havoc on them. They interrupted one of my best dreams by far, starring Layne, until it became a nightmare when I was forced to wake up. The sudden jolt caused me to fall out of bed. I heard the other two groan at the interruption of sleep, and I didn't blame them. *Someone upstairs had a death wish this morning.*

I reluctantly get up and get the door, since I was the closest, giving the guys my best sour face through the window. I'm in the midst of yawning when I hear *Royals* playing, yet again, on the TV. *It's like every time we turn this station on, the video is playing.* I unlock the sliding door and let the guys in.

"Really, this is starting to get old. Don't they play anything else?" Chase comments as he passes by me. Apparently, I'm not the only one noticing this irritating fact.

"Really, you can't use the front door, like normal guys?" I huff as I walk past them and drop back onto my bed. They're not the leading men in my dreams, so I don't care what they have planned for the day. I have a date with the sandman to get back to. Too bad I know that it won't happen while the lover boys are still around.

"Good morning ladies." Jason says while walking over to sit at Jen's feet on the bed. He grabs her foot and gives her toes a squeeze. "Rise and shine, sleepyhead. We wanted to take you out for breakfast this morning, if you're up for it."

"You two go ahead. I need more beauty sleep since the beasts woke us up," is my grumpy reply to their invitation.

"Oh come on, it's already ten in the morning. Daylight's wasting away. Let's go do something exciting today." Evan says as he runs over and jumps onto the bed I'm on. I reach out and try to kick him but he laughs and moves before I make contact.

"No. Go away. I'm tired. Plus, we have a lunch date with this couple from our hometown in a couple of hours. So, unless you want to chill with our oldie-but-goodie friends, then you'll just have to make do without us today." *Okay, I'm being super moody today. Sue me.*

"Just ignore her. We would love to go out to breakfast with you. I'm sure we can eat a little later with the Frosts," Jen reassures them before turning her *be nice* face on me.

"What? So I'm cranky in the morning. Especially when my dream was killed off."

"Maybe we can postpone with them for later or something—"Jen trails off.

I'm about to remind her that meeting up with them was her brilliant idea when my cell phone dings. Sighing, I roll over and grab it off the floor to see that I have a text message from *Hubby*. Apparently, at some point yesterday, Layne added his number to my phone making his name show up as Hubby. The joke instantly puts a smile on my face, and when I look up, everyone is staring at me as I've changed from moody to happy in two seconds flat. Ignoring them, I tap open the message.

Hubby: Good morning, Sunshine. Hurry down to the lobby. Your hubby awaits your presence.

Hollie: I just woke up. Can you give me 20?

Hubby: Sure. Are you hungry? I wanted to take you out to breakfast. Plus, Miller was hoping Ava would want to join us. By the way, he says to get a move on . . . he's starving and is about to eat the plant sitting next to him. That's how hungry he is.

Hollie: LOL! Tell him to can it, you can't hurry a woman. And if you keep texting me, it will take me longer to get ready. As it is, the lover boys from upstairs are here. They crashed our pad again by way of the balcony. Don't boys know how to use the door properly anymore?

Hubby: What's your room number again?

Hollie: 208

I wait a few more minutes but he doesn't reply, so I toss my phone onto the nightstand. "That was Layne. He says he's in the lobby with Miller and they also want to go out for breakfast. How about we just make this a big group thing?"

"Sounds good to me," Ava shrugs her shoulders and heads to the vanity to fix her makeup and hair. I scurry off the bed so I can rummage through my suitcase for clothes, and the guys decide it's best that they go back out to the balcony to give us some privacy. As soon as Jen shuts the curtains and locks the door, I rush to the bathroom to take the world's quickest shower. I can't go anywhere without one, or I'll feel gross for the rest of the day.

I'm just getting my clothes on when there's a knock at the door. Rushing through the rest of the dressing process, I step out of the bathroom. I hear Ava telling whomever it is to hang on a minute. Walking further into the bedroom to investigate who's here, Jen rushes by me and into the bathroom to get ready. I see that Ava is decent and tell her, "I'll grab it." Then I cross the room to the door, checking the peephole first before opening it.

"How's my beautiful *wifey* this morning?" Layne asks the minute the door is open, causing my cheeks to warm, but also bringing a smile to my face.

"Much better now," I say as I move out of the way to let them pass.

"Oh yeah, now she's good. You missed her about fifteen minutes ago. She woke up on the wrong side of bed. She was mad that the guys ruined some dream she was having." Ava tells Layne and Miller. "Speaking of, what *were* you dreaming about?" she asks, turning a curious look at me. *Right, like she doesn't know.* I bet she's trying to goad me into spilling the beans.

"Now that you mention the guys, where are the lover boys at? And why, exactly, are they climbing down to your balcony?" Layne wants to know.

"Don't worry. They don't have any designs on your girl, and she only has eyes for you. Jason has it bad for Jen, and the others are lot of fun to hang with, too." Ava says as if it's not a big deal, but I bet Layne would disagree.

"Okay—" Miller says, "But where are they?"

"Oh, they're on the balcony. They were leaving us alone to get ready. They wanted to take us out to breakfast too, but now that you're both here, we can all go together." I tell him as I walk over to let the guys back in before heading to the vanity area to finish getting ready.

"Hollie, I think you forgot something." Layne calls to me.

Frowning, I look over at him, "What's that?" I ask.

"This." Is all he says as I give him a questioning look while he walks over to me and wraps his arms around my waist, lifting me into a bear hug. He places a kiss to my lips, where I can feel him smiling as he pulls away, then sets me back down. "That's what you forgot, wifey." He says through a grin that lights up his face, and then winks at me.

"Wow. A girl could get used to that," I tease him before I turn back to getting ready. At this rate, we won't make it to lunch with the Frosts anytime soon.

"I think we're going to have to cancel on the Frosts," Jen says as she heads out of the bathroom, completely ready to go.

"We could invite them to eat with us now. By the time we get out of here and make it anywhere, it would give them plenty of time to meet us." Ava suggests, and just like that, everything and everyone is neatly wrapped up into our plans for a morning feast.

Jen calls Mrs. Frost and sets it up as we finish getting ready. Layne sits on the edge of the bed, watching my every move. I keep sneaking peeks at him, and when he catches my eye, he gives me sweet little smiles.

Finally, we're all ready to go, and Layne immediately claims my hand as we head out into the hall.

After exiting the hotel, we end up hitching a ride on a public transit bus, as they run about every seven to twelve minutes, depending on the time of day. Luckily, we don't have long to wait before the next one shows up. The Frosts were staying at the *Halekulani Hotel,* which was about twelve minutes from us, and fourteen minutes away from the *Cream Pot,* which is where we're headed for brunch. Also lucky for us, the Frosts were cool with having a bunch of extra people tagging along.

In the end, I'm glad the guys joined us for brunch. Mr. Frost wasn't surrounded by women only, and he was able to talk about sports with the guys. We girls had a great time with Mrs. Frost, and everyone got along well, enjoying each other's company and sharing a lot of laughter. Layne made sure to sit by me, and would alternate between letting his hand rest on my leg, and resting his arm on the back of my chair. If the Frosts' noticed, they never made any mention of it. *Thank heavens,* as that's the last piece of gossip I want to go around town while I'm away.

After brunch, we say goodbye and wish the Frosts well as we part ways. They are headed to Pearl Harbor to explore, and we're all left standing on the sidewalk, trying to decide our plans for the day. Layne wraps his arms around me and hugs me to his chest.

He dips his head so he can whisper in my ear, "*I would love to spend the day with you. Do you have any set plans?*"

"*I'm free, and wouldn't mind spending more time with you. What did you have in mind?*" I whisper back, enjoying the fluttering butterfly feeling in my belly, and the closeness of his lips to my ear.

"I thought we could check out the *International Market Place.* Have you been there yet?"

"No, but I know Ava would love to tag along. She's been itching to get over there."

Layne looks over my head at Miller and makes a subtle head tilt-type of maneuver toward Ava. Miller gets the hint, and lightly bumps his shoulder against Ava's. She looks up at him, giving him a little smile.

"Are you up for an adventure at the *International Market Place?* I can teach you how to haggle."

"I would love to go over there! I'm so excited." She widens her smile at Miller.

"Sounds good, then. Should we ask Jenifer if she wants to go?" I ask, motioning towards our other friend.

"Hey Jen, what's your plan for the day?" Ava asks.

"I was just planning on spending time with Jason. We haven't decided on what to do yet. Why, what were you thinking?"

"We're headed to the *International Market Place,* and you're all welcomed to join us," Miller offers, but I think he and Layne secretly hope they decline.

"Thanks man, but we're going to hit the waves today." Chase says with a polite smile and a wave of his hand before he and Evan take off down the street towards the bus stop.

"We'll have to decline, too. I want to spend time with Jen today, on our own. Thanks for the offer." Jason adds before departing with Jen, promising to check in later with us.

"Well, sunshine, it looks like it's just the four of us." Layne says as he releases me from his warm embrace and reaches down to interlock his fingers with mine. He looks over to Miller and signals that it's time to go, then we make our way over to a different public transit bus. I'm glad we have the local boys with us to show us how to get around.

"I wish I had known how to use the transit system the first day we ran into each other. I had to hide out in the *ABC Store* until a cab showed up. I was so worried you would be outside waiting," I admit to Layne as we make our way to a bench to wait for our ride.

"Why were you hiding from me?"

"I was embarrassed about how I looked, and I was just starting to feel decent again after being so sick."

"I thought you looked beautiful, like you weren't trying to impress anyone. That was the best part for me." He says, giving our joined hands a squeeze. "Why should it matter how I saw you? As it was, you ran away before I could get your name. I wasn't exactly happy about that, just so you know. So, no more running while you're here," he lightly scolds me, then kisses the side of my temple. "Besides, if I didn't like what I saw, I wouldn't have tried to talk to you. And I certainly wouldn't be sitting here, holding your hand now."

He has a good point, so I tell him, "You're right. I was just embarrassed. I'm not used to running directly into men, whom I've never met, that want to talk to me when I look like a hot mess. Does my dad count?" I joke.

"Hollie," he says as he runs the back of his fingers down my cheek. "You're a beautiful hot mess." Then he kisses my nose, making the butterflies take up residence once again.

Our bus shows up shortly after that and he leads the way, pausing to help me climb up the steps before finding us a seat halfway down the aisle. We sit down, and Miller and Ava find a seat of their own to occupy. Once everyone is onboard, the bus pulls away from the curb, and it's off to the market we go, with Layne's hand in mine on his right thigh and my head resting comfortably on his shoulder.

There's a big sign welcoming us to the *International Market Place,* hanging outside of the entrance when we arrive. It feels like we're about to enter a theme park here. One could also assume that we are by witnessing how excited Ava is to finally go shopping.

"Alright, we'll see you two later. I have some haggling 101 to teach Ava, here. I'll text you so we can meet back here later." Miller tells Layne then grabs Ava's hand as they walk off together, disappearing into the market.

Linking my arm through Layne's, we walk into the open-air market and immediately we're assaulted by all kinds of noises, colors, shoppers, and vendors at their little individual places of business. Almost like, if you could name it, it could possibly be for sale here. From where we stand I can already see stalls full of trinkets, woodcrafts, leather goods, knick-knacks, swimwear, sarongs, grass skirts, t-shirts, jewelry, sunglasses, and food. *So many choices, how do you know who to buy from?*

The market has drawn a large crowd today, making me feel a bit claustrophobic, as everything is a little too close for comfort. We find ourselves bumping into passersby as we walk around, window shopping and admiring many different items.

Layne leads me over to another area where there's a stall selling sarongs. The fabrics are so pretty, all in vibrant colors. "Choose one, sunshine, and I'll buy it for you, as long as I get to see you in it at the beach later," he winks at me.

I start looking through all of the material, trying to find that one perfect cover-up, when we notice a couple trying to bargain with the merchant. He's not budging though, and that causes Layne to perk up and pay attention. After a few more moments, the couple walks away, empty handed. Layne places his hand on my elbow and leads me away. I don't understand what's going on.

"What's wrong? Did something bad happen with that other couple?" I question him.

"No, sweetheart. He didn't want to work out a deal, and I know for a fact that we can find the same items elsewhere for a better price. That's why I pulled you away, and now we're going where I know those better deals are. There's nothing to worry about, Holls." He reassures me as he takes my hand and we walk in the opposite direction of where we just were, which happens to be the same way Miller and Ava went earlier. As we venture further into the market, we see that there's a place for a live band to perform, and a food court. Good thing, because I'm not a big shopper, and if he planned to keep me here all afternoon, food would be a must on my list of to-do's.

This place is amazing, and so full of life. Like nowhere I have ever been before. There are so many things to see and so much going on all around us. I feel like I'd better keep a tight grip on Layne's hand so we don't get separated. We eventually wind our way through the crowd to another stall where I can buy a sarong. Layne leads me over to the selection of beautiful colors and fun prints. I can't decide with so many options, but eventually I do settle on a white one that has purple hibiscus flowers strategically placed throughout the material. It's beautiful, and looks very feminine. As soon as I came across it, Layne agreed that it was the right choice. We made our purchase after a little haggling back and forth, then set off to look at other places and items for another hour.

I find a pretty set of wooden turtles, which I fall instantly in love with and decide to buy. We shop around, finding many useful and useless items, and we're having a blast the whole time. I even managed to get Layne into a grass skirt and a coconut bra. With one glance at that sorry getup, I was in hysterics. He was a good sport when I asked him to pose for a photo, telling him that he made one hideous chick. I like that he has a good sense of humor, playing along with my scheme of dressing him up like a woman and then laughing about it. Military man or not, he can be a big goof, it seems, and isn't worried about his ego taking a hit or what others think about a man dressing up like a woman as a joke.

In the end, Layne and I both picked up a new pair of sunglasses, and eventually decide to text Miller. We tell him to meet us at the food court so we can grab a bite to eat at the *Noodle House.*

After a late lunch, Miller and Ava decide to stick with us for a while, so Ava could make sure that she picked up everything she deemed that she needed while we were here. Really, she is just buying more junk that she really doesn't need, and where in the heck does she think she can store it all in her suitcase? But, for Ava's sake, the guys agree to stick it out a bit longer with the promise that we will head to the beach for a little bit of water play afterwards.

As we keep walking, I notice there's a tarot card and palm reading hut nearby. I elbow Layne in the side and point to it, shaking my head. *I don't believe in that mumbo jumbo.* It's all a bunch of hoopla, and none of it ever comes true. Ava hones in on a jewelry stall, making the guys groan. But they follow behind us anyway, acting like dutiful boyfriends. I sigh to myself. *If only.*

"Should we stop there and have our fortunes read? Who knows," Layne says playfully, "maybe you'll be the future Mrs. McKay, with three girls chasing around some prankster boys." Layne laughs as he leads us over to the fortuneteller, while Miller and Ava keep moving to the little shop.

His statement makes my whole body shudder with terror. "Don't even joke like that, putting the fear of miniature Layne's, with girls chasing them and causing mayhem all over town, into my head." I lightly smack him in the arm. "Besides, I think you're putting the cart before the horse here, soldier boy. Was that some kind of whacky proposal? If it was, I will have to respectfully decline your offer." I laugh at his fake pouty face before reaching up on my toes to kiss his puckered lips. "Ok fine, I demand a redo at least. Wait—let's try a redo in like a year from now." I say with a smile, attempting to ease the sting of my rejection.

"Oh, so you do find me charming and irresistible. Especially since you can't keep your lips off of me. And look, it's only day two, and you've already fallen into that insta-love category that women hate so much in books and movies," he teases me.

"Oh my gosh," I laugh. "How do you even know about that, anyway?"

"Hey, I pay attention to women and what they say. They're not all just pretty faces to me." He's cracking me up, but I still elbow him anyway.

"Let's not forget that you're the one talking marriage, kids, and already calling me wifey. I'm just playing along, here. Not that I don't mind it." I duck my head, trying to hide the smile that instantly formed on my lips at the thought.

"Ah-ha! I *knew* you loved me, the moment you set your eyes on me. Come on, Bruiser. Let's go see what Ava and Miller are up to, since you refuse to hear about how awesome our future will be together." He looks down at me with his fake pout again. "That breaks my heart, just so you know."

"Uh-huh, sure. Let's go, you big softy, before the others find out that you have a heart." I tease him while tugging on his hand, pulling him over to the jewelry stall that Ava drifted off to. I see she has a string of jewelry laid out before her. "Oh boy, we could be here awhile at the rate she's going. Might as well see if we can find some early Christmas gifts." I tell Layne then head over to where Ava is while he hangs by the counter with Miller.

"Hey, try not to buy out the store on this trip, Miss Money Bags." I tell Ava jokingly. "While you decide on more items that you don't need, and it looks like we'll be here for another year or so, I think I'll look for a necklace for my mom."

"Oh hush it, woman. You're wrong, we'll be here just half a year more," she laughs. "You know I can't go anywhere and not find something when it comes to jewelry. And who says it's all for me? Maybe I found your *birthmas* gift."

"That's what I love about you, Ava. You know how to make a girl feel special with the two most important events in her life, combined into one."

"I knew that's why you loved me. I'm just classy that way." She says with a big smile on her face then continues to browse the wares on the table. I shop a bit longer, finding a pretty gold necklace with a red coral pendant. It's the perfect gift for my mom for Christmas. Not too flashy or spendy. It's exactly right for her, and she'll love it. I'm just completing my purchase when I hear Layne.

"Sunshine," Layne calls out to me, nodding his head to walk over to him. From where I stand, I can see that he's looking at pieces of jewelry lying before him on the counter. I'm curious as to what he wants to show me, so I walk over and stand next to him. He steps back, then wraps his arms around my shoulders, hugging me firmly to him. "What do you think of these bracelets?" he asks as I eye some beautiful decorative pieces and a few charm bracelets.

"I like them. Are you buying a gift for someone?" I ask, raising my eyebrows.

"As a matter of fact, I am. Would you help me choose one? I'm never good at this kind of thing."

I'm curious as to whom this gift is for, and I experience a few moments of green-eyed envy over a woman who may be the recipient to the gift I have to now help choose. "Is this someone special to you? I would hate to pick out the wrong thing," I say, frowning a little. But I have no right to be jealous. After all, he's not my boyfriend, and we're just having fun together while I'm on vacation, pretending to be a couple, when we really aren't.

"Sweetheart, I don't think you can possibly pick out the wrong gift," he tries to assure me. *Easy enough for him to say, he's the one leaving all the pressure on my shoulders.*

"Okay, if you think that's true, then I'll pick something that I would love and pray this person doesn't hate me for it." I say while fingering a pretty beaded bracelet with a turtle charm hanging from it. The bracelet features glass beads in a rustic shade of red. The turtle is a distressed turquoise color, and dangles from the bracelet. The chain and clasps are silver, and I'm instantly in love with this beautiful piece. "This one right here," I point to the bracelet, "is the perfect gift for any lady. Whoever she is will be lucky to have it, especially if it's from you."

"I think you're right, my little sister will be on cloud nine with this piece. Thanks, sweetheart." He shows his appreciation by planting a kiss to the back of my head. "Why don't you wrap that up for us, ma'am," he tells the local woman behind the counter. "*Now,*" he whispers into my ear, "what do you say about making this pretend marriage official? I can't have my wife walking around without a ring on. I can't have the other guys trying to steal my girl."

"Ma'am, can we see your rings, please? My wife would like to pick one out for her pretty little finger." He says, resting his head on the top of mine.

"What?" I say, turning around in his arms so I can look at his face. "You can't be serious, right?" I ask, as I feel a bit embarrassed that he's calling attention to us like this.

"Sunshine, I may joke and tease a lot, but I'm not playing right now. Remember what I said yesterday, on the beach? You're here now, and you can be whoever you want to be for the week. You promised me that you would let yourself be carefree and live for you. So, right here, right now, I'm asking you to be my wife for the week," he says, staring into my eyes. "How about it, Hollie? Will you be my fake wife?"

He's right. I did promise I would live carefree this week, going with the flow and just being myself around him. *So, why not do something crazy and live in the moment?*

I decide to take the plunge. "Yes, Layne, I will be your wife for the week." I tell him as I stare deep into his hazel-green eyes. For a moment in time, we both just stand there, caught up in the rush of it all. This time there's no hidden humor behind the statements exchanged, and there's no playfulness in his eyes. The mood suddenly becomes deep, and is as real as real can be. I feel the natural shift of something happening between us. In that moment, with Layne looking at me with so much affection, I felt the conviction of his words and the things that he wasn't saying out loud, but was expressing from the depths of his eyes. There was this sense of freedom around me, and I felt as if I was soaring to great heights on these emotions.

He raises his hands and brushes them down my face and my neck, then lightly takes my head in between his hardworking hands and gently guides my mouth to his, where he kisses me firmly, and then more tenderly. When he finally lets go, I'm out of breath and smiling like a fool up at him. He gives me the most genuine smile in return before reaching behind me and taking a ring from the vendor. With his eyes firmly locked on mine, he takes my left hand and places the ring on my finger, before raising my knuckles to his lips to seal it with a kiss.

We're thrown out of our serious moment, that we both got a little too carried away with, when Miller decides to clap us on our backs with his big hands. "Well, that was interesting. I guess congratulations for you two crazy kids are in order?" he says, then punches Layne in the shoulder before squeezing me into a tight hug. "How about we go take a walk down to the beach now?" he asks.

"Great!" Ava excitedly exclaims. "Let me just pay for these, then we can go lay out."

And just like that, our intense moment is brushed to the side, but not before a noticeable shift takes place in what's really going on between us. *It's so strange.* I really like Layne a lot, yet I don't know him well enough to grow the kind of feelings that I just experienced for him, to this extreme extent. *I think I'm in serious danger here.* The question is, *do I care?* I'm not that sure I do. I want to hold on to these feelings for as long as I have left on this trip. Hopefully I don't break my own heart when it's all over and I have to fly away home.

"Hollie, are you with us?" Layne asks as he examines my face a little worriedly. "You look a thousand miles away."

"I'm good." I say as I wrap my arms around his middle, hugging myself to him. "Just thinking about how happy I am at the moment."

"Well, that's a relief. I was a little worried that I might have scared you away. There's just something about you, Holls, and I can't get enough of it," he says, while wrapping his own arms around me, bringing me in for a tight embrace.

"Alright, love birds," Miller teases us. "It's off to the beach we go." He turns his narrowed eyes on Ava next.

"Ok, woman, your purchasing window has now closed. Step away from the counter," Miller orders Ava, causing her to grin at him, and making Layne and I laugh.

"I think we should call Jen and check in on her and Jason. The boy has it bad for her. She might need a breather at this point," Ava says as she loops her arm through Miller's and we start to walk away from the jewelry place.

"I'll text her." I volunteer, as I pull my phone out of my purse. It was a wise choice to throw on our swimsuits under our clothes this morning. Now that I have my new sarong, I can just use that to lie on at the beach. And the girls don't know it yet, but I bought them each one as well. My token to them as something to remember Hawaii by.

Hollie: Hey, Jen. We're headed down to the beach. Meet you there in 20?

Jen: We're already there. The guys found a pickup game of football. See you in a few.

Hollie: Sounds like you are in need of company. See you shortly.

"Jen's already there with the guys. She's a little lonely, as the guys have found an impromptu game of football," I inform the group.

"Football, you say? Well, I think we better hurry down there, don't you ladies?" Miller asks.

"Oh, does that mean we get to see you shirtless?" Ava flirts with him.

"Would I deny you the rights to this ripped chest? I should think not, woman!" Miller smirks at Ava.

"You two are sweetly sick." I laugh at them. "Let's make it to the beach before I have to hear anything else that I may not want to hear. We'll text Jen when we're closer to see exactly where she is."

The beach was a lot of fun. Jen wasn't really lonely, as it turned out. She was catching up on her latest novel, while watching the guys toss the football around, not too far from her towel. She had an awesome view of a bunch of good-looking guys. But once we arrived, Miller and Layne convinced the guys to head out into the ocean and play football on the sandbars. Apparently they played like that all the time, at a place closer to the Army base, and it's a real hit with their friends.

Needless to say, Jen wasn't overly pleased by their change of venue. Ava and I were okay with it though, as it gave us a chance to catch up on the day's events and see what Jen had been up to. I was trying to avoid the whole ring thing, and I was hoping that Ava would keep her big mouth shut for a while longer. Although, Jen was in high heaven when we got here, so I'm counting on her head still being on cloud nine.

After spending a few hours on the beach, waterlogged and tuckered out from the heat, we decide that it's time to eat. Layne tells us about a great burger joint nearby called *Teddy's Bigger Burgers*, and everyone agrees to go there for a late dinner. The lover boys decide to hang out with us for dinner too, and hey, they're guys, they can't pass up a burger. So we all headed out that way for a tasty dinner and a nice walk down Kalakuala Avenue that runs along the side of the beach.

It turns out; *Teddy's Bigger Burger* is a 1950's themed diner with fantastic food. Nothing compares to it, not even the *McDonald's* we passed on the way here. The garlic fries were delicious, and the burgers piled a mile high, it seemed. Plus, you can't go to a 50's-style burger place and not have a shake as well, even if you feel like a roly-poly the whole walk home. I mean, who would pass on a thick, chocolate shake? *Not me, that's for sure.*

Chase and Evan head back to the hotel to meet up with some girls from their school, while Jason hangs back with Jen. Ava walks along with Miller behind them, while Layne and I snail-pace our way behind the group.

"Why don't you hop on my back, Bruiser? I know you're dragging after all that food, and you did manage to polish off that big shake," Layne says as he bends down to one knee on the sidewalk.

"Are you saying I'm a heifer?" I reach up and try to smack him on the back of his head.

"What? Of course not!" he acts as if he's outraged. "I'm trying to be a gentleman, here."

"*Mmm-hmm.* Well, that was an interesting way to go about it, soldier boy."

In the end, I decide that a free ride is not something to say no to, so I climb onto his back and up he goes. He loses his balance for a second, emitting a small scream from my lungs and causing me to hold on for dear life. He stumbles for a moment before he gets it back under control, and I burst into a fit of laughter.

"What are you two doing back there?" Miller yells back to us.

"Don't even say anything," I laugh out, thinking that he's going to blame me with a teasing remark about why he stumbled.

"Oh, you think that's funny, do you?" Layne says, as he tries to tickle my sides, thankfully leaving out any wisecracks.

"Not so smooth there, are you, Casanova?" We hear Ava call back to us as we try to make our way up the street. I'm still laughing, trying to push Layne's hands away.

"Ah—I see what the problem is. It was that shake she just *had* to tack on to her order. I would've fallen over, too!" Miller laughs. "Or maybe it's that gold ring you put on her finger, combined with the shake's weight. I bet that's it."

"What ring?" I hear Jen ask. I look over in time to see that now all of them are waiting for us to catch up. I look back to Miller, who seems confused that she doesn't already know.

"Oh, it's nothing. Just Layne staking his claim on Hollie for the rest of the week, so all other guys will cease to exist but him," Ava laughs. "It's not even a real ring, right?" she asks Layne.

"Oh, don't be so serious about it, Jen. It's just for fun." I cut her off before she can make a bigger deal of it. Bending my head down slightly, I whisper in Layne's ear, *"Right, soldier boy?"* He gives my thighs a squeeze, where his hands are holding onto me. But what I notice he doesn't do is actually answer the question.

"It's been a great day, let's not ruin it. Just let it rest, and let's enjoy the rest of our walk. Pretty soon I'll have to relinquish my rights to hold this beauty until I can see her again, tomorrow." Layne says, a little perturbed but trying to be as nice as he can to the group.

"I agree," I say, planting a kiss on his cheek. "Onward, rickshaw." I command as I settle in for the rest of the trip back to the hotel. The conversation changes, and Jenifer lets the ring conversation slide, for now.

As soon as we enter the hotel lobby, Jen and Jason depart, calling out their goodbyes as they walk over to the elevator, leaving the rest of us to find our way over to a set of couches off to the side of the front desk. Layne lowers me down onto a cushion before he sits on the other side of me, reaching out to slip his fingers into mine. He's rubbing his thumb over the back of my hand as we sit there quietly, just enjoying each other's company.

"Did you have a good day, sunshine?" he asks, as he rubs his finger over the gold band on my finger. He seems content in the moment, and I'm mesmerized by his fingers stroking my hand.

"I did. Thank you for spending the day with me." I reply, as I snuggle my head into the crook of his neck, curling my legs up onto the couch. "What should we do tomorrow? Or do you need to get back to work?" I'm not so secretly hoping that he says that he can see me tomorrow.

"I'm still on leave, sweetheart. I'll be with you until you're sick of me," he reassures me.

"So, what should we do tomorrow?" I ask him.

"Let's take the girls on a scenic trip to the North Shore tomorrow." Miller says, injecting his two cents into our intimate conversation.

"We could do that. What do you think, sunshine, want to take a drive with me?"

"I don't think you have to twist her arm too hard to get a 'yes,'" says Ava.

"I'll take all the minutes I can get with you, so to the North Shore tomorrow, it is. Is your vehicle big enough for five of us?" I ask him.

"You may want to plan for six," Ava states. I give her a questioning look, and she says on a sigh, "Jason?"

Lifting my head, I look over at her to agree, "Right. He wouldn't go anywhere without her. Looks like she's got a keeper on her hands. He's smitten." I look up to Layne and give him an intimate smile.

"Is that such a bad thing?" Layne questions me with a face full of both affection and seriousness. His hazel eyes appear to be swirling with other colors as they stare intently into my blue-grey ones, trying to peek into the windows of my soul.

"It could be a very good thing, with the right person." I say as I try to transmit my feelings back to him.

Leaning in, Layne places a soft kiss on my lips, and then leaves a kiss on my forehead, caressing my neck before he brushes some wild wisps of my hair away from my face. All of his care leaves me with a soft smile on my face, causing Layne's eyes to move back to my lips. I watch as he smiles at me, right before laying my head on his shoulder. I know that we have a small audience observing us, but I can't bring myself to think or worry over them or the alarming rate of my growing feelings or Layne's. There are some people who you meet in life, and you just know that you are meant to be in their lives. You have an instant connection, and you can't fathom letting it go. So for now, until I have to, I'm holding on to what we have, and am enjoying living every minute of it.

Eventually, all good things must come to end, and it's about that time for this evening, as it's getting late. The four of us have been sitting down in the lobby for a couple of hours, not wanting to leave each other.

"I hate to say it sweetheart, but we do have a long drive back to the base. Before we turn into pumpkins, we'd better get back." Layne gently reminds me of the time.

"Well, that's our cue," Ava says, poking Miller in the chest. They get up and walk to the entrance of the lobby, giving us privacy.

"Thank you for one of the best days I've had in a long time, Hollie. I really wish I didn't have to leave, but we both know staying isn't an option. I'll look forward to seeing you tomorrow, though." Layne tells me, wrapping me tighter into his arms.

I hate to leave the comfort that I feel and his warmth. I pull away and look into his face for a moment before placing a kiss to his lips. However, he has other ideas, and deepens the kiss, while sliding his hand up to the nape of my neck. We linger on the couch for a long while, just holding onto each other and exchanging a few more kisses, neither one wanting to break the moment. Finally, Layne pulls us up from the couch and we walk, hand in hand, towards Miller and Ava outside.

"What time do you want us to be ready tomorrow?" Ava, the voice of clarity, asks the guys. *At least one of us is thinking straight.*

"I was thinking we could swing by around ten?" Miller asks.

"We'll meet you in the lobby." Ava confirms.

I turn to Layne and give him one more, long hug, and he rubs his hands up and down my back before fully kissing me one last time. Then he pulls away, leaving me with a face full of longing but a beautiful smile.

"Sleep well, sweetheart. Sweet dreams. I'll see you tomorrow."

He whispers in my ear while giving a kiss to my temple. He pulls back and starts to walk away, but not before he leaves me with a nice little reminder.

"By the way, sunshine, we still haven't gotten to the bottom of who the real Hollie is yet. Don't forget! Tomorrow on our trip to the Shore, you owe me a story." And this time he really does walk away, with a little bounce in his step.

"Later, Killer. Later, Bruiser," Miller calls out to us. And then they're gone, and my heart misses Layne already.

"Come on Juliet, Romeo will be back tomorrow. Let's go see what Jen and Jason are up to. Maybe they need a chaperone." She wiggles her eyebrows at me suggestively, making me laugh.

"Yes, mom." I say as I swing my arm around her shoulder and we head back into the lobby and up to our room.

Chapter Five

Day 4

THE NEXT MORNING, Jason uses the door like a normal person, and he leaves the rest of the lover boy gang behind. Turns out, they actually found someone to take them deep-sea fishing for the day. Jason, I'm sure, couldn't bear to be apart from Jen, and so here we all are in the lobby, making our plans over bagels and juice at 7:30 in the morning.

"Whose bright idea was it to get up this early?" Miller complains through a yawn.

"Knock that off. It's catching, and now I want to yawn." I say right before I end up doing it myself. "See?" I say as I scoot closer to Layne.

Sitting here, snuggled into him, brings back memories of our time together yesterday. Just thinking about how well we clicked and how much fun we had the day before brings a smile to my face.

"I believe it was yours, genius." Ava scowls at him. "I could be sleeping in right now."

"Or, we could be listening to *Royals* again." Jen chimes in, and Jason laughs. "I'll pay you to never turn the TV back on for the remainder of our trip." She directs that comment at Ava.

"I'll second that, and throw my own money into the pot. But, you'll have to get Chase and Evan on board with that." Jason pitches into the conversation.

"*What's going on in that mind of yours, sunshine?*" Layne whispers in my ear. "Whatever it is, I hope it has to do with me," he says as he places a kiss on the top of my head.

"I'm sure any smile donned by Hollie this week will in some way have something to do with you, soldier." Ava chimes in. *Of course she would overhear us.* She's sitting on the other side of me.

"What about you, Ava? Any ideas about us floating around in your memory?" Miller wags his eyebrows at her, causing her to blush before she playfully punches his arm.

"I'll take that as a 'yes,'" he says smugly, with a lopsided grin.

"What's this? Was there something you've neglected to share with the class, Ava?" I tease her as I lightly kick her with my foot. But she just bats it away and plays it off like there's nothing to discuss.

"Okay, let's get back to the subject at hand," she says.

"Don't forget, I have to be back for dinner on this side of the island tonight." Jen reminds us.

After we got back to our room last night, Jenifer let us know that Jude was cashing in on his bet the next day. After Jason dropped her off at the hotel room door, Jude showed up, asking about her plans for the next day.

"Dinner?" Jason gives her a questioning look. "Are you meeting with the Frost couple again?" he asks her.

"Why don't you tell lover boy what your plans are, Jen?" Ava eggs her.

"Why? So you can deflect the attention off of you?" I laugh at her.

"That must be one good story you're trying to cover up." Layne taunts her back.

"We're not talking about me, remember?" she shoots back.

"It's not that big of a deal, really." Jen cuts in. "I have dinner plans with a friend from school," she evades as she looks anywhere but at Jason.

"Oh, for crying out loud, I'll tell him." Ava continues. "She has a dinner date with Jude. He's just a friend, and it's not that big of a deal."

"Is that why you tried to make it one?" Miller points out.

"Look here, Sean—"*Oh boy,* this is the second time I've heard her call him by his given name, and not his last. *This must be some story.* "Are you trying to get me in trouble? I was trying *not* to embarrass you with having to share our little sordid affair the other day."

"The only *sordid* thing we did yesterday was hold hands." Miller laughs, pulling her into a headlock. "And maybe exchanged a few kisses." He proudly states through a big smile.

"Now who just embarrassed who?" Jen says.

"If Jude is just your friend, why didn't you tell me?"Jason frowns at Jen but also brings the conversation back around. He seems a little upset, and who can blame the guy?

"I really don't want to go, and I wasn't sure how to get out of it. I thought that maybe Ava and Hollie could tag along so it won't be so awkward. He is a good guy, and really, there's nothing there between us. I just didn't know what to do."

"I'll tell you what you can do. If it helps, we'll all go out to dinner tonight, and make it a group thing." Miller suggests.

"He'll probably assume you'll bring us anyway, as we never seem to go anywhere very often without each other." I put my two cents in.

"There. It's settled. All of us will be there, which gives me another opportunity to be with you tonight, as well as today." Jason looks pleased by this little turn of events.

"Great. It's settled. Now, let's get back to making our plans for first part of our day. We're burning daylight here, folks." Miller reminds us. "It's a good hour or so to get to where we want to go."

Basically, the planning took place between Miller and Layne. They were the most native among us, after all. The rest of us just nodded when they told us what we were doing. I reminded them that we were just the tourists and they were our guides, so as long as they didn't lead us off a cliff or into some deep jungle to ditch us in, we would go wherever they suggested.

We're all packed into Layne's truck like a bunch of sardines: three of us up front, and three in the back. *Okay, it's not that bad.* Just a bit of a tight, fit but we make it work. I'm the lucky one in the group, as I have my permanent place right next to the driver for both parts of the trip. Jen and Jason decided to sit together with Ava in the back on the way to the North Shore. For the way back, it was decided that Miller would switch out with Jen, so that he can sit by Ava in the back.

Sighing, I feel perfectly content while holding Layne's hand on his muscular thigh, as I rest my head on his right shoulder. There's a country music station playing on the radio as we drive along the highway.

Miller nudges me about 45 minutes into our trip, pointing out the window to my left.

"There's *Castle Grayskull.* Well, in that general vicinity, anyway," he says.

"Why do you guys call the base that, anyway?" I ask.

"Schofield always seems to be surrounded by dark clouds. Do you remember that 80's cartoon, *He-Man?*" he asks

"I've heard of it, yes." I reply.

"Well, in that cartoon there was a place called Castle Grayskull, and it was always surrounded by dark-looking clouds as it sat up high on its mountain top. That's how it seems Schofield is. Anyway, it's a nickname that the soldiers use for the base. I'm not even sure when it started. It's just a reference everyone recognizes now and uses. If you were to stand on Waikiki beach, facing the direction of Schofield, you would see it surrounded by dark clouds."

"One day, sunshine, I'll have to bring you by the base to brighten it up." Layne says, giving my hand a squeeze.

"Wait, we're passing where you work and live, right? Did you guys drive home, then back to get us this morning, just to come back up this way again? That's a lot of backtracking, don't you think?" I ask.

"Actually, we didn't go home last night. We slept out on the beach, and then washed up in the ocean this morning." Miller informs us.

"What? Oh my gosh. You two are crazy. For one, isn't sleeping on the beach illegal? And for two, it had to be freezing in the water that early." Jen says, sounding a bit outraged.

"It's fine, we do that from time to time. No big deal, and no harm done," Layne says.

"You should have told us. You could have bunked in our room."

Jason tells the guys.

"Really, it's not that big of a deal. There was no point in driving all the way back home, and we're used to sleeping in worse places than on the beach, so really, it's all good." Miller tells him, officially ending the conversation on their sleeping accommodations.

Finally, we get to the North Shore neighborhood, where Layne pulls into a surfboard shop.

"Miller and I have boards being made that we wanted to check on. Since we were coming out this way, we figured we could make a quick pit stop and see how things are going. Do you want to come in? We won't be very long." Layne asks.

"Hey Jason, there's a soap shop on the other side of this building. Why don't you take the ladies over there?" Miller suggests. "It's called *North Shore Soap Factory,* and we'll meet you over there in about 20 minutes. The factory's supposed to be like that *Bath & Body* store that women love so much."

"Sold!" Ava exclaims. "We're all over it." She smiles at Jen and I.

"I figured as much," Miller says, as he shakes his head, but is still smiling at her.

"Sounds like a plan, then. I'll see you in a bit, sunshine." Layne says as he kisses me soundly on my lips.

"Watch Killer for me, would you?" Miller asks all three of us. "I'd hate for her to buy out the whole shop, forcing the people of Oahu to buy their products online and needing to wait for weeks before they can smell fabulous again." He winks at her.

We separate, going in two different directions. I feel a little bit of a loss not having Layne by my side, but I make the best of it. I really wouldn't have minded going with the guys, but I knew they would be talking shop, and I wasn't ready to be bored with talk of surfing. Plus, who could say no to bath soaps and body sprays? *Not this chick, that's who.*

"Let's go do some early Christmas shopping!" Ava says enthusiastically.

"I'm pretty sure we all know what will be under the tree for us this year," Jen comments.

"So, Killer, huh?" I hip-check Ava with my own hip. "What's that all about?"

"Apparently that's my new nickname, as I seem to be an awesome bargain shopper and haggler now," she muses. "That's what Sean says, anyway. He thinks I'm good at sniffing out a sale anywhere, and then finagling the prices down even more. I think I showed him the art of shopping 101 the other day, not the other way around. He had no idea what he was getting into when he met this chick!" she laughs.

"Well, let's go, Killer! Come show us how to attack those sales, then." I go to hip-check her again but miss, somehow, and stumble, making the group crack up.

"You know, this sure seems to be the happiest, most smiley, and funniest group of girls I've ever met," muses Jason.

"That's us!" Ava and I say at the same time. Jen just smiles up at him as she loops her arm through his. "I think it's time to sniff out the bargains, and lots of soaps, lotions and sprays."

"Maybe I should have thought more about being the only guy in this group at the moment. I may want to rethink that and head to the board shop." Jason narrows his eyes at us and then back at the surf place we just left.

"Don't even think it, mister!" Jen tightens her grip on his arm. "You're definitely with the right group. I don't see any other guys with a group of the best-looking tourist girls walking around here. You'll make the other guys envious."

"That's because you don't see any other guys around for one, and secondly, they aren't crazy enough to set foot into one of these shops." He shoots back.

"Oh, you'll love it, and you know it. You're just trying to hold onto your manhood at the moment. It's okay to touch base with the softer side of you." I laugh at Jason when he gives me a look.

"All I know is, your men better not be pulling my leg, and show-ing up when you're all done shopping. And I also know that I better not come out of there smelling all pretty because you decided to use me as the human spray tester." He says, cracking all three of us girls up again.

Eventually, the guys did make their way over to us, and we managed to leave the store with only a couple of bags. It was tricky, but with all three guys involved, they were able to head Ava off at the counter before she could buy out the place. Jason reminded her that she would have to pay for extra-heavy luggage, and Jen noted that the lotions she bought could open up in her suitcase, causing Ava to rethink her purchases.

I can't say that any of the guys walked away without one scent, at least, left on their skin. At some point, our noses started losing the capacity to smell everything. It was a bit overwhelming, and we were running out of room on our own arms to leave a scent, so it was up to the guys to take one for the team.

"You know what I've always wanted to get?" Ava says out of the blue, after we had just climbed back into the cab of the truck.

"What's that, Killer?" Miller takes the bait.

"A piercing." Is all she says.

"What?" I ask, surprised.

"Yep. I want to get my belly button pierced. How about it, soldier? Do you know of a place around here?" she asks Layne.

"We could take her over to *Pa'u Tattoo*. I bet they would do it." Miller says.

"Sweet, let's go over there right now!" she says giddily.

"Are you sure about this?" Jen asks. "What about your parents? They'll flip a lid!"

"I'm of age, and I'm about to go off to college. I think I should have a say over my own body," Ava informs her.

"All right, if you're sure, then I'll drive us over there right now." Layne tells her. "I know a really good place for lunch that's close by there anyway. We can hit it up afterwards."

After we arrived at the tattoo parlor, Jen opted to stay outside. She's pretty squeamish, so Jason decided to stay with her and keep her company, which we all knew that he would.

"What can we do for you?" a heavily tattooed man with a pierced lip asks.

"My friend would like to get her belly button pierced. Do you have time for an appointment?" Layne asks the guy.

"Yep, sure do. Why don't you take a look at the jewelry and find something you like. You'll need to sign a form that you're of age, and then we'll get started." He tells us.

Ava starts to browse the selection of rings with Miller, while

Layne and I take a seat.

"Are you going to watch when she gets it done?" Layne wants to know.

"Sure. I'm curious as to how this works."

"Are you going to get one yourself?"

"No. That's one thing I know for sure that I don't want to try. Why? Do you think that I need this experience as part of my living in the moment promise?" I wonder out loud.

"No. I was just curious, that's all. A tattoo or a piercing is a personal decision, and not one to be made on a whim. It's your choice, but not one I would ever push at you to try." He assures me.

"Good to know. Do you have any piercings?" I ask him. Might as well get the curiosity-based questions out of the way.

"No, I don't."

"What about tattoos?"

"Do you?" he avoids answering my question by asking one of his own.

"No, and even though I do think they look awesome on some people, it's not something I plan on trying, either. So, are you going to answer me?"

"Would it bother you if you dated a guy who had one?"

"No."

"Good."

"That's it? That's all you're going to give me in way of an answer?"

"Sunshine, you've seen me without a shirt on. You tell me." He says.

But I just sit there trying to think back to the day before, and if I noticed one or not. *It's possible I missed it.* I was being a little too shy to fully check him out.

"I'll let you figure out if I have one or not," he toys with me.

"When did you say we were going to the beach again?" I ask him. Honestly, as much as I had allowed myself to check him out the other day, when his shirt was off, I didn't notice a tattoo. But that doesn't mean that he doesn't have one somewhere else on his beautifully tanned skin.

"That's just cruel, you know. Playing with me like that. I think you're enjoying this because you know that the next time we hit the beach, I'll have to check you out like an organism under a micro-scope."

"Are you trying to tell me that you wouldn't enjoy it? Because, sunshine, I don't buy it for a split second." He coolly replies.

"We'll see." I say with a shrug, even though I know he's right, and I'll gladly scope him out, and enjoy every minute of it, too. *Doesn't mean I have to tell him that so he can feed his already healthy ego.*

"Alright, who's coming with me?" Ava asks, breaking up our little moment.

"I believe we all are, Killer." Miller says to her. *Oh my gosh.* It just dawned on me that his nickname for her rhymes with his last name. I stifle a giggle.

"What?" Ava asks as the guys turn a raised brow on me.

"Nothing," I laugh, because seriously, I can't help it.

"Nah-uh. Spill it, sister." Ava orders.

"It's stupid, really. No big deal." I insist.

"Nope. I'm not going in there until you tell us. And it's starting to become a big deal the more we have to keep asking you about it."

"You're the only one badgering me. The guys don't even care." I say, trying to confirm my response with the guys. *Crap.* They look curious, too. "Geez. All right. I'll tell you." I say. "I just noticed that Miller's name rhymes with his nickname for you, Killer. See? Stupid. I told you. Now, let's go get that piercing. What do you say?" I try to act all pumped up over the state of her belly button.

Ava shakes her head and starts walking to the back room, follow-ing the tattoo artist. But I still hear her chuckling. I know it was really stupid, and I just couldn't help but laugh.

"Are we calling you Miller the Killer now?" Layne jokes with his friend. Miller just rolls his eyes at him and walks away, but he, too laughs a little.

"I know. I'm a big dork. Just tell me now so we can get it out of the way." I say to him, slightly embarrassed.

"If you're a dork, then you're my cute dork, and I wouldn't want you any other way, sunshine." He can be so sweet, even when I make a fool of myself. Obviously, case in point.

"Come on, soldier boy, we have a piercing to watch." I say as I grab his hand and lead him down the hall where our friends just went.

We enter the room and see Ava getting her belly button swabbed.

The tattoo artist sure is taking his sweet time on her belly button. It's making me a little uncomfortable with the amount of attention he's paying it. Layne squeezes my hand.

"He's cleaning and sterilizing her so she won't feel too much when he sticks a surgical needle in her." He whispers in my ear, sending shivers down my spine. *A surgical needle? Oh heck no. Maybe I don't want to watch this.*

Next, the guy takes a marker and makes a dot above her belly button before he takes this giant clamp and pinches her skin. Now it's my turn to squeeze Layne's hand. Once the clamp is in place, he pulls a long, thick needle through her belly button and leaves it there before pulling the clamp off. I hide my face into Layne's chest, not wanting to watch any more.

A few minutes pass, and Layne whispers that it's okay to look now. I glance up in time to see Ava's new, shiny toy on her stomach and a big grin on her face. *Well, at least she found something that put a spark in her eye,* I think to myself, as I watch her grinning like a mad fool up at Miller. He's a foot taller than she is, so it's quite the neck strain.

"All right kids, time to pay and head out." Miller says, steering Ava by her waist to the front of the parlor. "I'm starving. Where were you thinking of going for lunch?" he asks Layne.

"The *Grass Skirt Grill,*" he replies.

"Perfect. Let me pay for this, and we'll meet you out at the truck." He tells us. I raise my eyebrows at Ava, knowing a fight of the wills will ensue. So I tug on Layne's hand and move us out the front door.

"Jen, be grateful you weren't in there. The clamp they used on her, and that big needle? That's all I could handle before I couldn't watch anymore." The words rush out of my mouth.

"Wow. I'm so glad I missed *that* happy joy-joy moment. Where is the happy camper, anyway?" Jen asks.

"Umm, you probably don't want to know. But I'll tell you anyway. Miller is in there, trying to pay for her new jewel. I think his nickname for her is about to fit the moment," I laugh.

"Oh boy," she says. *No kidding.* Ava is strong-minded and extremely stubborn. If he manages to pay for this, I'll be shocked. I pray that it doesn't take too long before we can eat. I'm starving, but those two seem to be like two bulls, and I know their heads are butting at this very moment.

"Let's climb in the cab and get ready so we can roll out the moment they decide to give it up and one of them gives in," Layne says. So we all climb in and it takes a good 15 minutes before we see an irritated Ava and one happy-go-lucky Miller walking out of the parlor.

Miller gets in the front of the cab and Ava climbs into the back. "I'm thinking 'Killer' is a great nickname for her at this moment," Miller beams back at Ava. She just shakes her head at him.

"Really Ava, it was nothing but pocket change. Let it go, sweets." He gives her a serious look.

"Who's up for some garlic fries and fish?" Layne tries to change the subject.

"Fish? I sure hope there are other choices," I say.

"Are you allergic?" Jason voices his concern.

"Yes, yes I am." I try to play it like I really am. I hate fish, and I really hope that Layne won't try to get me to eat any.

"Sunshine, I can read that lie all over your face," he laughs. "You're not fooling anyone. But don't worry—I won't make you eat any fish, if that's what you're worried about."

I let out a sigh of relief, which he catches right away, but smiles at me anyway, before he pats my knee and puts the truck into reverse, leaving the parking lot. We drive a minute or two down the street and then pull into another parking lot. Layne wasn't joking when he said this place was really close by.

Walking into the restaurant, I notice right away how tiny and cramped it feels on the inside. We arrived at the right time, as there are a couple of empty places and we snatch them up right away. After looking at the menu, I settle on teriyaki chicken, rice, and garlic fries. If the group thinks my food choice is gross, no one comments. Jason has his head in the sand where Jen is concerned at the moment, and Miller is too busy trying to woo back his Killer. That leaves Layne, whose busy jotting our orders down so he can place them at the counter.

After our orders are placed, Layne decides to play the get to know you game.

"Alright, Hollie, I believe you owe me a story. It's time to fess up about the real you." Layne looks at me pointedly.

I let out a nervous semi–laugh as my face flushes a bit. I'm truly embarrassed, and I don't want to spill it to the whole table, though it seems I have no choice. "I'm sorry. It was really stupid and childish of me." I apologize. "Though, you know why I did it."

"Yes, that part is true," he says. "And it's a good thing you've got your looks going for you," he teases me with a grin. "All right, so you're not really a farmer's daughter, as hot as that sounded, and you're not homeschooled, or being reared to help raise a basketball team. So, who is Hollie Reed?"

"Okay, at the risk of sounding repetitive," I begin, "there really isn't much to tell. The truth is, my parents own a pharmacy back home in Oregon. I'm the only child. I'm 18 years old. We really did come to Hawaii on a trip with our graduating classmates. I plan to work in the pharmacy and attend a local college in town." I fill him in as I feel like I'm giving an interview on the story of my life. I really don't like to be put on the spot like this. But, I know I kind of owe it to him. So, for him, I'll endure it. Plus, I want him to know the real me.

"I don't have a boyfriend, not that you were really wondering." I duck my head, feeling shy again as those words decided to slip out of my mouth. If I dwell on it, I suppose I don't want him to think that I have someone at home waiting on me while I play a game with him. I want him to know the true me, and to be honest with everything from here on. So, I may as well tell him that I'll be 19 in six months, too. *What can it hurt?* Maybe it will help me a bit. *What do I know?* I'm not one for chasing men, and my dating life thus far has a lot left to be desired.

"I'll be 19 in December, too. That's about it, really." *There. That should do it.*

Layne reaches over, placing his hand to the nape of my neck, pulling me in closer until our noses are touching.

Softly, with sincerity written all over his face, his says, "Thank you, Hollie. I'm sure there is a lot more to you that's just waiting to be discovered, and I can't wait to explore those moments with you." He says as he closes the miniscule distance between us and seals it with a soft kiss on my lips. Both of our eyes remain open as we stare at each other, getting lost. It's one of the most intimate and hottest moments of my life.

He pulls back first, giving me a reassuring smile, and pats my thigh. Then he turns back to the table just as our food arrives, silencing the group as we prepare to dig in. The garlic fries are calling my name, so that's the first place I dive into, emitting a humming noise from me. *It's just that good.*

"Don't overeat. We still have dessert to get. You can't leave this area without a milkshake." Layne informs us. "There's a place called *Kono's* just down the street. We'll stop there to grab shakes for the road before heading back."

Lunch goes over well as everyone calms down. We were able to get back to a relaxed state of mind, just enjoying the food, the company, and being on vacation. Ava was finally no longer miffed at Miller. *Thank heavens.* That could have been a disaster, otherwise.

As promised, Layne took us down to *Kono's* for a milkshake to go as we drove back down the highway to the Waikiki area. And also as promised, Miller booted Jen to the front seat, so he could spend quality time with Ava in the back of the cab, now that she was no longer upset with him.

It's the middle of the afternoon by the time we get back to the hotel, and everyone seems ready for a nap. Weird, I know, since we could have just done that in the truck on our scenic drive back. Then again, who wants to sleep when they are in Hawaii for the first time? Checking out the landscape, talking to friends, and enjoying the company of some seriously good-looking guys were better plans in my book.

The whole group follows us back to our room. No one is in the mood for the beach or more sightseeing, it seems. It's time to veg out for a bit before we head out to dinner with Jude. Speaking of Jude, I guess it's time to find out what's on the menu for dinner.

Ava and Miller claim one bed, as I flop down on the other. Layne comes over to sit next to me, as Jen and Jason take up residence between the two beds, near the foot of each.

"Can you tell us exactly what the plan is for dinner later?" I ask Jen.

"I'm not sure, to be honest. We decided to try the *Hard Rock Café*. It sounded like a fun new place to try out," she replies.

"Are you telling us you've never been to a *Hard Rock Café* before?" Miller asks incredulously. "Please don't tell me you all are living under a rock, in a tiny Podunk town!" he goads Ava.

"Oh come off it, Miller." Ava says, as she lightly pushes him.

"Not everyone has the chance to live it up like you, Mr. Military Man. Just because we haven't been to a place like that before doesn't mean we've never heard of it."

"You know what I like about you, Killer?" Miller says with a grin. "The easy rise I get out of you. It makes it all the more fun to tease you. Now," he continues, "it's a shame you weren't born with red hair like your friend over here," he says as he points in my direction. "Who knows what kind of spitfire you could have been." He laughs as she attempts to shove him off the bed.

"Aren't you the clown of the group," she huffs.

"Well, that sounds like a great plan to me." I say with a bit of excitement. I've always wanted to try this place out, but never been anywhere that had one. "Maybe you should call him and make sure to confirm the time and meeting place. Then we can take a nap or veg out with a movie?" I suggest.

"How about I call and check in with him." Jason offers, making me fall into a fit of laughter.

"Jealous?" Ava taunts him.

"No, I'm just trying to be helpful." He tries to play it off.

"Sorry man, you're not fooling anyone in this room. The BS meter just went sky high." Miller laughs, which makes Jason turn beet red.

"Okay, fine. I don't know anything about this guy, and Jen, she's my girl. I don't want to share. Is that a crime?" he asks the room at large.

"Nope." Layne throws in. "I know how you feel." He directs his comment at Jason, but his eyes are locked on me, causing me to squirm a little.

It looks like it's time to take control of the situation. "I'll call him and get it all worked out." I say as I grab my phone and dial Jude's number.

It's all set after a few moments of speaking with Jude. We'll meet him and his buddies in the hotel lobby in a couple of hours. I did let him in on the fact that we have friends who will be with us. He seemed cool with it, so I'm not sure what the big deal is. If Jen says that she's not into him, and he wasn't upset that she wasn't going alone, *and* he has his friends tagging along also, then are we all just a bunch of idiots? *I don't know.* It really did seem like they were into each other.

Maybe we were just hoping for something that wasn't really there, and we played it up in our imaginations. Lesson learned? *Possibly.*

"All set. We'll meet him and his friends in the lobby." I throw a look at Jason, as I continue on. "We'll meet up around five and walk over as a big group, totally not drawing attention to ourselves at all like a gang of tourists," I joke. "Now, let's see about ordering a movie. I'm beat, and I just want to lay here and think about nothing."

Jen decides to take the reins on this one and orders some cheesy romantic comedy. At this point, no one really cares. We're all tired. I set an alarm on my phone, just in case some or all of us end up falling asleep. Grabbing my pillow, I fluff it up against the headboard and lean back. I'm not even there one minute before Layne has his arm around me, and my head rests comfortably against his shoulder. I snuggle close to him as I prepare to watch the movie. I don't even get 15 minutes into it before its lights out for me.

As it would turn out, pretty much everyone dozes off, and thankfully I saved the group with my alarm. Otherwise, no one would have woken up in time for dinner.

After everyone's awake, we head to the lobby and meet up with Jude and his crew, which consist of a few of his good friends from school. We make nice pleasantries and introduce our new friends, then head over to a public transit bus to catch a lift to the restaurant.

It's nice outside at this time of evening; however no one is in the mood to walk tonight. "I think I've had more exercise on this trip than I've done all year. Thank heaven we're taking the bus. I'm definitely in a lazy mood," I comment on our choice of transportation.

"From where I'm standing, you look pretty good to me." Layne gives me a wink. He seems to be doing a lot of that lately.

"Is that so, soldier? And what do you see that you like?" *Okay, that was beyond crossing the boundaries.* "Wait, hold up. Never mind." I nervously check out the eavesdroppers who are staring at me like I've grown a second head. Yes, I just realized who's standing in our group, and it's definitely a shocking thing for me to say, as evident by the looks of my school friends.

"Can we start over? Or take a walk, maybe?" I ask hopefully, trying to laugh it off. This is exhausting, trying to be a new me, but not cross any boundaries that would make someone think twice about my actions or the things I've said.

"Sunshine, I don't care what anyone else thinks. Your opinion is the only thing that matters to me right now." He grabs my hand and pulls me a little ways away from the group. "*You know,*" he whispers in my ear. "You looked pretty hot in your shorts today. Now, you have two choices," he eyes me with great intent. "I can kiss you now, or when we're sitting on the bus. But I don't think I can stand here much longer without kissing those sweet lips of yours. You're too cute for your own good, and sweetheart, it's distracting me."

"I'm in such deep trouble—"

Oh no. I realize that I just said that out loud.

"One of us is in serious danger, but I don't know which one will walk away with their heart still intact," he says. "Now, which is it, sunshine? The bus or right here?"

"Here." I barely manage to get out. It's the first and last thing I want to do. I want to kiss him so badly, but I don't want to do it in front of people I know from home, and who all happen to know my parents. But it's too late. I made my decision, and it's time to deliver the goods.

His lips are on mine in a flash, and they feel so good. He wraps his arms around me, pulling me into him as he deepens the kiss. This isn't a sweet, chaste kiss, or soft in any way. This is definitely an all-out emotional punch of kiss. A little bit of time passes, and I realize that I've grabbed on to the front of his shirt, holding on for dear life. I reluctantly end the kiss, resting my forehead against his lips before looking up at him. "*Wow,*" is all I can think to say in this charged moment.

Gazing down at me, he quirks his eyebrow. "Planning on letting go, Bruiser? Or are you permanently attaching yourself to me for good?" he playfully smiles. Feeling embarrassed and emboldened at the same time, I slip my arms around his waist and lay my head on his chest.

"And if I decide to never let go? What would you do then, soldier?"

"Hold you right back just as tight." He says seriously as he places a kiss on my forehead.

"Hate to break it up, lovers, but the bus is here." We hear Miller calling out to us amongst some whistles and hoots from the peanut gallery.

Rolling my eyes, I look at Layne with a big goofy grin on my face. He slides his hands down my arms to my hands, then brings them both to his lips as he places a sweet kiss there before grabbing a hold of one. "If you're lucky, we'll pick up right where we left off later." He says with a twinkle in his eye.

"We'll see." I singsong back at him.

"You bet your cute tush we will," he says confidently. "Now march, woman, or you'll owe me ten push-ups!"

"Tush? Really?" I laugh.

"What? I can't say tush? Am I supposed to be too manly for that word?"

"Oh come on, soldier!" I say through my laughter. "You can't tell me that you really walk around base talking like that."

"I hear enough language from the guys on a regular basis. I see no need for other words. What would make you stop laughing at me?" he asks through his own laughter now.

"Tush is just fine by me." I say through a big, teasing grin.

"Besides," he continues on. "I wasn't raised to speak otherwise, nor would I in the presence of women and children. Even if that weren't the case, I still wouldn't call you a donkey," he teases me. "And another fact, I know plenty of military men, who are non-religious, and don't swear. Don't get me wrong, there are plenty of foul-mouthed men in the military, I just prefer to choose smarter or more intelligent words." He says, concluding his feelings on the whole *tush* statement.

"Feel better about justifying it, do you?" I tease him some more.

"I'll never live this down now, will I?" he laughs.

"Nope!" I say a bit gleefully.

"All right, you. March, or you'll owe me ten push-ups, and not the girl kind either! I can be a mean Drill Sergeant." he warns me.

"After hearing you say *tush,* it makes me disbelieve that you can even be a mean Drill Sergeant," I continue to taunt him.

"Woman." He slightly growls.

"Did you just growl?" I crack up.

Layne just gives me a look.

"Sir, yes sir." I salute him on a giggle.

"Don't tease me woman," he warns, as he pulls me towards the bus. "Or we will never make it to dinner."

"I think you are secretly trying to give me mono." I joke as I let him lead me to the bus where our friends are just starting to step aboard.

I hear him chuckle behind me as we catch up to the rest of the gang.

Layne rests his arm behind my chair while we're all sitting around the table chatting and enjoying dinner. Everyone keeps an eye on Jen and Jude, as well as Jason, to see how this all plays out. It's still a mystery why he would even bother to make this bet and then make sure that Jen follows through with it.

"Okay, I'm beyond curious as to why this bet took place and how you lost?" Jason says as he turns to look at Jen.

"Honestly, I don't know how I lost. I'm usually the best guesser out of anyone I know. And I know Hollie pretty well. I was surprised that Jude would take the cake on this one." She pouts a little.

"What was the bet about, anyway?" Layne asks the table at large, not knowing what's going on here. But there is no way that any of us want to say that we think Jude has a major crush on Jen.

"Well, we were in the ocean, and Hollie was sitting up on the beach, people watching. We were betting about how long it would take before she decided that we were more fun than watching random people." Ava fills Layne and Miller in.

"Jude guessed how long it would take her before she finally gave in, is basically what happened. But—" Jen looks at Jude with a confused look. "That's not like you to bet at all." She says to him.

"You're right. It's not normally like me." He replies a bit sheepishly.

"What possessed you to bet in the first place, and especially to challenge Jen who no one ever dares to go up against?" I ask.

"Easily explained," says Eric, one of Jude's friends who was also in the water with us. "We all know that Jude is a good, quiet, reserved guy. He's popular, sure, but he doesn't go out of his way to be. Now, he has plenty of dating opportunities, but I bet what you didn't know is that he never asks anyone out. You see, he's a big chicken when it comes to that." He shares with us.

"And I'll be the first to state it, since I doubt anyone else will."

Raising his eyebrows, Eric is daring someone to speak up, but when no one does, he continues on. "We've all wondered for the last year about Jude and Jenifer." He continues to eye everyone around the table from our home town, before sharing the rest of his thoughts. "We all believed that Jude had a secret thing for Jenifer."

This revelation causes an uncomfortable moment of silence at the table, as all eyes turn to Jen, Jude, and then finally Jason, to see what his reaction will be. However, Jen is too busy looking embarrassed and downright uncomfortable to do much else.

"I thought you said that there was nothing between you two?" Jason asks Jen in a state of confusion. "What's going on here? Is this all a joke? What about the time we've been spending together this week," he rushes out, sounding upset. He looks over to Ava and I, as if we can shed some light on his questions. We both shake our heads, and I throw my hands up, basically saying *don't ask me,* as Ava shrugs her shoulders.

"I can explain," Jen finally says. "I like Jude, sure, but as a friend. He's a great guy, and really smart. We would get along well as a pair of good friends. We have a lot in common, yes, but I don't see Jude in any other way, except friends." She tries to reassure Jason before turning her gaze on Jude, giving him an apologetic look. "No -hurt feelings?" she asks.

"Well, why did you insist on going out with her then?" Jason asks Jude.

Before answering, it's Jude's turn to give Jen an apologetic look. "Sorry Jenifer. I did it because I was trying to be someone different while I was here in Hawaii. I was still being me, but I wanted to let loose a little. Does that make sense?" he furrows his brows.

"Boy, does it ever." I quietly state, gaining his attention. "Do you like her, then?" I want to know.

"I do like her, as a friend, just as she said about me. Sure she's pretty, sweet, and responsible, but we're in the friends zone, for sure," he smiles. "No offense." He says, trying to do some damage control.

"None taken," she reassures him. "So, why did you go up against the all-time betting champ?" Jen grins, as she does her best to lighten the mood.

"Well, and please don't be mad, but I was dared to by the guys. They didn't think I could ask a girl out and if I did, they didn't believe

I would follow through with the date. It just happened to work out nicely," he says. "You see, the idea was already formed when the bet had presented itself, which turned out to be a good way to put my plan into action. I wasn't even sure it would pan out. I just got lucky, is all. I really do think you're awesome to hang out with, as are your friends. I didn't see any harm in keeping the dinner date, and it would prove to the guys I *could* get a date on my own and keep it." He smiles proudly at the guys.

"I just didn't count on you finding a guy while we were here," he frowns. "I did almost cancel," he admits. "The last thing I wanted to do was cause any issues. No harm meant, man." He tells Jason sincerely.

"So, this was all about a bet that you couldn't get a chick on your own?" Miller chimes in, causing Ava to elbow him in the side. He gives her the *what did I say?* look.

"Okay, I get it now. I may not like it, but I understand it. Thanks for clearing it up." Jason replies, wrapping an arm protectively around Jen's shoulders.

"Awesome!" Ava exclaims with a clap. "So, no secret lovers' quarrel going on here." She beams at us. "Who's up for dessert?"

Leave it Ava to change the subject and lighten the mood.

After dinner wraps up, Jude apologizes again and takes off with his friends for the rest of the night. The rest of us decide to walk off the big meal we just ate, and I can't quite wrap my head around the cost.

"I still can't believe how expensive dinner was tonight." I complain to Layne, as we walk towards the beach. "In fact, I can't believe how expensive it is every time we eat, come to think of it."

"Hollie, you have to realize the many factors that go into the cost of food around here, amongst other things." Layne begins. "For one, there's the cost of shipping to get the food here from the mainland. Then there is the sales tax, just like you have in the rest of the states. Don't forget that you also have to think about the cost of land and rent for the owners, as well as the fact that, for instance, grocers have to carry a bigger inventory since everything takes time to be shipped over. That, my dear, is why things are more expensive here on the islands."

"Okay, I get it. But still, I feel like it's highway robbery." I pout.

"Holls, no matter where you go in life, it will always feel like someone's robbing you blind. It's just part of life, and you're used to not having sales tax in your small neck of the woods. Life isn't the same everywhere you go." He gently reminds me.

"I know. It's just surprising, I guess. I thought I was prepared, but it's definitely been an eye opener out here. It helps to further confirm my decision to stick around Holly Grove."

"You may change your mind one day, so promise me you'll keep your options open." He says, slightly more seriously.

"I'll think about it. Is that good enough?"

"Let's move on and talk about other things, more important things. For instance, where we left off before the bus appeared earlier." He smoothly throws me out of my funk and into a butterfly-inducing frenzy.

"You've been dying all night to get back to that subject, haven't you?" I teasingly ask.

"Don't pretend that kiss didn't affect you as much as it did me." He tells me this smugly, because of course it was something that I hadn't forgotten.

"Is that all you think I'm good for? Hand holding, cuddling and kissing? Maybe I should put a sign on my forehead." I joke as I try to push against his chest. Of course, he's like a dang rock that never moves.

"Yep! That about sums it up, pretty girl." He teases me. "I have an idea. First, I want one more kiss. Then you can hop on my back and I'll carry you the rest of the way home."

Before either of us responds, I decide to brave it as I step in towards him and reach up to kiss him. When slowly pulling away, I tell him, "Thank you for the wonderful day we had. I had a lot of fun, and I forgot to tell you how much it meant to me. So, thank you." I smile up at him.

"Anything for my sunshine," he vows. Then picks me up and carries me back to the hotel. Though we did make a stop by the beach as we chased each other for a bit, playing a silly, childish game of tag before Layne and Miller drop us back off at our hotel. They leave around midnight with kisses and promises of their return the next morning.

I fall into bed that night, exhausted from the day's events, and pass out with a smile on my face and thoughts of Layne dancing in my head.

Chapter Six

Day 5

I WAKE UP around eight in the morning, to this really irritating song that used to be on my favorites list on my iPod. Now, I'm not sure that I can listen to it any longer.

"What did I say about the TV, woman?" I groggily ask Ava and Jen. "I can't believe—no wait, I *can* believe that this song is on, yet again!" I huff.

"I'm starting to find it funny. We should have made this into a game. Dang it! We could have had fun with the lover boys over this. We should have been checking every time we were in the room if it was on. We could have made a wager with the guys to see who had the most documented viewings. I bet we could have finagled something out of them. Darn it. That would have been fun," Ava ends her diatribe a bit gloomily.

"Umm, I hate to burst your bubble but I probably would have broken the TV if we had played such a stupid game," Jen laughs.

"Fine, be a spoil–sport," Ava huffs. "I'm jumping in the shower first before we have an infiltration of testosterone in our room and I can't breathe," she says as she makes her way toward the bathroom, waving her hand back and forth past her plugged nose.

"We didn't make any plans for today," I remind Jen as I start to get ready.

"What should we do? We already know it's a given that three particular men will be showing up soon. Should we make the plans this time? If so, I vote we try snorkeling," I suggest.

"Oh, that sounds like fun. Okay, I'm in." Jen agrees as she goes to pound on the bathroom door. "Yo, Ava!" she shouts at the closed door. "What do you say to the idea of snorkeling?"

"Done!" she shouts back.

"Good, because you were already out–numbered," she laughs. "We just wanted to let you feel like you had a say, when really, you didn't." She laughs again, and then walks over to her purse, to search its contents for her phone.

"I'm going to text Jason and let him know. Why don't you let the uniforms know, too?"

"Oh, check you out! Uniforms, huh? I like that. Clever." I wink at her before finding my own phone to text Layne.

Hollie: Rise and shine, soldier-boy. If you're not up in 10, you owe ME push-ups, and you have to do them the girly way . . . out on the beach for all to see.

I toss the phone back on the bed, smiling to myself.

"What's the look for? Did you talk to the soldiers?" Jen asks, just as we hear the shower turn off.

"No, I sent him a text telling him he had ten minutes to get up here or he owed me girly push–ups out on the beach in front of everyone," I laugh.

"Nice."

"I thought so."

At that moment, my phone alerts me to an incoming text message. I snatch the phone up from the bed and see that it's from Layne.

Hubby: Sunshine, who's the man in this relationship? I give the orders.

Hollie: Someone thinks he's a funny one.

Hubby: We BOTH know who's in control here.

Hollie: Or did someone wake up on the wrong side of the beach this morning?

Hubby: Nope. We've been up since the sun rose. What about you, lazy bones? I bet you just woke up.

Hollie: Wouldn't you like to know? Anyway—grouchy, we decided the group will be snorkeling today, so get your cute rear in gear and get up here already.

Hubby: I would actually.

Hubby: Like to know, that is.

Hubby: And Hollie, you don't have to beg to see me.

Hollie: A big ego will only serve to further inflate that head of yours before it carries you off into the sunset.

Hubby: Who's the comedian of this relationship today?

Hollie: You know it and don't forget it, mister!

Hubby: Lucky for you, I'm impatient to see your gorgeous face this morning.

Hollie: Flattery won't get you everywhere, either.

Hubby: Would you stop messing around so I can put the truck in drive, woman?

Hollie: Sir, yes sir.

Hubby: Music to my ears. Well, in this case, to my eyes. See you soon, sleepy beauty.

Hollie: What now? You're my white knight riding in on your stallion? Ha. Ha.

Hubby: Now she catches on. Quit HORSING around. Go get your cute self in a bathing suit and I'll be there within the hour.

Hollie: Bossy.

Hubby: Quit talking back.

"Are you ever going to talk about the ring that you're sporting on the finger that's reserved for married people?" Jen tosses at me from out of left field. I wasn't expecting her to say anything about it. I really thought she would let it go.

"Now remember, I'm living by Layne's rules while we're here. He asked me to pretend to be his wife this week. I know it might seem strange, but I'm going along with it. And besides, who is it really hurting that we're having a little bit of dumb fun?" I ask her.

"*You*," she eyes me seriously. "But," she heads me off from any rebuttal, "you're right. We did talk about it last night. I'm just trying to be a good friend. I don't want to see you fall hard if it doesn't pan out. You know how I am. I like to think things through. Ava goes by the seat of her pants, and you are the cautious one, living in safety mode. So," she holds her hand up again to warn me off as I open my mouth," this is me shutting up and backing off."

"I understand your views, and I appreciate them. Thank you for being an awesome best friend and having my back." I say as I walk over and give her a hug before letting us both get back to dressing for the day.

An hour later we're decked out in our swim-suits, waiting for Layne in the lobby with Jason and his friends, when we see Jude walk by. He gives us a small smile and a wave as he walks past us, towards the elevators. Apparently there are no hard feelings or love lost between Jude and us. Thankfully, it seems that we won't have to endure any awkward moments of silence around him in the near future.

"Sunshine, I see you follow orders well. You might make a good soldier in the future." I hear in my ear, right before two arms circle around my waist. Layne pulls me back against him for a crushing hug before releasing me, planting a kiss on the side of my head.

"That's what you think." I laugh at him.

"So far, it's what I *know*. You are down here, in a suit, like I told you. Are you not?" he asks with a cocky grin. "And waiting for me?"

I elbow him in the ribs, as he hasn't completely let me go and his arms are still lightly encasing me in his body.

"I see someone still thinks he's the funny one."

"You know it, sweetheart. Why fight it?" he chuckles.

Resting my head against his chest, I ask, "Where's the best place to go snorkeling?"

"Someone is the worse planner in this relationship," Layne teases me.

"Hey! I only came up with the brilliant suggestion. I didn't realize I had to actually plan it, too. I figured you would know where to go, once you got here." I playfully smile up at him.

"See?" he says over my head to the Miller. "Didn't I say she was a lazy bag of bones earlier?"

"Point proven." Miller gives me a lopsided grin before placing an arm around Ava's shoulders. "What about you, Killer? Are you a planner?"

"Seriously?" is all she says, making Jen and me laugh.

"Who's not the bright one in the group this morning?" I tease Miller.

"Hey, one can hope, right?" he says. "And besides, no question is ever a stupid question. You remember that, Bruiser." He playfully wags a finger at me.

"Well? Any bright ideas, soldier?" I look to Layne. "Aren't you always supposed to be prepared?" I tease him.

"Of course." he says. "And it just so happens that I know the best place to go. Grab your stuff, sunshine. We have a little bit of walking to do."

"Is this some kind of payback? You do realize no one will want to walk back here afterwards, right?"

"Bag of bones," is his only reply. But he did say it with a small hint of a smile.

"Don't worry, Bruiser. We'll catch the bus on the way back," Miller throws in.

"There. It's all settled. Now, can we get a move on? Or are we going to sit here all day and watch the flirt-fest happening between the love birds?" Ava says as she places her hand on Miller's arm, which is currently hanging over her shoulder.

"I'm with Ava. I'm ready to get out and do something new and exciting." Jen adds to the conversation.

"How far is this place?" Jason asks the guys.

"Not that far. It's about a 15–minute walk. It's near *Diamond*

Head." Layne answers Jason as he laces our fingers together, before leading me toward the hotel's main entrance.

Once outside, he starts walking toward the parking garage, which only confuses me.

"Why are we headed to the truck? Did you forget something?" I ask.

"I was only kidding earlier, sunshine. We're actually going further out, to a place called *Hanauma Bay.*" He grins, as if he thinks he's pulled one over on me. "It's really pretty, and is a great place for snorkeling. The beach is this amazing white sand, and you can sunbathe, too. You know, just the perfect place to be when you're a lazy loafer." He pokes fun of me on a wink.

I let the 'lazy' comment go and ask about something else that I find more important at the moment. "Are you forgetting that all of us can't fit in one truck?"

"Nope. That's why Miller brought his truck. We'll split up into two groups. Now who's glad that I'm the thinker and planner in this relationship?" There's that smug grin again.

"Whenever you two decide to stop your love sick ways, we would like to head out." Ava fake gags at us.

"Don't be jealous, Killer. There's plenty of that to go around. All you have to do is ask." Miller gives her his best charming smile before gently pulling Ava along to his truck, followed closely by Chase and Evan. Leaving Jason and Jen to ride with us in Layne's truck.

Off we go, towards a new adventure.

I can't wait to try something new and hope for a memorable day to come my way.

"We're lucky we didn't head out too late. This used to be a beach park, but now it's considered a natural preserve. They only allow 3,000 visitors a day. Once this parking lot is full, everyone else is turned away. Or so they're supposed to be. You could always get around that by riding your bike out here." Layne educates us as he pulls into the lot and stops at a toll hut. There's a one–dollar fee that allows us to occupy our space all day, if we wanted to.

After driving around for a few moments, Layne finds us a spot. He pulls the truck into the parking space, puts it in park, and then shuts off the engine.

After getting out of the truck, we find ourselves over by a ledge, overlooking a beautiful, amazing body of water, accompanied with white sand. The lot just happens to be located on a ridge that's above the bay. From up here you can actually see where the coral reef begins out in the ocean—it's that clear from where we are standing. And it's also then that I notice *Hanauma Bay* is shaped like a 'U.'

"Wow. What a gorgeous sight." Jen comments, as she and Jason walk over towards us, holding hands.

"Well, thanks for picking this spot. The view is amazing. I'm excited to try snorkeling." I say, with heartfelt affection.

"This place has really awesome fish, and I hear that they are also some of the tamest around the islands," Jason surprises us. "I actually researched this place before we left home." He explains, slightly embarrassed.

"Nice. It's best to know where you're headed and want to do before you go," Layne says, pointedly at me, "on vacation. Right, sweetheart?" he asks me as he pokes me in the ribs with his elbow.

"Moving on," I grumble.

"I think you picked a great spot, then." Ava says, as she and Miller emerge into our view. "It looks amazing."

"This bay definitely has a high population of fish to see. It should be a lot of fun today. I'm glad you ladies came up with this plan," Miller chimes in. "One of your better choices. I'll take this over your shopping sprees any day." He says, shaking his head. "I know Layne and Jason can relate."

"Anyway," Evan throws himself into the conversation, forcing me to remember that the lover boys were with us as well. "Tell us more about this place." *How did I miss that? Oh, right. Layne,* I think as I smile to myself.

Chuckling, Layne takes a-hold of my hand and glides me along the path towards the equipment rental place, I'm assuming. What I didn't realize was how steep this path was going to be.

"*Hanauma Bay* is actually a dormant volcano crater." Layne continues to share with the group, who are all here now. "It's one of three *Koko Head* craters. The volcano actually collapsed on one side, crashed into the ocean, and flood itself, forming the bay you see now."

"I read that the bay is protected from some of the biggest ocean swells, making it one of the calmest places to go snorkeling," Jason adds.

"You're right. It is calm a good portion of the time. So, getting here early is a big deal as it's a popular place for tourists. A lot of people like to bring their children here, as well as beginning snorkelers, like all of you," Miller says.

Picking up the conversation, Layne tells us, "The water off of the shoreline is also pretty shallow, making it easy to wade out into the ocean gradually."

I'm trying to keep up as I walk down this steep incline, focusing on not falling on my face. I feel like my feet should take off at a full run, but if I did, I don't think my body would remain upright.

"What are you trying to do to me?" I ask Layne, breathing heavily.

"What are you talking about, sunshine?" he asks sheepishly.

"You totally knew we would have to go down this steep hill and then climb it again later, after we're all worn out. You do remember we're not some of your soldiers, right?" I say as I try to keep myself from being a runaway tourist.

"Here's the thing, she wasn't really big into P.E. in high school, either." Ava informs the group. "Hollie did the bare minimum, and even tried to get out of the mile- run every year." She continues to throw me under the bus.

"Thanks for that. Now I really do look like a lazy bum." I frown over at her.

"You're welcome!" Ava gives me her best innocent face. *Right, like I'll buy that act.*

"Don't worry—I'm sure there's some other gem about you that I can share with Miller, at some point today," I forewarn her.

"Well," Miller changes the subject, "before we can get our gear, we need to stop by the *Marine Education Center* first."

"Why is that?" Jen asks.

"The goal is for all visitors to treat *Hanauma Bay* as a living museum. There's a short video that all visitors must watch first about how to protect the bay," Layne explains. "After that, we can rent our gear, shower, and head out into the ocean."

"Sounds good to me," I say.

"Didn't you two just give us the educational lecture?" Evan points out.

"I'm thinking we could probably skip the real version," Chase comments.

"You could, but then you would have to promise to come back to visit in the next 365 days. Any plans of that, in your near futures?" Layne asks them, as they shake their heads no.

"Bummer for us." Ava throws in.

"Looks like we're all headed toward the *Center*, then," says Layne while we walk hand in hand down the hill.

"Just don't let me land head first onto this road." I plead with Layne, causing him to laugh at my clumsiness.

"You'll be fine, as long as you don't let go of my hand," he assures me.

Miller leads us down to the *Center* where we watch the video, and then rent our gear. After we're all ready for the ocean, Layne snaps a selfie of us, on his phone, tosses it back into his day -pack, and then heads out into the ocean.

My next big step in living life to the fullest is about to begin.

The reef wasn't too rough, so we didn't need to bother with wearing water shoes, and the fish were pretty dang cool. We were able to check out a lot of the crevices and caves once we passed the coral reef area.

And lucky for all of us, Chase had brought an underwater camera along that we all took turns using. I'm sure there will be a lot of silly photos of us, and of the living creatures, which seemed pretty oblivious to the humans swimming around them and their homes.

Gratefully, this place featured a concession stand where we were able to purchase lunch. And luckily for all of us, not just me, we caught a tram back up to the parking lot, where we ate our food in a grassy picnic area. The view was still as impressive as ever, overlooking the ridge, but I was ready to fall into a coma- like sleep after all the exercise and excitement was over.

All in all, I would say this was one of the best days of the trip so far, other than the day I met Layne.

It was still mid-day when we finally made it back to the hotel. Layne and Miller tell us they have some stuff to do today, but will meet us back here for dinner later on.

Layne kisses me soundly on the lips before they part, leaving me staring after them.

"Why the long face?" Jen questions. "They'll be back in awhile. Let's go upstairs and get ready for the evening."

"I vote for a nap," Ava states.

"I'm with you." Chase says, and Evan agrees.

I must be losing it, or am spending too much time in La La land over Layne, because I keep forgetting about Jason's friends.

"Sounds like a good plan. We'll meet you around seven for dinner?" Jen asks Jason.

"See you then, dollface." he kisses her on the forehead leaving us gawking in his wake.

"Dollface, huh?" I bump her with my hip, turning my frown into a small smile. "*Hmm,* I like that."

"All right, Bruiser," she hip checks me back. "Time to freshen up, and take a nap. By the way," she eyes me, "I think that's a great nickname for you. I'm pretty sure we'll both have bruises on us by tomorrow if you keep hip checking me like this."

"And that's not a joke," Ava affirms.

They're right, I do bruise easily, and being somewhat of a klutz at times, I'm sure I'll see a few marks on me by the time I go to sleep tonight.

Layne and Miller came back around six that evening and crashed on the beds while we did our hair and makeup. We had all slept, showered, and changed earlier, and only needed to do some last-minute preparation by the time they showed up in fresh clothes.

Now it's dinnertime. No one really wants to spend a lot of money, so Jason suggests we find a local *Deney's.* Now, *Deney's* and I are not the best of friends. Every time I eat their *Moons Over My Hammy* sandwich, I get really sick. I need to stick to something that will sit better in my stomach this evening. The last thing I want to be is sick, especially when this is one of our last nights here in Hawaii, and with Layne.

Our group gathers in the hotel lobby and decides to walk there, as it's a nice night and the weather is still seasonably warm. The restaurant is roughly about five blocks away, and it doesn't take us long to get there or to be seated.

We're able to order our meals pretty quickly, despite the size of our group, and before long we are sitting back and just enjoying the company of the new-found friendships we've formed.

"I'm going to miss this," Jen says, waving her hand around at the group. "Our time here has been a blast, and we've met really good people, as well as some special ones." She says the last part as she gazes at Jason, a tiny smile on her face.

Our food arrives a short time later—thankfully, as we're all starving by this point. Half-way through the meal, I decide to call it quits. I'm afraid that it will mess with me later, so I throw in the towel and call it a tie. While everyone else is still eating, I lean back in my chair, slouch down a bit, and rest my head on the back of the headrest.

As I'm looking up at the ceiling, the others are eating and chatting—obliviously, I might add, as was I until this very moment—I start to gag and jump out of my chair. I'm beyond disgusted with myself at this point.

"Sunshine?" Layne calls out to me.

"What's up, Bruiser?" Miller asks.

"Oh, she's probably sick. The food here usually does that to her," Jen chimes in.

"Do you want me to run down to the *ABC Store* for Pepto?" Ava chimes in with an innocent enough offer, and a voice full of concern. If I wasn't feeling sick to my stomach over something else, I probably would have died right there on the spot from embarrassment.

"Ugh," I manage to choke out. "I'm so grossed out right now. I don't even know what to say."

"Oh come on, it's not that bad!" says Ava.

"No, it's not even the food." I tell her, as my body involuntarily shudders. Then I point up to the ceiling. All eyes move upward to where I'm pointing as I hear a round of their own disgusted noises.

"What the–?" Chase asks.

"Are those *cockroaches?*" A disbelieving Evan asks the whole group.

Finally, someone states what I had really hoped wasn't true.

"Whoa! That is so nasty, and there are a lot of those suckers too!" Ava exclaims.

"Everyone, check your food." Jen says in a disgusted tone. "And whatever you do, don't finish what you have left." She points out unhelpfully.

"Jen, I'm sure that's an obvious *duh* statement," says Ava.

"I'm getting the manager. We have a violation of the health code here, people." Jenifer says, becoming increasingly more outraged. Meanwhile, the rest of us collect our belongings, trying not to throw up what we just ate. *Though, that might be the best resolution for this horrific situation.*

"I'll see about getting our food compensated," Jason adds.

"Ladies, why don't you all go outside and wait with Evan and Chase." Layne gently prods me towards the entrance. "We'll clear up the bill and be out shortly. No need for us to draw more attention to ourselves."

He has a good point, so we go outside where there's a nice cool breeze and no threat of cockroaches hanging above our heads. Just thinking about it again makes me want to down some bleach. I'm sure we didn't really eat anything gross, but just the thought of what we saw won't go away, especially knowing how close we were to those pests. The knowledge sends more shivers down my spine.

Moments later, the men spill out of the entrance onto the sidewalk. Layne walks over to me, wrapping his arms around me.

"Everything's taken care of," he tells the group.

"What did you do?" I seriously want to know.

"Nothing you need to worry about. Just know that it's been handled, and that's that."

"What if I really want to know?" I ask him.

"Well, you'll have to ask me on our first anniversary, then." He says on a laugh. Though, somehow, I don't think he's really joking. I'm not even remotely prepared to go there, so I let it slide.

"Fine. I'll let you boys maintain your secret circle on this one." I decide it's best to pick my battles, and this is a pointless one to try to win. "What's our next line of strategy?"

"Are you trying to pull out a military term on us?" Miller laughs. "I don't think any of us has gotten past the food portion of the night."

"In-case it has slipped your mind; we unfortunately have only one day left after tonight." Jason pipes up with this dreaded information.

"I have an idea," Ava waves her hand in the air. I feel like we're in class and she's saying 'pick me, I have the answer!'

"Why don't we camp out on the beach tonight?" she continues.

"Perfect. Now Layne and I will have some company," Miller says cheerfully.

"I hope you have something to keep you warm, sunshine." Layne lightly squeezes my arm.

"It's not terribly late. We could swing by a store somewhere, I'm sure?" Jen asks hesitantly.

"Sorry to break it to you, Jenifer, but we're guys. We're not prized shoppers like Killer, over here." Layne gently bumps Ava with this foot. "I know where the convenience store is and the *Market Place.*"

"Where do you buy your clothes?" I question him.

"We have our uniforms and whatever other clothes we've managed to pick up along the way, but really, we're always either in the ocean, on duty or working out. There isn't usually a need to spice it up. Well, not until you pretty ladies came along." He glances over at Jason and his two friends. "No offense."

"None taken," Jason assures him.

"I think it's safe to say that we're all on the same page," Chase confirms as Evan nods his head.

"Well, there you have it, Bruiser." Miller shrugs his shoulders at me. "I'm clueless as to where to go, though."

"I'm sure we have something that will work in our bags. Let's go back up to the hotel room and scrounge through our stuff. I also want to make it over to the *ABC Store* for snacks. I need a replacement meal for that terrible dinner." Jen says, shuddering.

"I figured it out." I tell Layne, very proud of myself, I might add. I don't know why, but I am.

"And what's that, sweetheart?" he asks curiously.

We're all bundled up, out on the beach, in blankets and sleeping bags that were stashed in Layne and Miller's vehicles.

Earlier in the evening, when we got back from our day of snorkeling, we parted ways for a short time to clean up and rest. Our night out on the beach wasn't originally in our plans, but after the disaster that was dinner at *Deney's,* we had all agreed that it was a good way to end our thoroughly adventurous day.

After everyone changed, we headed to the *ABC Store* for some late night snacks before ending up where we are now, huddled around a campfire. It's a cove of beach slightly off the beaten path, and not noticeable by many, especially local law enforcement.

The guys totally had this planned out, likely hopeful that we would join them here. I can't really blame them, since it is our last night on the island to do something to this extent.

"About that tattoo," I reply coyly.

"And?"

"You don't have one."

"You're right. I don't. Do you know why?"

"No. I know it's not because you hate them. Does it have to do with your job?" I ask, more than a little curious.

"You're right, I don't hate them, and it doesn't have anything to do with the job. For me personally, I don't want to have anything that shows I'm an American when I'm deployed in another country. Really, it's just about my own preference. I know plenty of guys, like Miller, who have plenty hidden under their uniforms, so no one really knows, unless we're surfing or working out or something along those lines."

"I can see how that makes good sense. You don't want to be identifiable while working in case you're compromised, right?"

"Pretty much, sunshine."

"So, do they ever send you to other countries?" I ask. I want to know as much as I can about him when it comes to his job, or as much as he is safely allowed or feels comfortable to share with me.

"I do go away when I'm needed. I can be deployed to other countries, or I can work within our government in different parts of the United States. Really, anywhere they decided that they need me, I have to go."

"Don't you ever get scared?" I know I'm scared just thinking about him going to strange places and what bad things could happen to him there. Not that I have any real right to worry about him after I leave.

Or do I? There could be something real happening between us, but I don't want to jump that hurdle too fast and land on my face in the mud if it's all wishful thinking. *But surely we are on the same page here?* It certainly *feels* like it. I don't think I'm misreading the signals he has given me . *Then again, I'm still young and inexperienced with guys, so do I know for sure what the signals even are?* He has a dangerous job that takes him to different parts of the world, and he could just up and leave at any moment. Even his housing here isn't permanent.

His answer to my question snaps me out of my silent reverie.

"Sure, in the beginning. When I was first deployed and everything was brand-spanking new, I was clueless as to what to expect. Yes, they might try to prepare you, but you don't really know anything until you're actually in the thick of it all. Now, it's not so bad. It's actually pretty exciting to head off to somewhere new, with no real advanced notice at times."

"What's the worst thing you've experienced during one of your missions?" I'm really curious, but also nervous to hear this answer at the same time.

"Hollie, are you sure you really want to know? You might not like the answer," he quietly warns me.

I think about that for a moment, as I'm sure he can read the emotions running all over my face. In the end, I decide that curiosity and living for the now take precedent over any other feelings, and I nod my head for him to proceed.

"Okay. Don't flip out, though."

"I'll try not to." *I'm pretty sure I wasn't very convincing.*

Layne eyes me one last time before sharing with me something I know I can never un-hear.

"I've been shot at, blasted by rockets, mortared, had missiles launched at my plane, and I've been on bases during ground attacks."

Each time he added something new, my eyes grew bigger and bigger.

"Are you serious?" I ask in disbelief.

"Would I lie about something like that?" he says, deathly serious.

"No. It's just, wow—I just don't know what to say. It's all so crazy."

"It *is* crazy. But it's also real life, sweetheart, and it's mine."

"You're right. But I'm glad that you're sharing this part of your job with me. I'm also glad that I didn't know you before you went off to do these things. I would have worried over you, and I don't think I could have handle knowing that my–"

I stop my rolling thoughts, suddenly feeling more than a little embarrassed. Instead of continuing, I close my eyes and count to ten, hoping he will let it go.

"Well, now you know me." He says, causing me to open my eyes and look over at him. "And my last deployment wasn't the last time that these things could happen to me, either." He tilts his head to the side to gaze at me for a moment, as if he is trying to figure something out.

"Why did you stop? What were you going to say?" he asks, curious now.

I duck my head, feeling shy that he wants to pick this part of the conversation back up. I'll look like a fool if I tell him what I'm thinking and he isn't on the same page.

"Umm–So, you see." I begin, stumbling over my words.

"I might see, if someone would let me in," he interjects reaching over and stroking the side of my face. "Why don't you make me see? Or maybe *I* already do, but do *you?*"

I know he's hinting at a deeper meaning here, but I decide to answer his initial line of questions first.

"I was going to say that *if* you were my boyfriend, I don't think I could handle you being away, knowing the dangers that you face. I would be worried if you were coming back to me or not." I'm certain that my cheeks have been stained a deep red color after this admission.

"Sunshine, I don't get nervous about those things. When I'm out in the danger zones, I'm fully aware of what I've signed up for. I accept my own mortality."

He gazes into my eyes, searching for an answer, I assume. *But what is the question? What does he want to know when he looks at me that way?*

"Of course, in the past, I have never had anyone to come back home to, other than my parents and siblings," he tells me.

"Oh no?" I raise my eyebrows. *What's he saying?*

"That's right, sweetheart. You were mine the moment I laid eyes on you."

Shoot. He's good. And that's not at all what I thought he would say.

He leans in toward me and whispers under his breath, as he places a soft kiss on my lips.

"*You always were.*"

Chapter Seven

Day 6

WAKING UP IN the sand the next morning, with the sun on my face and a breeze in the air, is really not a bad way to start the day. Though it is bittersweet to rise and shine, since it's our last full day on Oahu. It's also the last day we will get to spend with Layne and the rest of the guys.

Rolling onto my side, I look over to see if Layne is still sleeping, but I don't find him in his sleeping bag. Slowly, I sit up, and let my eyes scan the beach and then over to my friends. Everyone's still passed out except for Miller—he's missing, too.

From what I've heard, both Layne and Miller are used to being up extremely early, which goes along with the territory of their jobs. I'm assuming that they are both out in the water, taking a swim. My arms form goose bumps just thinking about it. It's too cold to be in the ocean this early in the morning.

Throwing the covers off, I get out of my warm, cozy, but not entirely comfortable bedding, and go off in search of the guys. A few moments later, I see two bodies out in the water.

Everyone else is sleeping, the guys are busy, and it's just me, awake and feeling melancholy. After standing on the shoreline, staring out across the vast body of water, I decide a walk is what I need, to clear my head and improve my mood.

Snuggling further into Layne's oversized hoodie, I start a leisurely pace as I leave a path of my own footprints on the shore. If they need to find me, all they'd have to do is follow the tracks.

I have a lot weighing heavily on my mind, and this time alone is exactly what I need to sort it all out.

First off, I'm fresh out of high school, about to turn 19, and I haven't decided what to do about college yet. Second of all, I need to figure out my hours at the pharmacy and when exactly I'll be starting back there. But right now, the only thing I really want to think about is what in the world is going to happen between Layne and I.

Worst-case scenario, we part ways, having had one of the best times of our lives together. *Well, I guess I can only speak for myself on that score.* Maybe we even part ways and stay in touch as friends. However, the best outcome, and the one I'd really prefer, would be that we part ways and decide to see what happens with a long distance relationship.

That's what I really want. Now, I just have to put on my big girl pants and do what Layne has told me to do since he met me, and that's to basically do whatever I want to do. A relationship with Layne is something that I want. *But why does it feel so scary to admit?*

I continue to walk aimlessly in the sand for a while, thinking about every possible scenario and how they could all play out, when I realize that I should really be thinking about important stuff like school and a job. I've always had a job since high school started, at my parents' pharmacy. I even worked there every summer and have a good savings fund saved up, since there's not a lot to spend my money on in Holly Grove.

My parents are probably excited that I've graduated and that I'm close to turning nineteen, likely thinking I'll be moving out soon. They probably already have plans for my bedroom, too. Maybe Dad will turn that into, well, who knows what. Or Mom will make it a sewing room or a shrine to her books. *Okay, maybe she wouldn't really do that, but still, it could happen.*

I'm so deep into my rambling thoughts that I don't even realize that someone has approached me until I feel my hand being lifted into the crook of a muscular arm.

Slightly alarmed, I look over to my right, and see Layne looking at me with a big, goofy grin on his face.

"Sunshine, I've been calling your name for a few minutes now. What's got you stuck so deep in that thick head of yours?" he chuckles.

I shake my head, sighing heavily, looking forward as we continue to walk towards nowhere in particular.

Layne takes my hand from his forearm, so that now he's grasping it as we slowly walk along the edge of the water, but not so close to the waves that my feet will get wet.

Thankfully, he doesn't push right away, and gives me this time to be in my head without interrupting any further.

I don't know exactly how long it's been, but I know it's been quite a while since he joined my walk. Layne had been supporting my silence, until we come to a sudden, unexpected halt. Layne spins me around until he has my arms pinned behind my back, with both of his hands now holding mine.

"Hollie, what's on your mind, sweetheart?" he firmly but gently questions me, clearly expecting an answer.

I shake my head at him then turn my face towards the ocean, watching the waves roll in and out.

Layne gives me a little shake as he continues.

"Sunshine, I know something is going on, and I won't rest until I know what's eating at you. What happened? Did something go down when we were out in the ocean? Is that why you were out here all alone?"

I shake my head *no,* but I have yet to meet his eyes.

"You know, you gave me a scare when no one knew where you were. Your footprints led me to you. Otherwise I wouldn't have come this way to look."

Ugh. Why can't I just say it? I thought I could, but this is even scarier than I imagined it would be. It makes me want to hightail it out of here and then talk about it over the phone where he can't see my face. My palms are sweaty just thinking about exposing my feelings to him in this way.

Maybe a text message would be even better, and then I wouldn't see his reaction, or hear it. *No, that's just stupid.*

"I see the wheels spinning behind your hazy blues. Come on," he coaxes, "what's going on in that pretty head of yours?"

"It's embarrassing," I tell the water.

"Haven't you figured it out yet that you don't need to be embarrassed around me?" he gently reminds me as he tugs at my chin, turning me back to face him.

"There's nothing you could say that would make me think anything different when it comes to you." He searches my eyes, trying to reassure me that it really is safe to tell him anything.

"Really, it's nothing." I try one more time, silently pleading that he will stop this line of questioning. Though, really, I *do* want to know what will happen with us once I leave this island. A big part of me is also sad, knowing that I will be on my way home in the early hours of the morning, and I'm really not ready for the big goodbye that will ensue.

"Sunshine," he firmly says, "I've given you a whole lot of head space for quite some time now. I know something is bothering you, and it's causing you to retreat." He raises his brows expectantly while he patiently waits.

"Layne," I shake my head sadly. "I don't know what to say."

"Just tell me what's making you like this." He kisses my forehead.

"I'm scared, and I feel embarrassed, too." I say as I duck my head to rest it against his chest. I can't bear to face him when I admit everything. I've never done anything like this before, and I feel slightly foolish.

"Okay. About what?" has asks, as he lets go of my arms and wraps his big ones around me.

"About us," I look back up at him.

Titling his head to the side, confusion written in his eyes, he asks, "You're embarrassed about us? Why?"

"No, I didn't mean I was embarrassed by us. That came out all wrong." My semi-tense posture deflates a little, as I take in a deep breath. *I feel like I'm messing this up.*

"Well, that's a relief. I thought my scary mug was the main cause." He teases me, trying to lighten my mood.

"I'm just scared when it comes to us," I finally admit to him.

"What about us?" he searches my eyes, then roams my face, looking for something to let him know that I'm serious about being scared of what might come next. Though, he doesn't know that last part. *Yet.*

"Are you scared that I've pushed you outside of your comfort zone?" he worries now. "I'm going too fast," he quietly states, more to himself than to me.

"*Is* there even an *us?*" I question, as it's now my turn to search his face for some sort of sign that there's more to us than just friendship, and that I'm not dreaming up everything that I've felt this week.

Though, I'm starting to doubt myself now, by the look on his face.

Placing his hands on my cheeks, he stares back into my eyes. "Of course there's an us, Hollie. I'm standing right here, aren't I?" he asks with an air of seriousness.

Looking at him, seeing a deeper emotion in his eyes that he clearly wants me to see, I realize that I have to go with the *no question is a dumb question rule,* as I realize I should have known the answer all along. Instead I let my fears get the best of me.

Inhaling deeply and exhaling, I take the plunge so I can put my fears at ease, once and for all.

"I know that, but after right here in this moment, what comes next?"

"Sky's the limit, sunshine. Our future is whatever you want it to be."

Okay. He gave me something, but didn't exactly help me to close a tight lid on the subject at hand.

"Is there something beyond the here and now, Layne?" I pause, taking a breath, working the nerve up to ask. "Are there more tomorrows, after today? Or is today our last day together forever?"

"Hollie, whatever gave you the impression that I saw you as a fleeting moment of hanging out and just having fun?" he furrows his brows.

"Do you honestly think I have been going through such leaps and bounds to be around a woman, such as yourself, to just then forget about her? Do you think this is all fun and games for me? That you leave, and I go search for the next woman? Is that what you really believe?"

He's upset now, thanks to my own self-doubt.

"I don't believe that about you, but can you blame me if I didn't think there was more to come? We never agreed to anything past this week, but now I can't bear to leave you, thinking it all ends here, on this shore, never to be heard from again. Or maybe it's better if we do stay in touch, as friends. I don't know, Layne. I've never done this before." I'm feeling frustrated and upset now, too.

"That's why I'm worried sick over, drowning in the unknown factors of our relationship." I really feel deflated now, and even more unsure after my emotionally charged speech.

Gripping my shoulders firmly, he asks, "Hollie, did you just hear what you just said?"

"Yes. I heard everything I said, as well as what you said. What does 'sky's the limit' mean, anyway? I thought I knew where this was going, but now I feel a bit confused. Do you want to keep seeing me after I leave?"

"Listen to me, Hollie. I'll repeat it again." He's definitely not playing around. "Did you hear what you said a few moments ago?" he stares intently into my eyes, willing me to get it, by the look he's giving me.

Coming up empty, he continues for me.

"You said, 'our relationship.' That's exactly what we have, sweetheart. We are in a relationship, one that I fully plan on maintaining until it's physically impossible to do so. Don't you believe in love at first sight, or fate? What about the love stories in the movies you've seen? Or in the books you've read? I'm sure you know many examples of couples who've met and know in an instant that they belong together, then live happily ever after. Or pretty dang close to it."

Now I'm staring at him in amazement, knowing that this beautiful man feels that way and isn't afraid to express it or share it with me.

"Never doubt that we have something special." He drives the point home as he winds one arm around my waist, holding me firmly to his chest.

"It may seem beyond crazy to our friends, and family, and heck, even to us, but I don't care. I've got it, and I'm keeping it. Remember what I told you recently? I said, 'the moment I laid eyes on you, Hollie Reed, you were mine.' Make no mistake about that."

"But, we never talked about the possibilities for us after this trip. Tomorrow will be here before you know it, and I don't want to walk away from you yet. I didn't know if you were on the same page as me. Can you blame me? I was so scared to say something, not knowing if you would feel it, too. I know, it sounds silly now, saying it out loud."

I shake my head about how clueless I can be sometimes. *Did I miss the boat on the signs he has shown me throughout the week?*

I didn't realize he was serious enough to take this relationship past this week and into the future. I mean, I knew he was taking this relationship to a whole new level for me. Showing me something I'd never had. However, a part of me thought it was all just a pretense between two people who had a whirlwind vacation romance and, a strong attachment to each other, but then parted ways, returning to our separate lives.

Sure, we were inseparable all week, and had this strong connection between us, but that's something you see in the movies and read about in books all the time. It's not something that really happens in everyday life. I don't believe in fairy-tale endings.

Or, at least, I didn't. I had hopes, and wondered about the possibility, but I knew that life wasn't built like that. Now that I've met Layne, I wonder if I could have been any more wrong. *I know this doesn't happen to everyone, so why did it happen to me?*

"Hollie, I'm not going to waste what little time we have left to spend together, trying to convince you of the why's and how's. I don't know those answers."

He places both hands on the side of my face again, tiling it up so he can make eye contact with me. "Believe me when I say that this is only the beginning of you and me. What comes next is many tomorrows. You are my reason for everything and now, I finally have someone waiting for me, when I come home from deployments."

He's right. *Why should I dwell on the how's and why's of Layne choosing me?* Though, I did have cause to stress over what was to come once we parted ways. Feeling loads better, I lean into him and rest my head against his chest as he wraps me up in his arms. We silently stand, rooted to the spot for a few moments, soaking in the morning air and everything that was just said between us.

"I'm sorry. I've been letting my fears get the best of me until I was going a bit crazy, and you basically told me everything on day one." I mentally shake myself.

"Better?" he asks.

"Yes."

"Any more doubts?"

"None that come to mind."

"Good, then we should get back to the group. That's if they haven't already gone on a manhunt, looking for you." I feel his chest vibrate against my cheek as he laughs.

Sliding his fingers through mine, we retrace my footprints back to our camp area, seeing that the group is still intact, making breakfast.

"Well, well, well. Look who finally decided to rejoin the group," Ava smiles at me.

"What happened to you this morning?" Jen questions.

"She needed a little timeout, but all is well. Isn't that right, sunshine?" Layne asks me, as he places a kiss to the back of the hand he's holding.

"It's not a big thing. I had a lot to think about since we return to Oregon tomorrow. I needed a bit of space to think about what comes next in my life, as you and Ava move on to college, and I stay behind. That's all. Nothing to worry about. Just having a pity party for one." I smile at her, letting her know that I'm okay. *Well, at least where Layne's concerned.* I still need to work out the rest of my life and my plans to join the adult world.

We walk over towards the fire, taking a seat on our sleeping bags, trying to warm up.

Layne pulls me over to him as he places his arm around my shoulder, allowing me to rest my head against him.

"So, that's it?" Miller eyes Layne.

"That's it. We had some wrinkles to iron out, but now Hollie knows what's up and we'll survive."

"Good." Miller smiles at me and Layne. Turning to the rest of the group, he asks, "Who wants some fish?"

All of us girls groan in disgust, making the guys laugh.

"Okay, that's out. Maybe something like bagels and fruit?"

"Now you're talking rationally," Ava beams at him.

We decide to make ourselves useful and help get breakfast going, with whatever it is that Miller has in a big brown sack, and the group goes back to playfully chatting.

All is right in the world. For the time being, that is.

The next big obstacle really comes when we have to leave tomorrow. I'm not even going to dwell on it for anymore of my time here. I'll wait to see where the chips fall tomorrow, when it actually comes to fruition.

We spend the rest of the day being bums on the beach and going out for lunch and dinner before we return to our hotel to pack.

Packing for home is the worst part of a vacation. We'd tried to keep all of our stuff in our suitcases this week, but we all know how that goes. Miller and Layne joined us in our packing party, which eventually included our famous balcony climbers, coming down for a final visit. Jason was probably feeling left out, or maybe he was experiencing the withdrawals of not having Jen around. Regardless, we put the guys to work, checking drawers, looking under the beds, and searching all of the little hidden places to make sure that we didn't forget anything.

After packing, we decide to spend the rest of the evening in our room, making up games to play and telling more funny stories from our childhoods. We needed to have a fun evening together before the heavy stuff went down in the morning.

Miller and Layne decide to camp out in Jason's room so they could be around when we went to the airport the next day, which I was grateful for. I hated to say goodbye when it was time to kick the guys out of our room, even if it was just to send him up the elevator, one story above me.

Before the guys left us for the night, Jen decided that it was best to exchange personal information with them then, as opposed to in the morning, when things could be a bit hectic. So, now there's no reason that we can't all stay in touch.

Layne kissed me unhurriedly that night before he left the room, and it took me hours to finally go to sleep, knowing that he was one ceiling away.

Day 7

Waking up today *sucked.* End of story. Today we fly home, away from our newfound friends, and dare I say, boyfriends? I suppose that's what Layne is now, though it feels like more than that, and the term 'boyfriend' seems so inadequate to describe it.

It's fast, but I'm not even going to question it. I'm going to live in the moment, enjoy what we have, and see how it works out. There are no guarantees in the line of work he's in, so sitting here, questioning how crazy I am, and how young I am, is really not that important, considering the bigger picture. Sometimes life throws you a fastball, and you either swing at it, or you miss your chance. If you're lucky, you'll hit it out of the ballpark and score big, and that's the side of the coin toss that I'm banking on.

We've been up for an hour now, getting ready and making sure that we have all our belongings in our suitcases. Though, I feel as if I don't have *all* of my belongings, and I wonder if I could squeeze Layne into to my bag. I'm so not ready to leave yet, or ever, to be quite frank about it.

I breathe deeply in and out, trying to release the stress that I'm feeling. I wish there was a way to extend our tickets, however, that seems impossible, and we all have responsibilities to get back to at home.

There's a knock at the door, and Jen goes to answer it while I apply my makeup and continue to think about the rambling monologue in my head.

"You look good without it, sunshine." Layne says as he kisses the back of my head.

I lean my head back against his stomach and look up at him through the glass mirror, giving him a small smile.

"Good morning to you too, soldier. Sleep well?"

"Not as good as in my own bed, but I've slept in worse conditions on harder areas, so the cot served its purpose. And really, who could sleep knowing that you were a floor below me?" he winks.

"Did Miller steal all of the covers, or something?" I tease him.

"Or something. Who's trying to be the funny one this morning?"

"The one who's trying to be brave enough to leave alone in a couple of hours."

Layne wraps his arms around me, giving me a sad smile. "No frowning faces this morning, sweetheart. You're stealing my sunshine."

"Do you think you can fit into my luggage?" I ask him seriously through the mirror. "Or send me a life sized cut out of you?" I attempt a laugh. *Dang, this is going to be tough.*

"I wish I could go with you, too. However, with work, it's impossible. You know what, though?" he asks, with a little more cheerfulness in his voice, trying to be upbeat about what's to come next.

I shake my head, not knowing what he's thinking.

"Technology these days is pretty awesome, right? We can call and text at any time. We can also email each other as well. But," he says, as he looks back at me in the mirror, "my personal favorite would be letters through the mail. I love a good old fashion letter." He kisses my head one more time.

"Layne's right. You are fortunate to have a lot of communication lines open to you." Jen, the ever-optimistic and positive one, says.

"So, enough of this sadness. It's time to grab breakfast then head over to the airport," Layne finishes for her.

After checking our room one more time, the guys help us carry our luggage down to the lobby. We meet up with Jason, Evan, and Chase before checking out at the front desk and going out to Layne's truck. He places all of our luggage into the bed of the vehicle and secures the lock on it. He has a bed cover so he can store his belongings safely, such as his surf board and the camping gear. We find a place close by to eat at before we find ourselves back in the truck and on our way to the airport.

Evan and Chase caught a ride with their classmates in one of the hotel's big vans, as Jason opted to have as much time as possible with Jenifer, riding in Layne's truck. Though, it turns out, he's on our flight, too. I have no doubt that one of them will be switching places so they can be by each other.

After everyone is loaded into the truck, with seatbelts on, we drive to the airport in complete silence. No one, it seems, is in the mood to chat. I'm sure everyone else is feeling as blue as I am at this moment. Just thinking about leaving this beautiful place, my new friends, and my now-boyfriend causes my eyes to water. With nothing else to do, I place my head on Layne's shoulder and enjoy the warmth of his touch for as long as I can.

And just like that—it feels like—we're at the airport, and Layne pulls into the short-term parking lot. I really don't want to get out, so I hold onto him a little tighter while everyone else vacates the vehicle, leaving us alone.

"*I know, sweetheart. I hate this, too,*" his voice is a whisper against the top of my head.

"I don't want to leave, Layne." My eyes start to water a little more. I've never felt this way in my entire life, and it's horrible. I feel physically sick about being separated from him.

"Life is unfair sometimes, you know that?"

"I know, sweetheart. Though, we are lucky that we can keep in touch so many different ways. Imagine, had this been twenty years earlier, we would be stuck with phone calls to the payphone on base that would have a mile-long line, which even to this day, still does. Or, we would have to deal with snail mail letters. So, we should count our blessings and look at the positives." He gives me a squeeze, and then pats my knee.

Still pouting, he adds, "Come on, sunshine, don't be so gloomy. Please, for me?"

How can I deny him when I'm about to board a plane in an hour?

"Let's get you checked in so we can spend a little more time together before you walk out of my life. Thankfully, it's not permanently." He smiles sadly at me.

I finally let go of him, so he can climb out of the cab of the truck. Once he's out, he reaches in and hauls me out, before hugging me to his side with one arm. Towing my suitcase behind us with the other arm, we make our way to our friends, who have already entered the airport.

After we check our bags and get our boarding passes, we find an area to hang out in that's right before the security checkpoint. After the events of September 11th happened, security has cracked down at all American airports, and non-passengers can no longer enter the airport past the checkpoint. So, we make the best of what time we have left together in that area, and spend it huddled up in a group.

I'm snuggled up to Layne, as best as I can while sitting in the hard airport chairs, holding hands, and quietly talking amongst ourselves and our friends. We didn't have anything special to talk about, having gotten our serious conversation out of the way the day before, so everything is just basic chitchat as we count down the time before we have to part.

Layne rubs my arm as I lay my head against his shoulder. I can tell that he too needs to touch me as much as he can before he has to let go.

Our time comes to an end almost as fast as it started. We have about thirty-five minutes before our plane leaves, and we need to be at our gate within the next twenty minutes so that we aren't bumped for not being on time. Apparently, this happens a lot, and our parents made sure that we knew not to be foolish and goof off, or oversleep and miss the boarding call. After all, dawn was barely breaking when we made it to the airport. I'm glad it's not very busy here this early in the morning, as it looks like we can make it through security pretty quickly.

Miller walks with Ava over to the checkpoint to say goodbye as Jason, his friends, and Jen make their way to the line to get through it. They know that Ava and I will be along as soon as I can unwrap my arms from around Layne. I have the urge to miss my flight on purpose, but that wouldn't be the responsible thing to do.

"Sunshine, as much as I hate this, just like you do, we have to say goodbye." He holds on to me tighter. That says to me right there that he's going to have it just as rough as I will when we finally break apart.

"Text me when you land safely in Oregon, sweetheart. I want to make sure my precious cargo makes it there in one piece. Can you do that for me?"

I can't even speak right now, so I just nod my head into his chest, fighting against the tears. I'm trying to hold it together until I get on the plane, where I don't care if I fall apart, silently in my seat.

"Good. I look forward to it." He kisses the top of my head as I squeeze him tighter.

"A few things before I let you go, sweetheart. I want you to make me a promise, and I'll make you one as well."

"Okay," I manage to get out, around the lump quickly forming in my throat.

"Every day, no matter what, even if you're sick, I want you to text me a picture of your beautiful, smiling face. I need to see my sunshine to make my day complete. Can you do that for me?"

"*Yes.*" I whisper into his chest.

"Good," he quietly replies. "Now, I in turn, promise to write you a letter every week. So you have something to always look back at when you need a piece of me. I'll also promise to send you a photo every day. Does that work for you?"

I only nod my head again.

"All right, sweetheart, I want you look at me now."

I slowly raise my head to look at his tanned face, trying to memorize it one last time before I absolutely have to let him go. My eyes roam its oval shape, taking in his sandy brown hair and multicolored eyes, which still mesmerize me when I stare into them, moving down to his full mouth and narrow jaw.

He looks back at me, memorizing all of my features as well before he lowers his head and our mouths melt as one. There's no beginning and no ending right now as he slowly kisses me. His hands roam my back as I round his neck with mine, pulling myself closer to him, praying that this moment never ends. At some point, his hands make their way into my hair and he holds me tightly.

Sighing, he pulls away a little bit and stares intently into my blue-grey eyes, showing me his feelings in the deep depths of his own eyes. I hope he can see the same thing when he looks back into mine. It's all that needs to be communicated between us. We promised that this wasn't a *goodbye,* but more like a *see you later,* so words are not necessary at this given time.

I hear Ava calling to me through the background noise of the airport.

I close my eyes for a moment, and Layne leans his forehead against mine, before opening them again, meeting his hazel-greens.

"This is it, baby. It's time to go." He takes my hand and places it over his heart. "I want you to know that you will always be with me in my heart, as you own it. Completely."

I take his hand and place it over mine. "You have mine, too." I search his eyes one last time, as my own eyes start to well up. I can't stop the rush in time as a tear trickles down my cheek. Layne reaches up to wipe it away with the slide of his thumb before placing a kiss along the path where the tear fell.

He pulls away and looks over my head, taking in a deep breath. He nods his head, to who I can only guess is Miller, before looking back down at me. He kisses me one last time before he pulls away again. "It's time to go, sweetheart. I don't want you to miss your flight. Well, that's a lie, but it wouldn't be wise. We don't need your parents to send the big guys from my job after me." He jokes, trying to lighten the mood.

"They would, too." I smile.

"I'm sure. I know I would, if I had such a beautiful daughter."

I lean in one last time and hug him as he holds me back just as fiercely. We pull apart too soon, and I lean up to kiss him on his nose. "I'll text you when I land, soldier. In the meantime, be good, and make sure to keep an eye on Miller for Ava."

"Don't worry, his mother made me promise the same thing," he laughs.

"I bet she did." I know what we're doing here. We're both stalling and trying to lighten the mood, so I can leave on a happy note.

I know that I'd better walk away first, or no one will. So I start walking backwards, while I keep my eyes firmly trained on his the whole way. I get to the security line, and finally swallow the big lump in my throat.

I can't do this.

As if I was watching the action from somewhere up above, I find myself running back to him and leap into his arms.

"Hollie, baby, I wish I could hold you forever, but you have to make your flight." He says as he rubs my back with one hand, trying to soothe me while I cry into the crook of his neck.

"I know, I know." I keep repeating.

"We'll talk every day, I promise. And the days I'm out in the field for training, or away on a mission, I promise to think of you when it's safe to do so. Before you know it, sweetheart, we will be back together."

"Okay." I say through my tears.

"Can you promise one more thing for me?"

"I'll try."

"Be strong, for the both of us. I know you can do it, Hollie . You're a strong woman, and behind every soldier, he or she has a strong partner. Right?"

I hope he's right, so I nod my head, calming myself down.

"That's my girl. You can do this. *We* can do this. Just have faith and believe in us. It will all work out, you'll see."

I unravel myself from Layne as I slide down to my feet. We hug one last time and he leaves the sweetest of kisses on my lips before he gently prods me along to the line for the checkpoint. He plants one last kiss on my forehead, then starts walking backwards, watching me the whole time, as I move forward through the line to catch up with Ava.

Miller waves to both of us with his own sad smile, and I return one to him. *I know how he feels.*

My eyes search out Layne one more time, and by the time I've gone through the metal detector, I can no longer see his handsome face, and my heart breaks a little. But I manage to hold it together a bit longer as we make our way to the departure gate.

Ava wraps her free arm around my shoulders as we walk towards our friends and find a seat. By the time the gate agent calls us to board the plane, my whole body is sick and I'm feeling emotionally numb.

But this time, I'm not scared to get on the plane and head back over the ocean for the second-longest flight of my life. No, this time I'm physically not feeling well, and I'm not sure what's going on.

Is it because I don't know when I'll see Layne again? Or what's going to happen from here on out? Or is there some other force at play here?

Eventually, we make it on to the plane and slide into our seats. Chase comes to sit by Ava and I while Jen takes his seat further back, next to Jason. I'm grateful that this time I'm sitting in the aisle. *Something is just not right.*

Maybe it's just nerves, and that's what I chalk it up to until an hour into the flight, I have to rush to the lavatory. That's how I spend the rest of my flight home—in the bathroom, sick as can be.

I can't even count how many times I was up and down over the course of the seven-hour trip, but I did know that I felt bad for Chase and Ava who had to deal with me.

I wish I could say I got some rest on the flight, but really, I didn't. I was grateful to Ava who got the Pepto-Bismol from Jen, along with some Tylenol, as I was in bad shape.

The moment we land, and it's safe to do so, I turn on my phone and text my mom, telling her that I'm not well, and to please buy something for me at the gift shop before I reach her.

Then I text Layne, letting him know I made it safely but I was sick, and I hoped that he didn't turn up sick as well.

Hubby: Miller and I are both fine and we're both glad you and Ava and the rest made it back safely.

Hollie: Are you sure?

Hubby: That we're glad you made it home? No, not really, as we would rather you were here. Otherwise, yes, because we wouldn't want anything bad to happen to you.

Hollie: I wish I didn't have to leave you either. But I meant about not being sick.

Hubby: Baby, I'm just fine, I assure you. It was probably something you ate.

Hollie: I bet you're right. Stupid *Deney's*. Every time I eat there it makes me sick. Maybe it was food poisoning.

Hubby: There you go, sweetheart. Go find your mom and get some rest.

Hollie: That's the plan, soldier.

Hubby: Good. Miller and I are about to head to dinner, so I'll check in with you in a little bit.

Hollie: Okay. I miss you.

Hubby: I miss you too.

Hollie: I bet you're already bored without me.

Hubby: How can I be when I can drive you crazy with photos and text messages? However, you're right, it's not really the same, and I'm going crazy not seeing you. I miss your face.

Hollie: I'll drive you crazy with our new way of communication so that you won't have time to miss me. Well, not completely at least.

Hubby: That's what I'm banking on.

Hollie: Me too, soldier. Me too.

Hubby: Now, quit holding up the plane and get that cute 'tush' off.

Hollie: Lol. You had to find a way to bring that back up.

Hubby: Maybe. Now, why are you ignoring your commander's orders, woman? March.

Hollie: Yes, sir.

Hubby: That's what I like to see, but prefer to hear. I'll call you later. Go take care of yourself, please.

Hollie: I will. Talk to you later, soldier-boy.

Hollie: PS, Ava says to tell Miller hi and to be on his best behavior or she'll have to fly back over there to kick some butt.

Hubby: He says to tell her to dream on. Now, quit stalling and move out like a good soldier.

Hollie: I'm going, I'm going. Don't rush the sick and weary. We can only go so fast.

Hubby: Smart aleck. But a cute one.

Hollie: Goodbye, Layne.

Hubby: Bye, wifey.

Chapter Eight

June 22, 2013

IT'S BEEN A week since I left Hawaii, and I'm suffering from withdrawals from the beautiful weather and breathtaking scenery, but most of all, from the gorgeous Army man I left there, along with my heart.

How is it that I barely know this man, yet I feel so connected to him, as if a part of me is missing? You hear about things like this sometimes, and yet you never really believe that they could be true. Now, I can stop dwelling on the subject, as I've seen my own personal storyline falling into the pages of one of those love stories where you wish to be the coveted heroine.

Since I've been home, Layne and I have been able to keep in touch via phone calls, texts and email. And true to his word, he sends me a picture of himself every day, and since I made the same promise, I too have sent him one, no matter what.

It helps to see each other every day, even if it's just through the photographs. People change constantly, and this allows us the security of seeing each other's faces regularly. It makes the miles apart go down a little easier. It's almost as if we aren't in two different places, at least for a single moment in time. I'm graced by his presence in that moment, where I can capture it in a still-shot and see his picture whenever I need a pick-me-up, or whenever I just miss him.

Also, I love the photo idea he came up with, as it allows us to see what's going on in each other's lives—where we are, what we're doing, or how we look. He made me swear I wouldn't dress myself up unnaturally just to take the photos. I have to be myself, and act as such in whatever setting I'm in when I snap the shot and send it to him.

As for the phone calls, he tries to save those for special times—morning wakeups, or goodnight's before dozing off. We try to have Instant Messenger conversations as well, whenever we can both be on a computer at the same time. I think it would be too hard to hang up the phone during the week if we spoke that way too often. I doubt either one of us would ever get to sleep.

I'm starting work again at my parents' pharmacy in a few weeks. My parents have been generous in giving me extra time off before Jenifer and Ava leave for college. They know I'll have a lot of free time then, forcing my focus to be at work and not on what plans we can make to hang out. What they haven't realized is that all of my attention will still be taken up and preoccupied by thoughts of Layne.

I haven't decided what to do yet about my education. I know I'll go to college, but *when* is the real question. *Will I take a year off? Will I do online classes now? Or should I actually attend the local school nearby?* I'm not sure, and I don't even want to try and sort it all out any time soon. I just graduated from one school; no way do I want to think about diving back into another one in the near future. *My parents may have other ideas, though.*

Today is Saturday, and I'm waiting for the girls to come over. We haven't made any real plans, except to veg out and watch some sappy romcoms, like *P.S. I Love You* and *The Notebook.* Maybe we'll even throw in *Fried Green Tomatoes* for old time's sake. Whenever we get into one of these moods, my dad vacates the premises and goes hunting, fishing or heck, maybe even goes off to chop wood. *Does anyone really know what a man does when he's out communing with nature?* Whatever a manly man would do, he's off doing *that*. My mom's at her local book group drinking tea, eating sweet treats, and enjoying the local gossip, I'm sure. I wonder if they just call it a book group so that they have an excuse to get out and have a ladies' day away from their brooding husbands. I doubt there's any real book talk going on, or reading the books at all, for that matter. I think it's all just a ploy to escape the house. Who can blame her? I wonder if I'll be like that in my later years. *Hmm, maybe I shouldn't get too far ahead of myself here.*

I'm pulled out of my thoughts by a loud honking coming from my driveway. I walk over to the big picture window in our living room and peer out through the sheer curtains, seeing Jen and Ava as they pour themselves out from both sides of the car.

Can't they show up without making a big deal? I think Ava does it to irritate our nosy neighbors. *Whatever.* They just need to get their butts in here before I give them each a swift kick.

A few moments later, they both come strolling through the front door. They're practically family to us, so knocking went out the window years ago. It also serves to tick my dad off, as we love to outnumber him in the female department. He has a thing or two to gripe about when we're all here with my mom. He's really not a grumpy old man, he just likes his privacy, and we tend to never give him any, so he has to seek solace elsewhere, which is usually with his buddies. Sometimes he takes off to go camping, leaving the house to us women, and boy do we all have a blast, including my mom.

"Any news from Layne?" Ava asks as soon as she sits down next to me on the couch, settling her legs casually onto the coffee table.

"I talked to him briefly last night before bed, when he called to say goodnight." I inform her. "He's been pretty busy since we left, but nothing seems to be new on his end. He's just working and hanging out with Miller."

"Good. Someone needs to keep him out of trouble now that I'm not there to chaperone his field trips out in public," she smiles to herself.

"What is the deal with you two anyway?" I ask her, out of curiosity. "You two seemed to get pretty cozy back on the island. Is there anything you want us to know?"

"We're just friends." She tries to assure me without a real ounce of believability in that sentence.

"Uh-huh, right," I laugh. "I know you were pretty chummy with him. There has to be more to it than that. Spill it, sister!" I kick her foot playfully with one of mine.

"No, honestly, we're in an open-friends relationship."

Furrowing my brow, I give her a frown. "A *what?* That's nonsense. I've never heard of such a ridiculous title. Just admit what you two really are." I try again to pry it out of her.

"I'm not sure how to really state it any other way. We're just friends," she maintains.

"We feel something towards each other, but let's be realistic for a moment, ladies." She continues on, "I've known him all of six days. How can it be anything more? Yes, we had fun. Yes, we exclusively hung out together *and* with our friends. Do we like each other? *Heck yes!* Do we want something more? *Definitely.* But I'm off to college, and he's in Hawaii at a military base, of all places. Let's be real. If we were in the same state and town, we would probably be getting to know each other by casually dating. But, we're not, and we know that we wouldn't want to hold the other person back if they found someone to date who happens to be living in the same place." She says with false bravado. She's trying to put up a front, but we know her better than anyone, and can see through the mask that she wears.

Jen and I let her have this moment, though. She can believe what she wants. If she thinks he's not head over heels for her, then she's a bigger fool than I am, with feelings for a man I barely know.

"Oh no, you don't." She waves her finger at me. "I know what you're thinking. You're giving me the pity look. I know it all too well," she reminds me.

"I am not. I just don't get it." I push my lip out at her. "He's head over heels for you, so I don't get what the hold up is. You can have a long distance relationship, like Layne and I." I cheerfully remind her of my situation.

"I know he is, and vice versa. He doesn't know what he'll be doing or where he will be. I'll be busy with college. How is that fair to either one of us? He wants me to get the college experience. We decided not to label ourselves as exclusive and just have an open-friends relationship. So, it's like we are together, but we aren't, and if I hear of him going on a date, I can't get mad. I agreed to this deal. He can't get mad about what I do, either."

"Oh right, like that will stop him," Jen says sarcastically.

"Whatever, you two. Let's move on to you, Jen. What's your deal?" Ava asks, quirking an eyebrow at her.

"Jason and I freely admit to liking each other. We also have agreed to working out something so we can have a relationship. He's thinking about transferring schools, so he can go to our school, Ava, and get the same degree. If he can't get in, then he will stick it out where he had planned to be. It's not like we are that far apart now, like you two," she says sadly. "We just had fate on our side, and will only be like two hours or so from each other's school as it is."

"Well, I, for one, am happy for you." I smile over at her.

"Can we just get to the love-fest of movies, already? Who has the chocolate, popcorn, and milk?" Ava demands of Jen and I.

"Take a chill pill. I'm on it, crazy." I kick her one more time before getting the goods, then setting up the movies. It was hard to choose what movie to go with first, as they all make us cry like babies. That makes me glad that Layne isn't here to seeing the waterworks. In the end, we save *The Notebook* for last, as it's the most hopeful of the bunch. Or maybe it's a toss-up. Either way, it happens to have the best looking man starring in it. *Yep, let's go with that thought.*

It's getting late in the day when the Mailman drops the mail through the door's slot. *I know.* We still have that old fashioned slot, where the Mailman can walk up to your door, without fearing for his life, to deliver the mail. *You have to love good ol' Holly Grove.*

Walking over to the door, I bend down to pick all the pieces of mail up laying on the floor, when I notice an envelope addressed to me. Frowning I take it, along with the other pieces of mail, over to the couch, dropping the rest on the coffee table.

"What's the matter?" Jen notices my expression first.

"I wasn't expecting anything, so it just seems weird," I tell her.

I flip it over, and that's when I notice who the sender is. The back has a return address, and the name on it says only one word, *Hubby.*

Ava leans over with prying eyes to get a peek at my letter, just as she sees his name. "Oh! Someone has it bad for you!" she laughs. "Your dad would probably flip if he saw his baby girl getting a letter that's from a man named 'Hubby.'" She continues to put her two cents in on the matter.

"Would you be quiet, already? Who cares about that part, I just want to know what it says. This is so romantic, and great timing before we watch *The Notebook,*" Jen gushes.

I carefully open the envelope, pulling the letter out.

"Read it out loud!" Ava commands.

Rolling my eyes, "Yes, queen of the house, I'll get right on that." Unfolding the paper, clearing my throat, I begin reading aloud:

My Dear Hollie-

Some may call me old fashioned, but so be it. I still think it's a timeless expression of the heart when someone sends you a love letter. So this is me wanting you to know that I couldn't get you off of my mind. Today, yesterday, the day before . . . dating all the way back to the day that you left.

I want you to know, sunshine, that whenever you need me the most, all you have to do is pick up this letter, and remember these simple truths about my feelings for you.

You are always with me no matter where I go. I hear your laughter on the wind. See your face in the sun, shining brightly for the all world to see. Smell you in the rain after a storm. Feel you when I see a kiss between lovers. Taste you in chocolates and sweets. Yours is the face of all that is beautiful in my world— the vibrant colors of a rainbow, the warmth of a fire, a child's delighted smile. Your eyes are as blue as the sky and as grey as the clouds around the base.

No matter where I look, I can always find a piece of you looking back at me.

Always,

Layne

I can't help the smile that spreads across my face as I crush the letter to my chest. I look up at my friends to find them staring at me in awe.

"Wow," Ava says. "Yeah, that's all I got."

"Who knew Layne could be so swoon-worthy?" Jen wonders aloud.

"I did," I say with a small smile.

I immediately grab my phone to send Layne a text, letting him know that I got his letter and how he brightened up my day. It also reminds me that I haven't sent him a self-photo for today, as well.

Holding the letter up, I plaster a big smile on my face and snap a shot. I attach it to a text message and push *Send.* Then I set the phone back on the coffee table with the letter and start up our next movie, settling in for the next two hours, praying I can keep my head together so I can pay attention to one of the greatest love stories of our generation play out on screen.

June 29, 2013

The following Saturday, I was hoping for, but not truly expecting, another letter from Layne, which I do receive. This time my mom is home. By now, it's week two of being home, and she's up to speed on who the man is that's calling on her daughter all the time, causing said daughter to always be distracted or busy.

The Mailman comes late again and pushes the letters through the slot. It's the only piece of mail and I go running for it before my mom can snatch it up.

Jen and Ava came by again to hang out, though they too had high hopes of reading another letter.

"I wish Jason would send me little notes, too," Jen pouts.

"So, just tell him what Layne is doing, and you know he'll step up his game." Ava replies.

"Maybe, but I want him to send me one all on his own." Jen makes a good point. He shouldn't have to be told; he should just do it, without any hints from her.

"Hurry up, Holls! We want to know what he says this week." Ava says impatiently.

I open the letter and slide it out, preparing once again to read it out loud.

My Dearest Hollie,

Saying hello to you was the best thing that's ever happened to me. I never want to say goodbye.

Missing you like crazy-

Layne

I look up at the group as a whole, and they are all in their own blissful state over this new letter.

I immediately pick up my phone and text Layne.

Hollie: Literally running into you was my happiest day.

Hubby: I miss you, Sunshine.

Hollie: Back at you.

Hubby: I'll call you later tonight to wish you sweet dreams.

I smile and shove my phone back in my pocket, but a few moments later it goes off again. I pull it back out to read Layne's new text.

Hubby: Of me, of course.

Hollie: You just HAD to spoil it, didn't you? Couldn't let me have this moment?

Hubby: We both know it's the truth. Later, Sweetheart.

Fine, he can have that round. There's always next time, I smile.

July 6, 2013

And so it begins, the Saturday ritual with my mom and my friends where we all gather around the living room, waiting for Layne's love note to arrive. I've also decided that every time I get a letter, I wait to take my photo until I'm holding the letter, with a big smile on my face.

Sometimes my friends get in the photo, or my mom, but I don't mind. I want Layne to see what a big deal his letters are to all of us, and to know how much it means to me that I share them with the ones I hold dearest to my heart.

Today, my dad is home. He eyes all of us, then shakes his head and heads out to his man-cave, which is the garage. He decided that he finally needed one, even though Jen and Ava are leaving in a month for college. That fact didn't stop him. He still thinks that after all these years he needs it, because it's the greatest invention ever, and why did he take so long to discover it?

The girls came over earlier in the day and we did manicures and facials, stuffing our faces with ice cream and gabbing with my mom about everything and nothing. She decided to skip book club to hang with us, citing that we were better company. I know she's serious when she says that, and also because she can't contain her giddiness that her daughter is living out her own love story with these letters. I'm sure she will report it all back to her book club eventually, and all will be swooning over my man. I pray this doesn't become a hot topic in the local newspaper, though. In a town as small as mine, you never know.

Finally the mail arrives, as mom is taking a lasagna out of the oven. She sets it on the stovetop and hurries into the dining area where we had set up shop earlier.

I open the letter and read it out loud.

Hey Holls,

I just wanted to tell you that I'm still wearing that smile you gave me. I never want it to go away.

-Layne

Picking up my phone, I send Layne a text.

Hollie: I need to see your beautiful smile.

Hubby: Anything for you, my sweet girl.

And just like that, life feels right, and everything is wonderful in my own world of blissful promises and smiles.

I put the letter away, then get back to helping mom with dinner, setting the table and all while wearing a smile of my own, Layne's gift to me as well.

August 3, 2013

Hollie,

Instead of missing you, I wish I could be kissing you.

Layne

Pulling out my phone, I take a snapshot of me with the letter and send it to Layne, because no way can he send me that note and I not respond.

Hollie: Trust me, I wish I could be kissing you instead of missing you like crazy, too.

Not even two seconds later, Layne replies while I'm still holding my phone. I was secretly wishing he would get back to me right away. I click on his message, and it's a picture of him making a kissy face at me.

I laugh, causing everyone in the room to give me a look, so I turn the phone around to show them. My mom smiles and the girls laugh at the silly face Layne is making. A moment later, my phone dings with a text message again. Of course, I already know it's going to be from Layne.

"I'm glad your dad isn't here. He might have tried to call that young man." My mom teases me. However, I'm really glad dad isn't here, either. When he meets Layne, it would be a given that he would never live this down.

I smile at her knowingly, then glance down to read the message.

Hubby: That's me kissing you from across the ocean. I have to get back to work, but I'll call you later.

Hollie: I'll be waiting.

Then I take a second photo of me making the same goofy kissy face, and send it to him.

Hubby: Now I have your kiss permanently secured in my phone. Whenever I think about your lips, and kissing you, I'll pull up your photo. Thank you, sunshine.

August 24, 2013

Like clockwork, the gang is all here to see what comes through the mail slot today. It's getting closer to the time when the girls have to leave for college, and I'm not even close to being prepared for my best friends to go off on their own, without me.

My parents have been great about giving me freedom for the summer, and the month after, to spend time with my friends before they go away. Just thinking of their departure brings me down a little. I hope that my work and Layne's weekly letters will get me through the lonely times.

Mom hands me the letter she just picked up off the floor, and I open it, all sets of expectant eyes on me.

I clear my throat and begin to read what Layne has to say this week, out loud for all to hear.

Dear Hollie,

The world is a better place, knowing you're in it.

Love,

Layne

September 7, 2013

Hollie-

I miss you so much! Probably not as much as you miss me; because lets face it, I'm amazing!

Yours,

Layne

"I see you're dating a comedian. Didn't you say he was in the Army?" my dad asks sarcastically.

We all bust up laughing at my dad's comment, even though Layne's words had us smiling like loons, knowing he's so full of himself, but also trying to make me laugh, too.

"When did you say we would be meeting this young man, again?" Dad continues.

"I didn't," I laugh. "And for good reason, apparently."

"No respectable man dates my daughter and never shows his face," he says stoically.

"Oh dear, pipe it down. You know he can't just hop on the next plane and be here. He has to get approved time off. That takes awhile. I'm sure he would love to come out to visit just as soon as he can," my mom scolds my dad.

"You women drive me crazy. I'm going to the cave." He huffs, cracking us up again as he leaves the room.

I pick up my phone and take a photo, but this time I try giving him a raised eyebrow look as I snap the shot. Then I send it to Layne, which gets me an immediate response.

Hubby: What's with the face, sweetheart?

Hollie: My dad wants to know if you're a comedian or in the Army.

Hubby: I'm a Jack of all trades. Didn't I tell you that I take my act out on the road doing USO tours?

Hollie: I knew you were pulling my leg trying to pretend you worked in CI or was it Infantry?

Hubby: That's classified information, ma'am. Remember what I told you last time?

Hollie: I don't know, maybe you need to refresh my memory? I think I'm forming Alzheimer's over here.

Hubby: I think I'd better show you in person, the next time I see you. That will refresh your memory and warm up your nights.

Hollie: Such a flirt. Aren't you at work? What if one of the guys sees your text?

Hubby: They'll be jealous of the hottie I'm thinking about kissing over here, wishing she wasn't mine.

Hollie: Oh yeah? Who's that?

Hubby: Oh, you don't know? She's an older lady down at the fish market. Sorry, sweetheart, I didn't want you to have to find out this way.

Hollie: I guess I better fly out there and let her know that she can't have my man.

Hubby: Don't get my hopes up.

Hollie: Sir, yes sir.

Hubby: Woman!

Hollie: Get back to work, soldier. That's an order.

Hubby: Bossy.

Hollie: Darn straight. I'll call you later tonight.

I toss my phone on the side table and flop down on the couch, next to Ava.

"That was like a marathon texting session you had going on. What's that goofy grin on your face for?" she elbows me.

"Oh, just a little flirting, that's all."

"I'm sure she'll be up late on the phone with him, like she is every weekend." My mom rats me out.

"I should have known." Ava says as she shakes her head.

"I think the whole town knows what Hollie is up to every Friday, Saturday, and Sunday," Jen says through a teasing smile.

"I bet it will be in the Monday paper." My mom adds, deciding to get on the poking-fun-of-Hollie train.

"We're lucky she graces us on any of those nights at all. Of course, you know that the phone is permanently attached to her head the moment she gets a call," Ava jokes.

"Pretty soon, we'll have to take her to Dr. Peters to get it surgically removed." Laughs Jen, causing the others to laugh as well.

"Ha ha. You all are hilarious. Now, let's find something to do while the old man is in the garage."

"I like your thinking. What do you have up your sleeve?" Mom asks.

And just like that, I've successfully changed the subject.

September 21, 2013

The girls left for school a week and a half ago, and I've started back at work. Holly Grove isn't the same without them, but somehow I manage to keep putting one foot in front of the other. The world didn't stop, so neither can I.

Today I'm looking forward to the one thing that gives me my high at the end of a long work week.

I hear the slot squeak open and close. I quicken my pace to the door and sure enough, without fail, is a letter addressed to me from *Hubby*.

I don't know where my mom is and I don't want to wait, so I tear open the letter and let my greedy eyes drink in his words.

Hollie,

Thinking about you makes me smile.

XOXO-

Layne

After sending him a photo with the letter, as per usual, I sit down and send him a text along with it.

Hollie: Thinking about you gets me through each day, one at a time.

I know Layne can't always get back to me right away, but it doesn't mean that I'm not always hoping each and every time that he will be fast on the draw. Eventually I set my phone down, and pick up the book I was reading. I've picked up this hobby again since the girls have been gone.

If Layne can't be here, nor I there, then the next best thing is reading about someone else's happily ever after. I need a substitute boyfriend when I can't see or talk to my real live one. With books, you can have as many boyfriends as you want, and no one gets upset, jealous or calls you out for cheating. *It's a win-win.*

Layne understands. Even if he thinks I'm a little crazy.

October 12, 2013

Mom has decided to pick back up with her so-called book club recently. She still gets the scoop on Layne's letters from me, but it was time that she went back to being her own age. It was fun while it lasted with Ava and Jen home, though.

With her absence, I now realize how nice it is to savor Layne's words and keep them mostly to myself. Mom doesn't ask for full details, so I pick and choose what I want to share, or sometimes just confirm that yes, indeed, he had written to me that week.

Today, another letter comes through the slot, so I place my new book on the side table and go to pick it up. Before I can get to it though, my dad happens to walk through the front door a moment later, just missing the Mailman.

He sees the mail and bends down to grab it, then stands back up as he thumbs through the bills and junk.

"Hollie!" he semi-shouts, even though I'm not that far from where he's standing.

"I'm right here Dad, no need to shout."

"Oh, well. You have a letter." He says as he turns it over to see who the sender is.

"'Hubby?'" he gives me a stern look. "And who would that be, not the comedian-Army fellow you say you're dating?"

"Dad, it's just a joke that he has decided to keep up. It doesn't mean anything." I say, a bit embarrassed that my dad finally, after all of this time, has found out about it.

"So you didn't secretly get married in Hawaii and forgot to tell us?"

"Ha ha." *That's all he's getting from me.*

"All right, all right. Here, take your letter. Is your mom home?"

"No, she's at her book club tonight. She made enchiladas for us before she left. Check the oven." I say as I snatch the letter out of his hand and go back to the couch.

Opening the letter, I soak in every detail he has written.

My Hollie,

You can't see them, but I kissed this paper 20 times, then mailed my kisses to you.

XOXO-

Layne

Hollie: Here's a new kiss photo to add to your collection.

Hubby: Can never have too many.

Hollie: I didn't want you to feel lonely, having only one kiss.

Hubby: Careful, the men might start texting you for their own kiss photos if you keep this up.

Hollie: Always trying to flatter me.

Hubby: Just ask Miller. I have a pool of guys waiting for me to bite the bullet. Not literally, hopefully.

Hollie: Not going to happen. You've got this one in the bag.

Hubby: That's what I'm counting my lucky stars on.

Hollie: No need. Let fate work her magic.

Hubby: Are you reading sappy love stories again?

Hollie: Maybe.

Hubby: I'm the only sappy love story you need.

Hollie: And one day, when we can be together, I'll kick all of my other boyfriends to the curb.

Hubby: I'm not sharing my girl.

Hollie: Not a fat chance.

Hubby: The guys want to go out to eat. I'll call you when I get back. In the meantime, be good.

Hollie: Sir, yes sir.

Hubby: Woman!

Smiling to myself, I place the phone on the floor by the couch and get back to my book. I need to find out more about this *Four* character.

November 2, 2013

Dear Sunshine,

Whenever you're having a hard time, I want you to remember how proud I am to call you mine.

Love-

Layne

November 23, 2013

Hollie,

Just the thought of you keeps me awake at night. However, it's the dreams that keep me asleep.

I know it doesn't make sense, but it's the truth. Basically, my dearest girl, you are never far from my mind.

Love always,

Layne

December 21, 2013

Hollie,

Happy early birthday, my love. May all of your dreams come true this year.

Love always,

Layne

Hollie: Thank you, Layne. I miss you.

Hubby: I miss you too. I'll call you later when we have time to chat, sweetheart.

December 24, 2013

Hollie's First Birthday with Layne

The phone rings, waking me from a deep slumber. I just about fall out of bed trying to grab my cell phone off of the bedside table, not bothering to check the caller ID as it's already on the last possible ring before it goes to my voicemail.

"Hello?" I groggily answer, but get no response. I try again. "*Hello?*" This time, I hear someone whistle a tune over the phone. I pull the phone away, looking at it in the dark, trying to figure out who is calling me at seven in the morning on Christmas Eve.

Is this a joke?

Then I hear the most wonderful sound ever, Layne's voice.

"Happy Birthday, Sunshine."

"I'm so glad to hear your voice, baby. Thanks for calling me. I miss you like crazy." I rush out as I flop back onto my bed and bury myself deeper into the covers.

"I miss you too, sweetheart. What are your plans this year?"

"I'm not sure what the day has in store for me, but my friends usually put together a birthday party. Luckily, this year Ava and Jen decided to come home for the break instead of going on some crazy road trip. I think their parents would have had their heads over that one," I laugh.

"I wish I could be there with you, Holls. You know I would if I could have had the time off, right?"

"I know, Layne. It sucks, but we'll make it through. There's always next year, right?"

"That's my girl," he says proudly. "I don't have a lot of time before I have to go to PT. So, I just wanted to let you know that I have two gifts for you."

"Babe, you didn't have to get me anything. Just the sound of your voice is enough. Really, it makes my entire day."

"I'm glad, sunshine. But it's too late for the first gift, because it will always be true, and the second, well, you'll have to see your parents for that one." He informs me before continuing.

"My gift to you this year, Hollie, is the most important one of all time. Are you listening? I don't want you to miss this, sweetheart." He pauses before continuing, "I love you, Hollie." He says the words with so much emotion in his voice, I have no doubt that he's speaking the truth.

This is the first time I've heard him tell me he loves me. He might sign his letters with 'love,' and he might even write about it in his letters or texts, but to hear him say it? It brings tears to my eyes.

"Hollie, I've been waiting to tell you how much I love you until this special day. It's the staying kind, sweetheart. As long as I walk and breathe on this Earth, you will always be mine. You own my heart and soul, and I want you to know that you are always with me in my heart. Wherever I am now or down the road, you will still be in my heart, no matter what comes our way."

I don't even have to think about what I'm about to say next, because I feel what he does too, and it's time I put myself out there and let him know it.

"Layne, I want you to know how much I love you, too. This is now the best gift I've ever received, and it ties in awesomeness with the gift of hearing your voice."

"I want you to know that you are truly my sunshine and you make me so happy. I love you, Hollie."

I sniffle into the phone, trying to hold myself together. He is just so sweet, and I miss him like crazy, I *need* him like crazy. Yet, I can't have him physically, and that hurts my heart.

"I didn't mean to make you cry, baby. I just wanted you to know how much you mean to me."

"I know, Layne. It's okay. I just wish you could be here, or vice versa. That's all. I don't want to ruin this moment. We just shared the best thing to ever happen to me, and I'm so dang excited. I can't wait to share the good news with everyone."

My overzealousness makes him laugh. "Hollie, you always bring a smile to my face. You know how to brighten my day. Thank you for that, sweetheart."

"Only for you, soldier."

"I almost forgot the other part of your present. Now, I won't be offended if you laugh, but I'm doing this anyway. I want to always be the first one to wake you up on your birthday, wish you a happy birthday and to do this—" he says, before going into his-off key rendition of the happy birthday song.

"I know it was probably terrible, and I don't care that I just got laughed at by my roommate and a few others walking past our room. I would do anything for you, Hollie," he vows seriously.

"I know you would, Layne, and that makes me love you even more."

"I hate to break this up, because I love all the Hollie time I can get, but I do have to get going so I'm not late for physical training," he says sourly. "Make sure you check in with your parents for my second present. And Hollie," he says as he pauses, making sure he has my attention, "don't forget the most important thing today."

"Layne, babe, it's been six months. How can I forget the one thing I do every single day?"

"I know, baby, I just wanted to make sure you still send me a picture. But the reason I'm reminding you is for the fact that I want a picture of you with my present."

"Umm—do I want to open this gift in front of my parents?" I ask nervously.

He laughs. "Hollie, sunshine, what are you trying to imply? I would never send you something you couldn't open in front of your family. If I gave you something for your eyes only, we would have to be in the same room, alone, without prying eyes around," he teases me.

"Okay, then. I think I can accomplish the mission."

"Good. Now, I have to go, but before I do, I want you to wrap your arms around yourself, squeeze tight, and know that that's me hugging you, and to remember that one day, it really will be my arms around you."

"Only if you do the same, even if Sean harasses you for the rest of your life about it." I laugh, but I'm also serious.

"Sean has seen and heard me do worse things than this, so it's an easy task I can handle."

"Good."

"All right Sunshine, remember to send me a photo later, and I'll try to get a hold of you tonight to see what you thought of it. If I can't, I'll text you instead," he assures me.

"Wait, before you go, what was that song you were whistling?" I ask. Trying to hold on to him for a tad bit longer.

"That was *First Call*. It's just the song they play in the military, and they want you to hightail it out of bed the moment you hear it. Remind me to send you the words one day."

"Oh, I bet that's a joy to hear," I laugh.

"No. I hate it." He laughs back. "It would scare the heck out of me, and everyone else, just about, when I first entered basic training, causing us to literally jump out of bed. It definitely put the pep in your step to be ready before your Drill Instructor bursts through the door, yelling and screaming at you the whole time as you rush to get ready and then line up for inspection. *Ahh,* the good old days. But that's for another time, sweetheart. Thanks for trying to distract me," he chuckles. "Now, I'm hanging up, as much as I don't want to." He sighs heavily, "I love you, Holls."

"I love you too, soldier."

"Bye sweetheart."

"Bye Layne," I say, and then the line is dead. I'm left with an aching heart, but a giant smile on my face. I automatically jump out of bed and go running for my bedroom door. *I have a present to find.*

Later that day, I'm sitting on my bed, getting ready for my birthday party with the girls. But before that, I need to take a picture of me with my present, to send to Layne. I've purposefully waited all day until I was all dressed up before I sent a photo.

Earlier this morning, I found mom already up making breakfast as I ambushed her about my present, asking her how she could keep this package a secret from me. She just shakes her head and laughs, saying something about young love. I then inform her that Layne had just now called me and that he told me that he loved me. I'm sure she already knew this. But she just smiles at me and goes off to get the package.

I sit down at the table patiently waiting—*sort of*—for my gift. She brings it back and sets it down in front of me. Stepping back to give me privacy, but not going too far away, she patiently waits to see what's in the box as well.

I don't bother with pretenses. I just rip that sucker open so I can get to something that Layne has touched. I pull out another box that's wrapped up very prettily. *I'm sure he paid for it to be gift-wrapped by a professional.*

Upon unwrapping the present, I find a beautiful glass jar filled with tissue paper. There's a note on the outside and I pull it off, finding hidden words. The note had been placed over them. The jar is labeled: *The Kissing Jar.* Baffled, I decide to open the note that holds Layne's handwriting, yet another piece of Layne that I'll treasure.

I also decided I should read it aloud, because I know my mom is overcome with curiosity at this point.

Dear Hollie-

If you'll notice, the jar is labeled 'The Kissing Jar.' This is no ordinary jar; it's special. Now, I want you to open the jar, and there you'll find another piece of paper with your mission. Happy birthday.

Love,

Layne

I put down the paper and lift the lid from the jar, finding this other piece of paper. I open it and read this one aloud, too.

Hollie Reed-
This is your mission, should you choose to accept it.

First, fill this jar with one Hershey's kiss, every single day.

Your mission is to continue doing this daily until I am standing on your porch, with you in my arms.

On that day, your mission will be complete.

That will be the day that I give you a real kiss, plus one for each of the substitutes, until every single one of those kisses has been properly replaced.

This is your mission. Can you do this for me?

XOXO,
Layne

I put the note down and look in the jar, finding a bag already filled with Hershey's kisses. I look up at my mom, and we both smile like big loons at each other, right before I burst into tears. *I miss my soldier.* My mom wraps her arms around me and holds me tightly for a few moments before I pull away and swallow the hard lump in my throat. I wipe my eyes, then take out my phone to send Layne a picture and text.

Hollie: I accept.

Then I push send, knowing it will be awhile before he sees the message, and start right away on fulfilling my mission. Once the task is complete, I finish getting ready for the day, with a full heart and a bounce in my step.

December 28, 2013

> *Hollie-*
>
> *I love you now and always.*
>
> *Layne*

Hollie: I love you too.

Hubby: Remember, you're always in my heart. I love you, sunshine.

December 30, 2013

> *My Love,*
>
> *When did all of the love songs ever written suddenly become about you?*
>
> *Layne*

Smiling to myself, I pick up my phone and shoot off a text to Layne.

Hollie: Since the day I slammed into you.

Hubby: The best day of my life.

Hollie: So sweet.

Hubby: That's me, sugar and spice and everything nice.

Hollie: I thought that was little girls. I'll call you later tonight.

Hubby: Smart aleck. You better. I'm counting down the hours until I hear your sweet voice.

Hollie: "sigh"

Hollie: I'm so glad you're not made of frogs and snails and puppy dog tails.

Hubby: Who says I wasn't? You just get the sweeter part of me. The guys on base get the rest!

Hollie: Yeah, the gross parts, that is.

Hubby: Exactly, which are the best parts.

Hollie: Boys!

Hubby: Boys at heart, only. Hurry up and send me a photo of your pretty face so I can get some work done. I miss you.

Hollie: I miss you, and I love you.

Hubby: I love you too, Hollie. I'll call you later, baby.

Hollie: I'll be waiting.

Hubby: You better.

Hollie: Bossy.

Chapter Nine

2014 Love Notes

January 6, 2014

> *Hollie,*
>
> *What's that saying about the moon? Something like: I love you to the moon and back?*
>
> *Well, if that's how it goes, then I'll be taking that trip for the rest of my life.*
>
> *-Layne*

January 13, 2014

> *Sunshine,*
>
> *Every time I see the sun, it reminds me of you. If I could box*

up little rays of the sun's light, I would put them in this letter and mail them to you to brighten up your life, like you do mine. Instead, I left this paper out on the beach for awhile, collecting as much of the rays as it could. You can't see them or feel them, but just know that I tried to send a piece of the sun to you.

The sky to your sun-

   Layne

February 17, 2014

   Dearest Hollie-

   I love seeing you in photos. I love video chatting with you. I love the emails and the text messages. I love hearing your voice over the phone. But nothing will ever take the place of having you right next to me.

   Looking forward to the day when we will have the opportunity to see each other face-to-face, on a daily basis.

   Always,

   Layne

March 17, 2014

   Hollie–

   I know being with me won't be easy, and I won't tell you it is. But what I can tell you is, it's going to be worth it in the end.

   Stay strong and know you are never far from my mind, heart and soul.

   Forever yours,

   Layne

March 31, 2014

Name a star that shines so bright for the whole world to see: Hollie

-Layne

April 14, 2014

Hollie,

I like you, a lot. You make me smile. You make me laugh. And you truly make me happy. You're smart, beautiful, and I love how different you are. Sure you're a little crazy, funny and klutzy, but your smile alone, sunshine, makes my whole day and brightens my night.

-Layne

May 5, 2014

My Love-

The Army may have my body, but you will always own my heart.

Yours Truly,

Layne

May 26, 2014

Dear Sunshine-

You are my rock, as you stand behind me and support and encourage me. Whenever you're having a hard time, I want you to look back on these words and know how true they are and how proud I am of you.

Love-

Layne

June 9, 2014

Lovely Hollie-

Happy one-year anniversary, sweetheart.

A little poem to brighten your day:

Roses are red, violets are blue, my life is perfect, because I'm with you.

Love-

Layne

July 7, 2014

My sweetest Hollie,

Did you know that all of me loves all of you? Because, Sunshine, I do.

I miss you more every day.

-Layne

August 4, 2014

Dear Love,

The distance between us only makes me love you that much more.

Thinking of you-

Layne

September 22, 2014

One of your hugs would go a long ways right now. A kiss would go even further.

Yours-

Layne

November 3, 2014

My sweet Hollie-

I'm the guy who waits months to hold you in his arms while you're the girl who waits months for that first kiss all over again.

-Layne

December 1, 2014

Holls,

I can't wait to kiss you again and show you just how much I've been missing you.

Love you,

Layne

December 15, 2014

Hollie–

All I want for Christmas is YOU.

All my heart,

Layne

Chapter Ten

December 24, 2014

Hollie's Second Birthday with Layne

I WAKE UP to music playing over and over, and I reach out to slap the alarm clock, but it doesn't stop. It's not my alarm. As I slowly realize this, I feel a bit disoriented.

"Oh for all that's holy. You've got to be kidding me." I grouch, as I realize it's my cell phone ringing, and go in search of it in the pitch black of my bedroom. As I'm searching, I see that it's six in the morning. I do believe someone wants an earful. By the time I find my phone, tangled in my covers, the ringing stops.

"Seriously?" I exclaim, as I throw it back on the bed and then lay back down, only to be disturbed by the music again. If I had been more with it, I would have realized who was calling me and what day it was, but I was in a seriously foul mood for being woken up this early and, more than ready to let the person on the other end have it.

I hit the green button, ready to give the caller a piece of my mind, only to hear a whistling tune. I automatically feel my anger deflating and start to smile as I lay back in my bed, getting comfortable as I settle in for this awesome morning phone call.

"Happy Birthday, sunshine."

"I'm so glad to hear your voice. You're lucky though, soldier. I was about to let you have it for ruining my beauty sleep," I warn him.

"Well, I miss you too, sweetheart," He chuckles. "So, what's on the birthday girl's agenda this year?"

"I'm not sure what my family has planned, but it will probably be the same as every year. Well, mostly. This year, Jen and Ava won't be home, and I'm bummed out. But we do plan to have a birthday party still, by Skyping each other at the same time to celebrate. The plan is for each of us to have a cupcake, and then we'll probably spend it catching up and joking around. It won't be the same as being together, but it's the next best thing. It's a tradition that we don't want to ruin even if we are miles apart."

"I'm happy for you, sunshine. I wish, yet again, that I could be there with you."

"I know, Layne." I say a little gloomily. "There's always next year, right?" I try to sound upbeat, but my heart is just not completely in it. I really wanted to see him, but it just wasn't possible. I was able to see him over the summer again this year, but I had to go out there. Which was fine, because hey, *it's Hawaii, and who would turn a trip there down? Plus, Layne was there.*

"That's my girl." He tries to sound just as happy as I try to pretend to be. "I got up a little bit earlier this year so we could have some extra time to talk."

"Babe, you didn't have to get up so early just for my birthday." It makes me happy for the thought, but I also feel bad for him at the same time.

"I know, baby, but I'm glad I did. And besides, I really wanted to. So, there's another two-part present this year. But this year, you don't have to rush off to find your gift. It should be sitting on your dresser where I instructed your mom to leave it for when I called you this morning," he informs me.

"What? How did I miss her coming into my room? I'm a pretty light sleeper."

"Good to know, for future birthday surprises," Layne comments, and I can hear the smile in his voice.

"However, before you get up to find it, I want to tell you something." He says, but I have a feeling that I already know what the words are going to be before he even speaks them.

"My gift to you this year, Hollie, is the most important one of all time. *My love.* I love you, Hollie."

He pauses, so I can get the full effect of the meaning of his words, before continuing.

"It's the forever kind, sweetheart. There will never be an end to it for as long as I walk and breathe. You own my heart and soul. I hope you know that you are always with me in spirit. I want you to know that you are truly my sunshine. My *only* sunshine. I want you to know that you make me happy. So whatever you do, whatever we go through, no matter what, please don't ever take my sunshine away. I love you, Holls."

"I love you too, soldier."

"Now, your mission is to go find your present." He commands me.

"Sir. Yes, sir!" I say as I hope off my bed and dash to my dresser, flipping the light on as soon as I make it there.

"I have to say, Hollie, I really like hearing that from you. I think you should call me that more often," he laughs.

"Oh geez. Men." I say on a laugh as I discover my present, right where he said it should be.

"Find your gift yet?" he asks a bit impatiently.

"I did, in fact, find it. It's so tiny. It's not a ring, is it?" I ask a bit cautiously, but maybe even a little bit hopefully.

"Hollie, my sweet girl, I wish that were true, but would I do something that important over the phone, without my presence?" he asks.

"No, I guess not."I say, a bit bummed.

He laughs. "Don't pout, Sunshine, it's not a pretty look on you. Well, scratch that. You're always pretty. I just like you better when you're happy and smiling."

"Oh, you don't like me as much when I don't smile, then?" I try to pretend like I'm upset, but he knows me well enough not to buy into it, so he brushes it off and continues on.

"Woman, just open your gift before the apocalypse happens and I have to go fight the zombies," he jokes.

"Don't be so testy so early in the morning. It's not becoming of you." I tease him back, making him laugh.

I tear open into my gift and pull out a long box, which I hurry to open. In the box is a set of dog tags. I pull them out and right away, I see a picture. Upon closer inspection I notice that it's a picture of Layne and I from my last visit to Hawaii during the past summer.

"Oh, Layne!"I exclaim excitedly. "It's perfect. I love it."

"Did you see both parts?" he asks.

I look back at it and notice a second tag. I pull it up to inspect it and see writing and a little piece of a heart hanging off. The tag reads: *You carry my heart.* Then I look over to the heart and it says: *With you.*

"Layne, you are such the romantic. This is really sweet. Thank you so much, sweetheart."

"Anything for you, Hollie. Anything. Now, I want you to look in the box for the last part."

I reach in and pull out a tiny slip of paper. I unfold it and read aloud, *"Hollie, your mission, if you choose to accept it is: To get your butt back here! I miss you, and need my Hollie fix. Love, Layne."*

"Of course I accept. Can you get me on the next flight out?"

I hear him sigh. "Babe, you know I want to, but I couldn't get the time off myself. I'm sorry, sweetheart. I'll fly you out here after the New Year, though."

"This is so hard sometimes, Layne. I miss you and I just want to see you all of the time."

"I promise, Hollie, I will see you very soon. I put in for leave, and seeing as I really haven't had much time off, I hope it gets approved. And then, before you know it, I'll be standing on your front porch." He finishes, and just then, I hear the doorbell ring.

"Okay, that was really weird."

"What's that, babe?" Layne asks.

"Someone just rang my–,"my mouth slams shut and I realize what an idiot I am. I jump out of bed and go running to the living room. My phone is all but forgotten on my bed, as I dropped it in my haste to see if I'm dreaming, or if he's really here.

My fingers fumble with the locks, and somehow in my crazy flight to the door, I completely miss my parents standing in the entry-way, watching me. Finally, I manage to get the locks undone, and as I swing the door open to my elated surprise, there's Layne, standing on my porch.

My eyes immediately well up in tears, and I leap into his arms.

I can't stop crying hysterically as I maul him with kisses all over his face. He hugs me fiercely, never letting go, bravely enduring my crazy attack. After a bit we hear a throat clear, causing me to lift my head and see my parents. My mom's beaming at me, as my dad is staring with a cocked eyebrow.

Layne sets me down, but doesn't take his arm from around my waist as he hugs me to him. There is no way my father is going to make us separate after all these months of being apart. He knows how hard it's been. But I do understand that this is their first time meeting in person. Of course, they've met over Skype and have talked a few other times on the phone with me. They really hit it off in a way that only males can, but I'm not encouraging a bro-mance between them. This is *my* man. Dad can find himself a new pal to hang with.

"Sir," Layne says, holding out his hand to shake my dad's.

"Son, you know better than that. It's Carson, and what's with this handshake nonsense? A man can't hug another man these days?"

I smile like a big lunatic at my father before turning it on Layne. He smiles down at me, shaking his head, too. Then he lets me go for a moment to get a back-pounding hug from my dad, and a nice mama-bear hug from my mom.

"Ma'am, I mean Carol, it's great to finally meet you and Carson. Thank you for allowing me to stay in your home." He politely thanks my parents, while simultaneously imparting me with a little gem that I had no idea about. I would have assumed he would be staying elsewhere. This is definitely a shock.

Eyebrows raised, I give my dad a questioning look.

"Well, we couldn't have him staying alone, at Christmastime, all the way in town, now could we?" he asks.

"Of course not, I'm just surprised, but beyond happy. Thanks, Dad." I say as I hug him.

"Anything for my girl." He smiles proudly at me then turns it on Layne.

"Watch it, Layne might get jealous if you call me *your* girl," I tease my dad.

"Tough. He'll have to get used to sharing." And then he turns to go back into the house, snatching my mom's hand as he goes, dragging her along. I bet she would have tried to nose her way into this happy reunion even further, if given the opportunity.

"So—" he starts.

I don't even let him finish his sentence before I throw my arms around his neck and slam my lips to his. After a sufficient make-out session, he pulls away with a big grin on his face.

"I'll take this as a sign that you're happy to see me?" he says a bit smugly.

"You know it, soldier!" I say as I kiss him one more time.

"Wait. I thought you said you only got me two gifts this year? This technically makes three." I inform him, like he can't do the math himself.

"No sweetheart, this isn't your birthday gift. It's technically your early Christmas gift." He proudly informs me.

"I have to say that you are one lucky man, as I was feeling horrible that I didn't get your gift to the post office in time. It's sitting under my tree."

"Holls, you know you didn't have to do that. I would rather see your beautiful face and hear your sexy voice any day, over a present." He says as he pulls me into his chest and places a chaste kiss on my lips.

"Although, I would never turn down a gift from my girl," he winks at me.

"If you two are done making out on the porch for the whole neighborhood to see—" we hear my dad yell from inside the house.

Oops! Looks like they hadn't shut the door behind them.

"I believe that's our cue to be on our best behavior." Layne winks at me. "I know I'm pretty hard to resist, but you have to try to behave, Hollie. We wouldn't want to start a scandal around here. Can you imagine what the old biddies would print about us?" he mocks outrage.

"Oh, heavens no! We wouldn't want to be front page gossip in the papers later today." I joke. *Well, it's not really a joke—it could happen in this town.* Layne smiles down at me as he slides his hand into mine before walking up to the house and closing the door behind us, effectively closing us in and keeping any prying eyes out. If they want to gossip about us, then let them. Nothing is going to ruin my holiday cheer this year. I have Layne and my family, and that's all that matters in the end.

As I told Layne on the phone, Jenifer and Ava both decided not to come home for winter break this year. They had plans to go on a big ski trip with their new friends instead.

I let them off the hook with skyping later for my birthday. I wanted all of my free time to go to Layne. Now they can enjoy their trip, knowing I'm in good hands.

Yes, I was a bit jealous, but I knew they didn't totally forget me.

Later that night, we are sitting around the fireplace watching *A Christmas Story* on TV, my all-time favorite holiday movie. This movie is classic—*how can you not love it?*

On a whim, I lean over and whisper in Layne's ear, "*Happy anniversary.*"

"Well, now that you mention it, it really has been, what? Thirty years together already?" he jokes, and gets my elbow in his ribs for that.

"I'm not that bad, soldier-boy."

"No, but maybe you're just not that good," he laughs.

"Ha ha. Maybe Santa plans to take back your presents this year and just leave you coal," I huff.

"Come on, sunshine, you know you love it when I tease you. You didn't have a brother growing up, so someone has to school you in the male art form that is teasing." He winks at me.

"Did you forget I grew up with two best friends by the names of Jenifer and Ava? I think they imparted all of their firsthand knowledge of brotherly teasing on me, thanks to their older brothers."

"*Ahh,* well, seems I've been put in my place. It doesn't mean I'll ever stop harassing you, though. It's too fun to rile you up." He laughs, making my dad laugh, too.

"Whose side are you on anyway, old man?" I rib at my dad.

"Who are you calling old, *young* lady? I've got a lot of good moves left in this body," he says.

"Oh no, Mom, don't let Dad turn on his oldie music and shake a leg," I laugh. *That would be way too embarrassing.*

"Earlier, you told me that you were my early Christmas present,"

I say, turning to Layne. "Don't you really mean that you are my anniversary present?" I question.

"Nope! I meant what I said," he maintains.

"By the way, it *has* been eighteen months now that you've been dating the most awesome chick that I happen to know," I wag my brows at him suggestively.

"Says you. The way I see it, I've been dating this downright annoying hag—*ooph!*"

All of the wind is knocked out of Layne's chest as I elbow him with apparently too much force behind the throw.

"Sorry, babe," I apologize.

"That's okay, sweetheart," he says with a gleam in his eye. "Payback is always the best revenge," he laughs.

"Will you two pipe it down? This old man can't hear the boob-tube." My dad says as he pretends to be older than he really is, just to give us a hard time.

"Carson, you remember what it's like to be that young and in love. Leave the two lovebirds alone." Mom helpfully chimes in, yet it's still a tad bit embarrassing.

"Okay, how about we all go back to the movie now?" I say, trying to get the attention off of us and back on the screen.

"What's the matter? Too much heat in the kitchen?" Layne whispers in my ear.

"Really? Are you asking for a second serving of butt-kicking?" I ask him.

Leaning his head against the couch as he laughs, he tugs me with him and pulls my head to his chest. "Why don't you just be a good girl and watch the movie, sunshine." He says against the shell of my ear, sending the butterflies in my stomach to take off in flight. *He's so good at that.* I decide to shut up and relax while enjoying the view of the screen and of his chest as he casually plays with the ends of my hair.

Later that night, after we're ready for bed, there's a knock at my door.

"Come in," I call out, knowing who it is. It helps that he sent me a text first to make sure that the coast was clear.

"So, this is the room of the one-and-only Hollie Reed, is it? Tell me, do you have any secret stashes of things that you don't want me to know about? Like, stuffed animals from your childhood? Or maybe a poster of one of those famous boy-bands?" he laughs as he shuts the door behind him, scanning my room. "Maybe you have a secret diary hidden between your mattresses filled with all the reasons you find me irresistibly attractive," he teases me.

I take a throw pillow and chuck it at his head, which misses as he ducks, cracking us both up.

He comes over to my bed and pounces on me, causing me to fall back onto my pillow.

"I'm pretty sure this is going to get us written up in the gossip column," I tease him back.

"Don't care." He says simply, as he roams my face with his hazel eyes. "I've missed you way too much, and I need some uninterrupted moments with my favorite girl." He smiles as he leans in for a kiss.

"Besides, I have two reasons for breaking house rules to see you," he says as he sits up.

"Oh yeah? What are they?" I ask curiously.

"For one, I had to see you, Hollie. I've been dying to get you alone all day. Cut a guy some slack, will you?" he says as he lays down on the other side of me.

"I'm just giving you a hard time, soldier." I roll to my side to lay my head on his chest.

"But," I warn, pointing a finger into his chest, "if I get grounded over this, you're going down too, buster." I half-warn and half-tease him.

"Yes, ma'am. Being grounded with you wouldn't be a hardship, just so you know. However, if your parents try to ground you on the night you turned 20, then I'm jumping ship."

"Only if you take me with you. So, what's the second reason my man couldn't stay away?"

"Do I need a second reason? You're reason enough, baby." He says as he strokes my arm with the backs of his fingers.

"But you are right—I *do* have another motive for seeing you. Why don't you reach in my pocket and see what you can dig up?" he tells me.

I eye him suspiciously, but do as he instructs, pulling out a note.

My eyes light up as I look to him for confirmation.

"Yes, sweetheart, it's exactly what you think it is. Why don't you go ahead and read it so I can watch your beautiful face?"

Sitting up, I open his love note and read it, to myself.

December 24, 2014

Hollie my love-

I'm on my way to surprise you for Christmas, and I look forward to your reaction upon my arrival. I honestly hope I can contain myself in front of your parents. It's been unbelievably hard not to spoil everything. I'm surprised Sean hasn't already spilled it to Ava. I was sure that you knew by now. I'm not sure how we managed to pull it off.

I miss you so.

As I sit here on the plane, thinking about you, and life in general, I can't help but realize what a rich man I am. Do you realize I have the most valuable item in the entire world? Do you know what that is, my love? It's YOU.

Thank you for giving me you.

Love always,

Layne

Setting the note down on the bed, I take a moment to look at Layne with a dopey grin on my face, but with all of the love that I can muster shining out of my eyes.

"Thank you. You're the best gift I could have ever imagined. Who knew a small town girl like me would end up with a world class guy like you?" I scoot back into my spot, with my head on his chest and my arm around his waist.

"I think it's the other way around," he quietly says. *"I'm the lucky one."*

I decide it's best to not respond to that, and choose to just enjoy this moment that I have with him while I can, secretly knowing that he has it all wrong. I want to lay here, with him, and think back through the time we've been together, and how amazing it is that we've lasted this long with an ocean between us.

And that's what I do as Layne lightly rubs my back, as he too is in his own world tonight. It feels good to have his warm body here with me, where I can physically see and touch him. *It's been way too long.*

After a while, I start to fall asleep on Layne. I'm so warm and comfortable that I don't want to move, so I snuggle into him as much as I can and let my eyes start to drift closed.

"I love you, Layne. Merry Christmas."

I feel him kiss my head, right before I pass out.

The next morning, I wake up alone under my covers. I'm assuming that was all thanks to Layne. Maybe I'm really not that much of a light sleeper after all. I roll over onto my side and see that it's nine in the morning. I wish I could just snuggle longer into my blankets and go back to sleep, but there's a special someone here, waiting on me.

So, I climb out of bed, throw on my robe, slide on my fuzzy slippers, and go in search of a hairbrush and toothbrush. I know Layne's Christmas wish isn't to see a bed-headed girlfriend with bad breath first thing in the morning.

Once I accomplish these small tasks, I go in search of the smells of breakfast and hot chocolate floating in the air and straight to my nose, making my mouth water.

Stepping into the kitchen, I see my folks are up, and so is Layne. He sees me and sends a sweet smile my way, as he takes in my appearance.

"Good morning, sleepy." My mom kisses me on the side of the head as I stop at the counter for some cocoa.

"Morning," I mumble. I'm so not a morning person, but for Layne, I could at least try, right? *Maybe.* I don't think anyone can really take my love for sleep away.

Not even Layne.

"Good morning, sunshine." Layne plants a kiss on my temple the moment I sit down next to him at the table.

My dad laughs. "Sunshine, huh? I don't think this girl is any kind of light source in the morning. Sorry to break the bad news, son."

I roll my eyes at my dad, but he just smiles at me before he takes a big, heaping bite of eggs. *Dang, now I'm really starving.*

"Don't worry, Hollie. Your plate is coming. We've all had breakfast already, but your dad decided to steal your plate for a second help-ing. He didn't think you would make it down before dinner tonight," she laughs.

"So funny. I would have made it for lunch, at the very least."

"If you say so," Dad says with another mouthful of my breakfast.

"Food thief. I think Santa left you coal in your stocking this year." I wave a finger at him.

"Santa knows better, isn't that right, dear?" he gives Mom a mis-chievous grin.

"Right, now eat your food, before Santa puts you on the naughty list, permanently."

"And on that note, Layne, why don't we get out of this kitchen? It's too hot in here."

He chuckles, and places a hand on my knee. "Oh, leave the old lovebirds alone." He jokes, referencing the comment that was made to us just the day before.

"Old? I don't see anyone old birds in here. Do you, Carol?" Dad asks Mom.

"I only see two spring chickens." She replies as she finishes up my breakfast, then plates it for me.

"Well, I don't see you putting a pep in your step to bring that plate anywhere in my vicinity. I think we need to trade you in for a newer model."

"Just remember where you lay your head at night, who makes your food, and who does your laundry," she taunts me.

"I wouldn't try her, trust me. I learned that when we first got married. I'll forever remember the horror stories of your mother's pranks," Dad shivers. "Your mom, believe it or not, was a feisty one in her prime. She could get the best of you."

"What I really meant was, we should send you on a vacation to a nice resort," I giggle.

"Just eat your food, missy."

"Yes, ma'am." I mock salute her before tucking into my deli-cious, mouth-watering biscuits and gravy.

I look over to Layne, who's just shaking his head with a hint of a smile on his face. I wink at him, and go back to my food.

After breakfast, I decide to show Layne around Holly Grove. The best place to do that would be with a walk down Holly Lane. We get ready for the day, bundle ourselves up, and set out for a walk to my favorite place in town.

The distance from my house to the town's center is only about a half a mile, so we take our time, not in a hurry to get back home or really go anywhere, but just to be together.

"Remember I sent you something on your last birthday?" Layne asks.

"Yes, I believe I know what you're getting at." To be honest, I had wondered when he would bring this up. I'm definitely excited for the possibilities of what it means for us.

"Do you still have it?"

"I do. It's in my room, and filled to the brim. I have more than one now, in case you were wondering."

"I think I need to cash in on as many of those promises as possible."

"*Hmmm.* I like the sound of that. You can call those kisses my *birthmas* gift this year."

"How about we just see what happens as the day unfolds?"

"I hope you didn't go all out for me. I'm good with the kisses. You do owe me like, a lot."

"*Like,* really? How much is, 'like a lot?'" he teases me.

"I don't know. We'll just have to count them when we get home, and you can try to give me all the kisses you owe me before you head back to that island paradise of yours."

"I think we should start now. Every time we make it to the corner of a street, we have to kiss at least three times."

I laugh. "Three? That's it? I don't think I can stop at three. You're crazy."

"We can't make out on the corner every chance we get. I think three is a respectful number. Do you accept the mission, Miss Reed?"

"Yes, I do."

"Those words are music to my ears. Maybe next year you can say them for real."

"Maybe." I smile at him as we continue walking towards Holly Lane, stopping at every corner on our special kissing quest.

We walk, hand in hand, down the main street, admiring all of the shops decked out for Christmas, as Layne still keeps up the kissing game.

Since it's Christmas day, the shops are all closed, except for the diner. Some families like to head in to *Noelle's Café* for the holiday, especially the singles in town. I think Noelle secretly loves to stay open and celebrate with an eclectic mix of town folk.

We stop in there next and have some pie and more hot cocoa. I hear Noelle has the best eggnog, but I can't stomach the stuff. Of course, while we're there, I have to make the introductions for Layne to anyone who has entered the diner since we've been sitting in here.

What was I thinking? Oh wait, I wasn't. I was too busy being a silly girl in love to consider our small town filled with know it all's. Then again, he's a new face in town, and if I were them, I too would want to know who he was—*though I wouldn't go so far as to actually try to meet him.*

Once we finally get out of the café, I take Layne down to the massive Christmas tree at the other end of the lane, and we continue to admire the creative way that the town has dressed itself up with decorations. I personally love the red bows and ribbons wrapped around the trees and street lamps. Some have holly or mistletoe attached to them as well.

I think the town looks fabulous in its seasonal décor, and the tree is really beautifully decorated with white lights, round red bulbs, and a giant gold star perched on the top. It's simple, but still spectacular at the same time. *Classic Holly Grove Christmas.*

Once we stop in front of it, Layne positions me just so as he lets go of me completely. I give him a quizzical look as I watch him pull something from his pocket, which turns out to be a small, gift-wrapped box.

"Hollie, I have something important I wanted to give you this year. I wanted to make it something special, shared just between us."

He hands me the box, but I'm slightly hesitant to open it, wondering if he's about to do what I think he's going to do. I look at him one more time, but he's just patiently waiting for me to unwrap the gift, and I decide that I should probably oblige him.

I manage to get the paper off and open the lid, only to stop and stare at the shiny object looking right back at me. I glance back up to Layne then quickly look around to see if the gossipers are out, but confirming that we are alone, look at him intently.

"Hollie, will you accept this promise ring? It is a symbol of my intentions for you and our future together."

I'm rapidly blinking my eyes because now they're tearing up as fast as they can, and simply nod my head yes. He takes out the blue sapphire ring and places it on my left ring finger, above the ring from him that I have continued wear, which also sent the town into a feeding frenzy after returning from Hawaii the first time. My parents were not happy about it, but I've refused to take off the ring since he gave it to me.

Noticing my other ring, Layne looks up at me. "I see you still wear my heart around your finger. Thank you." He says, placing a kiss to my thoroughly adorned finger.

I help him back to his feet, and he envelops me into his embrace.

"I can't promise we will always be in one place for long periods of time." He warns me cautiously.

"Yes, I know." I quietly confirm into his chest.

"And I don't know where I'll be stationed next year, or the next after that, but wherever that is, Hollie, I want you to be with me. Do you accept this new mission?"

"Yes, wholeheartedly. I want to be where you are, Layne. Always," I sincerely tell him, as I go up on my tiptoes to kiss him.

He hugs me to him a little more tightly, and we stay that way for a good while, just basking in the promise I've made to him and loving that he wants me with him wherever he goes.

At some point, later in the day, we walk back to my house, getting there in time for an early dinner with my parents. But on our way back to the house, Layne points out something that I never caught, which was crazy silly on my part, since it's been in my face since I've lived here.

He noticed that the street we've spent most of our day on is called Holly Lane, and that it's a funny play on both of our names. We decide to take a self-portrait with our phones at the street sign, together. I love the way it turns out, and immediately decide that it's now one of my favorite new memories of us together.

We still have gifts under the tree to open, as I'm sure it didn't happen because they were waiting on me to wake up that morning, so we decided to finally head home to continue on with the holiday's festivities.

As we wander up the walkway to the porch, we see a present sitting on the top step. When we get close enough, I bend down to pick it up. I see a note attached to a box of Ho Hos and a box of Ding Dong Hostess Cakes.

What in the world? I give Layne a questioning look as we go inside the house.

"Mom!" I yell out the moment we cross the threshold of my home.

"In the kitchen!" she yells back as we make our way to her.

"We found this weird gift on the porch?" I question, the moment we enter the kitchen.

"Oh, it's probably a gift from the neighbors. Remember? They always do something cute or funny for people. But, yes this year it's a little strange, and definitely not the usual." She says upon further inspection of the boxes. "Was there a note?"

"Yes." I say as I set the boxes down and pull off the note.

Reading it aloud, I say, *"Ho Ho Ho. Merry Christmas, from the ding dongs down the street."*

I look up at my mom just as we both bust up laughing, along with Layne.

"Oh my goodness. That was a good one," Mom continues to laugh.

Very clever neighbors, it appears we have. I'm still smiling as Dad walks into the kitchen.

"What's so funny?" he asks.

I pick up the boxes and note then shove them at him, as he eyes the stuff questionably. He sets everything down, then opens the note. A moment later, we are laughing all over again, and this time with Dad.

After the goofiness wears off, I help Mom make dinner and set the table. Once dinner is over, we gather around the Christmas tree, and my dad hands out the gifts.

Dad hands me a present that's from Layne. "Another one?"

"Trust me, you'll love this one." He says, giving me a sheepish look.

"I already love what you gave me. But, just for you, I'll accept this one, too."

I rip into the packaging and then lift off the lid to the jewelry box. Never did I ever expect to find what was at the bottom.

A big smile forms on my face. "You sly devil, you. I can't believe you tricked me like that!" I laugh, as I punch his arm. "I can't believe you waited all of this time."

"So, you love it then?" *As if he has to ask.* "I'm glad. I hated that you thought you were helping me pick out a bracelet for someone else."

"Thank you, it's beautiful. I love it, and I love you."

My parents look at us questioningly, and Layne retells the story of the turtle bracelet and the shopping expedition.

After Layne finishes, my dad hands over a present to Layne from me. *I can't wait to see what he thinks.*

"Hollie, you shouldn't have, but doesn't mean that I'm not thrilled you did."

He unwraps his gift, lifting the lid off of the box. Inside, he finds a book entitled, *Our Love Story.* It's a book that I had specially made for him to take wherever he is, so he can look back on our life together even when we are very far apart.

He gently opens the book to see what it's all about, and I decide to share with him what I've done.

"This is a book full of our daily photos, text messages and emails. It's a way to keep the memories of our long distance relationship safe. We can look back on it in the future, and have fond memories of these hard years we had to endure in the beginning. Or, we can just laugh over everything, too. That works for me. I'm sure there are plenty of smart remarks in there made by you," I tease him.

"Hollie, truly, this is the best gift, next to you, that I've ever received. Thank you so much. I look forward to reading the things we've said over the last year and a half."

He gives me a kiss on my cheek before getting back to checking out his book, like the happiest boy on earth.

I look over at my parents. I forgot they were even in the room, as they've been so quiet. But they're actually nowhere to be seen. It appears that they have quietly left us to our privacy. I smile to myself, thanking them in my head, and think about how much I love my parents, and Layne.

Layne spends a few more days with us, and we continue our game of catching up on the promises of the kisses he owes me. My parents also spend some important time getting to know him better before we have to take him to the airport.

My parents come with me to take him to his plane. They give us privacy again—as they've been very good about doing lately—after they say their goodbyes to him, and I can't bear to let him go.

We stand still for a long period of time holding on to each other, both not needing to give voice to the emotional communication between us. We said our goodbyes the night before, and have already had a long talk about our future together.

So today, it's all about the promise of seeing each other again.

Though, I don't know when that will be. And I know I said I would not make this harder on him, but I can't help it. I cry like a baby, and I hold on to him as tight as I can until the very last moment before he truly has to leave me.

Wiping the tears streaming down my face, he gives me a sad smile. "Hollie, remember sweetheart, this isn't a goodbye forever. We're just saying, 'until we meet again.' Remember, my heart belongs to you, and *only* you. And also remember the promises we've made each other. This should be a happy and joyous occasion. You're breaking my heart, Holls." He softly kisses me.

"I really don't want to leave you either, and I hate to say it, but I have to go. The plane won't wait, and my bosses won't be happy if I'm not back on time." He hugs me to him one more time. "I love you, baby," he says into my hair.

"I know. I love you too, soldier."

He pulls away with one last look, then walks to the security line and out of my life for who knows how long, until we see each other next.

My dad drives us home as I sit in the back with my silent tears and my heart slightly broken, missing Layne.

Chapter Eleven

2015 Confessions of a Soldier

Layne

THE LAST TIME I saw Hollie was a few days before the New Year started. I left her behind, with tears in her eyes, and it killed me not to go back to her and hold her one last time. I knew I couldn't, for if I did, I wouldn't be able to leave her side.

This long distance romance has been one of the hardest things of my life, even over my career in the Army. Every day I wake up missing her, even though I try to stay upbeat and positive that I'll be able to have her in some form, and that we will find ways to actually see each other in person soon.

The only saving graces so far have been the letters, photos, text messages, phone calls, and when we can video chat together. We try to connect as regularly as possible, even with the time change, as we keep each other in the forefront of our own thoughts.

As much as I love having those special moments, just between the two of us, it's just not the real thing. I try to never let on to Hollie how hard it is for me. I know how much she struggles; I don't need her to know how much I struggle as well. So I try to keep it positive.

We made arrangements for her to come back to Hawaii this March to visit. One of my commanding officers, and his wife, offered to put her up while she is here. I am already excited to see my girl. Still, even with the knowledge that Hollie will be here with me at some point this year, it is way too hard for me to wait.

I need to make the best of our opportunities for communication even more so now, or I'll go crazy from the thoughts of missing her and from the ribbing the guys like to give me every now and then about my relationship.

Hollie isn't the only missing person from my life, however, as Miller is no longer here. The base doesn't feel the same without him, and I still can't believe he's gone. It doesn't seem real. Every day, I wake up expecting to see him, yet I don't.

He ended up being medically and honorably discharged last summer due to a back injury. He couldn't perform his job duties and needed rehabilitation, which I know he could have received from the Army. Though, there was no way he would ever be able to do his job like he used to. It was best that he find a civilian job and recover slowly, instead of trying to aggravate it and cause more damage by pushing on with his regular duties.

I think the only good thing that came out of that for Miller was that he and Ava were finally able to commit to an exclusive relationship. He was tired of their weird relationship status and firmly took control, taking the 'friends' part right out of the equation.

Miller decided to relocate to as close to Ava's school as he could get. He moved in with an old Army buddy of ours. There's still a bit of travel time for them, but nothing like a whole ocean to cross.

Since he's been home, he's made leeway on his recovery. I know he's a bit depressed about not doing what he knows and loves, but thankfully he was able to get an education during his time in the military that will hopefully lead him to bigger and better things when his body eventually affords him the opportunity to do so.

I have other friends out here, but no one will replace Miller. He always had my back, out in the field and on base. We had an easy camaraderie with each other, and really, he was like another brother to me. Life's not the same here, nor will it be when I have to deploy for another mission.

All of this is just depressing me further upon thinking of it. March can't come soon enough.

I need my girl.

February rolls around, and life isn't getting any easier. There's talk of a deployment in the works, and my fingers are crossed that it doesn't happen before Hollie's trip to see me. I haven't told her about it yet, as I don't need to add to her worries. When the time comes, if it actually does, we'll have to cross that bridge then. For now, I'm trying to focus on other things, like Hollie's happiness. No need to stress her out about it just yet.

As for Miller, he can't be any happier to be with Ava, but he's also struggling with being out of the military life. On a positive note, his treatments with his doctors have progressed nicely over the last six months. He's also been applying for jobs with companies as a Systems Engineer.

Life at the base is good, albeit lonely without Miller. Thankfully, Hollie fills my life up with her pictures, messages, and phone calls. I'll have to continue to live that way for one more month.

If I could only turn the hands of time to March already.

By the time March had hit, I couldn't have been any more thrilled that Hollie would finally be here. Too bad that good news came with the bad that I'd been dreading. Shortly after Hollie's visit, we were to deploy overseas, and with this mission, I wouldn't be able to give her a lot of specific information or have much regular contact. I won't even know for how long I'll be gone.

I hadn't planned to tell her the news until the very end of her trip. It was the last thing I wanted to focus on while she was here. It's a rare treat to see each other, so why color it with sadness and thoughts that might worry her if I don't have to? Yes, I was being selfish. Whatever time I could get with Hollie, without coloring it with dread, was what

I was going to focus on.

When the big day had finally arrived, I couldn't stop the permanent smile I had on my face that whole day. The guys had been teasing me and calling me Mr. Sunshine, as they know that Hollie is my sunshine. I let their harassing comments roll off my back, as I was just too excited to see my girl.

I had everything planned out for the four days that she would be here, right up until the moment she left. But first, I had planned to greet her with flowered leis the moment she stepped into my breathing space.

Earlier, my phone had alerted me to a text, showing the name *Wife,* which is how I had Hollie saved in my contacts list. She was letting me know that her plane had landed, and she would hopefully see me in ten minutes.

The moment I saw her, all my focus zeroed in on her only, as she casually made her way toward me, but not yet seeing me. Once she finally located my position, the biggest smile crossed her face, and tears easily flowed down her face as she ran straight into my arms. I swept her off of her feet and spun her around a few times before settling her back onto the ground, though I never took my arms off of her. I knew exactly how she felt, as I peppered her face with kisses. It still felt like a dream having her here, in Hawaii, and in my arms.

We were practically inseparable during her visit, except when the late night hours rolled around. Those were really hard times, probably the worst ever, because then she was mere streets away from me, instead of a whole ocean.

The temptation to sneak out and see her was so strong, but I would never disrespect my commanding officer, his wife, or Hollie by sneaking her out in the middle of the night. I'm not a perfect saint, but I'm not a jerk, either. I can respect her wishes too, even if it did kill me to lose sight of her for six to seven hours of precious shuteye.

I don't think I really got much sleep those nights, and I know the nights to come long after would be just as torturous, with what was waiting for me both abroad and at home.

That was the best and worst trip she could have had. I really dreaded having to tell her about my upcoming deployment. When she finally found out, she bawled her eyes out and my heart cracked with every tear. She has never experienced something like this, and I knew it would be hard, but this was the worst possible torture a man could suffer through. Well, so far, it was the worst kind of torture I've ever endured.

I promised to continue writing my letters, and would try to get word to her as soon as I could, as often as I could, but there were no guarantees in the field. I asked her to promise me she wouldn't give up hope, and to keep the Kisses jar going, until I could fulfill those promises as well. I told her how much I loved her, and thanked her for running into my life.

We might have started off on a whirlwind, and we were not living a conventional relationship, but somehow it works, and it would until my dying breath. People may think we were crazy, but I only know that I'm crazy about this woman, and that's all that matters in the end.

By the time she had to go back home, I made sure to hold her a lot longer and tighter than I think I've ever held onto her before. It felt like I was leaving part of my soul with her, as I was about to head off into the unknown, alone.

I know I didn't sleep much the whole week before we left the country and everyone we loved, everything we held dear, behind.

I could only hope and pray that this deployment wasn't a long one, and that we had luck on our side.

April 2015

I didn't realize how limited our communication back home would be until we arrived at our destination. It's a bit of a remote place, and we're lucky to even be able to stay in touch with our top commanding officers.

Every mission is different. On some deployments, you have downtime, where you can just kick back, play with video gaming systems, have access to the internet to check in more regularly with loved ones back home, watch movies, and so on. *Not this mission, however.* It looks like we'll be roughing it a lot more, and we're all just hoping that the letters we write, or even emails, actually make it to their destinations.

Sunshine,

I don't know when I'll be back, or when you'll see my letters, but for now, I'll continue to write when I can. Just know how much I love you, and that I think of you always.

Love,

Layne

May 2015

We made it through the first month, though we ran into some issues we hadn't seen coming. Other than that, patrols keep us busy, and downtime sucks. It's hot during the day, and downright freezing at night, and it's so dark that you can't even see your hand in front of your face if you tried.

I try not to think of Hollie until it's time to call it quits for the day or during my downtime. Nights are the hardest, and it's during those times that I wish I could wrap her in my arms and strengthen my body with her warmth.

Sunshine,

I haven't been able to write for some time now. But I wanted you to know that I'll be holding you in my heart until I can hold you in my arms again. This thought will have to tide me over until I can get through this mission.

Love,

Layne

June 2015

I really miss Miller's jokes, his sarcastic humor, and all that's good about the guy. I could really use a dose of moral support these days. It's pretty lonely out here without my wingman. He knows how to make time speed up and keep the guys smiling.

I wish he were here to give me a hard time about writing to Hollie, and to keep me on my toes.

I just have to keep thinking about the positive things in my life, and how much having Hollie to go home to is a treasure. Without Miller in my face 24/7, thoughts of Hollie invade my mind instead, and remind me that she's now my rock. I have to keep focused on my job, my men, the goal of this mission, and that I'll being seeing her as soon as we're done here.

Sunshine,

It's been written that "behind every strong soldier, there's an even stronger woman." That's you, sweetheart. You are my strength and my rock. You help me to push on when the days are long and lonely. You support me and make me want to be a better boyfriend, man, and soldier for my country.

Love,

Layne

July 2015

Right now I have a little reprieve from daily duties, and decide to take a rest, as it's hotter than Hades here and I'm beyond exhausted, though rest isn't coming easily for me today.

We've been running on very little sleep lately, with missions starting before the sun rises, most of the time. Even considering how tired I am, and how worn out my body is, my mind won't turn off. So instead, I lay on my cot with thoughts of Hollie floating around in my head.

What is she doing? How is she? Does she think of me as much as I think of her? What would we be doing if were together right now?

Sunshine,

As I lay here, thinking about you, I can't help but wonder if you can feel how much of me still belongs with you.

Love,

Layne

August 2015

At this point, I'm starting to feel homesick. This mission isn't going as smoothly as we had hoped, though no one is really surprised. I think this mission is tougher on me not having Miller at my side for moral support, or to watch my back.

Even though I'm with guys who I would trust with my life, nothing can replace the ease and sureness of having your best friend at your back.

Sunshine,

I'm homesick without you. I need to see you. I need to hear your voice. I need to feel your touch. I need my sunshine.

Love,

Layne

September 2015

This month has been a long one. I'm feeling alone a lot more as time marches on. I miss the daily photos of Hollie, her text messages, and our phone calls. We've been stuck in such a remote area that we haven't been able to send normal communications back home. They only know that we left, and would contact them when we could. I don't know how the other men are handling it, though morale is down in general, and I just hope that Hollie hasn't given up hope on me.

> **Sunshine,**
>
> **I can usually float by on the waves of this life, missing you. But sweetheart, tonight, I'm drowning.**
>
> **Love, Layne**

October 2015

> **Hollie,**
>
> **There isn't a day that goes by that I don't think of you. I miss you and pray that soon I'll be able to see your beautiful face again.**
>
> **Love, Layne**

November 2015

Morale is pretty low at this point, and that feeling of gratitude or being thankful for anything is pretty much out the window. We lost a few guys this month due to snipers in the areas we've deemed as hot spots around the sector we're in charge of.

It's been an awful month, but I'm still holding on to a thread of hope, and I thank my lucky stars every day that I have Hollie. I'm keeping a tight grip on that hope that this mission will succeed quickly and the rest of us can make it out of here alive.

Sunshine,

I feel like I'm going crazy over here. I don't know which way is up or down anymore. I only know that I need you, and I miss you like mad.

I love you.

-Layne

December 2015

HOME. THAT'S THE official word around camp today, that we have fulfilled our duties and have received orders to return stateside. *It hardly seems real.* I almost feel like it won't *be* real until I'm stepping off the plane and touching U.S. soil with my own bare hands.

Even if it doesn't seem real yet, just hearing the words and knowing that we have only one week left here has been the best news, for me, to date. It's been the longest nine months of my life, as it has been the loneliest without my best friend, Miller, at my back, and knowing that I finally have someone waiting for me back home. I've never been this excited about returning home—*ever*—in all of the time that I've spent deployed.

Though, the downside to returning is, Hollie won't be waiting for me when we arrive back at the base. In fact, no one will. *No Hollie. No Miller. No family.*

I'm feeling a mixed bag of emotions. On one hand, I'm excited, and on the other, I'm nervous. *Will Hollie still be waiting for me when I return? What will life bring for me back in the real world and on base?* I know I've only been gone for nine months, and this time it wasn't even that long of a stretch. Yet this time around, I feel like there are too many unknown variables in my life to return to.

Am I due for a base transfer soon? What about the guys, how will they take returning back to 'normal' life, this time around? How is Miller holding up? What about Hollie? Does she think I'm dead? Does she know I still love her and have missed her every single day of my life?

Knowing I have another week left, I remind myself that I need to make sure I continue to stay focused, not get sloppy, lazy, or anything else, so I can continue to keep myself and my fellow soldiers safe. All depressing thoughts are wasted time, and I need to shove them in a dark hole and bury them deep. There's no time for that garbage. I should be thanking my lucky stars if and when we make it back. It's not like I'm not already used to having anyone there when I return anyway, except for Miller. He was all I ever needed back when it mattered the most.

I think it's time to find a scrap of paper and write Hollie a letter, even though I can't send it. I know it will make me feel better to know that I tried this whole time to stick to my promise to her. It might be the one thing to ground me at the moment, and tamper down all of these thoughts swirling around my head.

Thinking about writing a letter to Hollie, it reminds me that I have almost a whole year's worth of notes that need to reach her, and I can't wait to hand deliver them to her door.

Sweetheart,

We just found out we're coming home.

<u>Home</u>.

I can't even imagine it. It feels like a dream. Do you know how happy that makes me feel? I can't even picture home anymore, but there is one home that will always remain true.

And that home, sunshine, is wherever I am with you.

I'll be there as fast as I can.

Love,

Layne

I had one final night patrol left, two nights before we were set to head home. Things were normal, with guys quietly joking around and talking about the first thing they would do when they got home.

We never saw it coming. One moment, it's a nice, peaceful night.

Then it morphs into a chaotic flurry of commotion and noise. All of a sudden, there are several explosions around us, coming from what appear to be an ambush of IEDs and RPGs. The blasts rip through the air, sending up smoke and a lot of dust, when all of a sudden I find myself flying backwards into a building, as my helmet flies off and my head slams into the hard wall of a nearby building.

As I lay here, I can just faintly make out the sound of shots being fired, and that someone's yelling, "Everyone okay?" But I can't seem to focus enough to call out a response, as my ears are ringing and my vision is starting to dim. The only thing I know for sure is that my body is in a world of hurt, I can't move, and I don't know what's become of my unit.

Eventually, my mind starts to wander to my life back home, and if I'll even make it out of this place alive. As the remainder of my vision gives way to the darkness, Hollie's face is the last thing I see, before it's lights out.

Chapter Twelve

December 24, 2016

WAKING UP ON this winter morning makes me feel like hell has frozen over. It must have happened, because hellish is how I feel. There is nothing joyous about this occasion, and I feel so much colder on the inside than any other given day so far this year. I can't get warm enough to melt, no matter how hard I try. And I *do* try, as I bury myself in layers of blankets. The best gift this year, the only one I really want, would be for everyone to forget what day it is, and let me stay in this bed, only to surface when the New Year starts.

When will the pain subside, allowing my heart to finally mend? Will it ever get easier?

I pray the weather turns bad and no one is able to make it out tonight to celebrate my 22nd birthday. Yes, I'm awful for thinking that, but the one thing I want this year won't come true just from making a wish and blowing out candles. There will be no phone calls bright and early today before the whole house is awake, to wish me a happy birthday. At least I will always have two birthdays full of memories to hold onto until I can safely deposit them in a box deep in the recesses of my mind, only to be brought out on this one day of the year. It's not a special day because it's my birthday.

It's special because of what Layne meant to me. The love we shared, and his selflessness in waking up extra early just to call me on my birthday before heading out into the field, extremely tired himself, made me cherish his effort.

Layne began the calls by whistling the military tune of First Call through the mouthpiece of the phone. His first words would always be, *Happy birthday, sunshine.*

He made sure to remind me that what we had was the staying kind of love, and that even if distance separated us, as long as he walked and breathed, I would be in his heart. I knew how much he loved me then, and how happy I made him.

Layne ended the call by singing happy birthday, talking to me for as long as he could before heading off to work. I loved him so much then, and I still love him so much.

I will forever cherish his loving words.

Thinking about these memories are depressing me more, throwing me further down the rabbit's black hole. My eyes are red and puffy, I'm sure, from all the crying I've been doing while the memories of Layne assault my brain, shattering the fragile wall I have built to help keep my emotions at bay. I thought I was doing a pretty dang good job 95% of the time. Apparently, December 24th will always be the catalyst in tearing that wall down. I really don't think time can ever fully heal the breach.

And this is how my parents find me. Good thing they have a key to my place, as there was no way I was getting up to let them in, or anyone else for that matter.

"Hollie, I know today is a hard day for you, but honey, you have to get up and get yourself together." My father says, in a loving tone. He hates to see his only daughter cry, especially because he doesn't know how to make it better. *No one can make this better.*

"Carson, I told you we shouldn't have let her stay alone last night. We knew this would happen." I hear my mom lightly scolding my dad. She doesn't really mean it, but she too is clueless as to how to fix this for me.

"Come on, honey, we know you want us to cancel your party, but so many people will be there. They love you too, and they want to help ease your pain and celebrate your life. Please lean on us for once and let us take some of your pain for a little while. You don't have to stay the whole time. Just stay for as long as you think you can manage, and if you want to leave, someone will see you safely home. Just give us a couple of hours, tops. That's all we're asking, Hollie," my dad pleads with me. I know, I'm being a miserable pain, so after I try a little more stubbornness, I finally succumb to my dad's pleas and get out of bed.

Slowly, I drag myself down hall into the bathroom and turn the shower on. Once it's hot, I climb in, standing under the jet streams for so long that my mom eventually worries about me. She sticks her head in to see if I'm okay. Once she realizes that I'm fine and closes the door, I decide to hurry my shower along. This is in hopes that time will fast-forward through the rest of this day as well.

The day passes by pretty uneventfully, even to the point that I'm bored to tears and wish my parents had let me stay home and wallow in self-pity until my party. I tried to help them with decorations, food, the cake—you name it. But my own mother would shoot me down every time. I was supposed to take it easy, rest, and cheer up as best as I could. Since I couldn't imagine the last one happening, my parents took it upon themselves to start dropping hints about my birthday present. However, I told them that I didn't want anything and that they've done enough for me over the years. Just raising me was enough. I honestly didn't need anything or want anything.

Okay, that's a lie.

I wanted *and* needed Layne, but since they couldn't deliver on that score, I couldn't imagine anything else. So, I played along and let them torture me with their cryptic hints about an awesome present, all the while letting them think that they were succeeding in distracting me.

Eventually the traitors—I mean, my best friends—show up to help with the finishing touches for the party and food. I'm still not over them pushing the party on me after all. *Couldn't they just let this one day slip by, unnoticed?* Since I wasn't in the mood to fill in the awkward void, I went upstairs to my old room and started getting ready. It was a family tradition that every year the birthday person dressed up really nice, so the attention could be focused on them in their finest that one day of the year. This being the case, I brought over the dress that my mom had bought me for this momentous occasion. *After all, you only turn 22 once, right?* I manage to get my hair curled, makeup applied, and dress on before I finally slip into my black heels. Double-checking my appearance in the full length mirror, I make my way back down the stairs and into the living room. I plant my butt in the loveseat sofa and don't leave it until the party starts.

By the time five o'clock rolled around, I was ready to get this show on the road. The faster it started, the faster I could run away like Cinderella at the ball. Maybe I would drop my glass slipper behind and my own Prince Charming would show up on his white horse, saving me from myself. Then again, we lived in Holly Grove. I really didn't know any guys left my age that hadn't moved away, were off at college, or married already. Who am I fooling, it didn't matter, because I only wanted one man, and he didn't want me back.

Even Jude was off and married. And Jason's friends were in hot pursuit of their sports dreams and didn't have time for serious relationships. Still, it didn't matter. I wanted the one I obviously couldn't have.

The doorbell rings as my mind starts tumbling down a dangerous staircase that it shouldn't even be on in the first place. I decide to fake it to make it, and plaster a smile on my face, shutting my mind down until my own private pity party that will surely come later in the night, and go greet the guest.

Ava's parents, Rick and Tilley Walsh, and Sean, come in, bearing gifts with happy birthday wishes and friendly smiles. Ava's parents are like a second set of parents to me, and they genuinely mean well. A few minutes after they arrived, Jenifer's parents, Tim and Judy Gustafson, my other set of pseudo parents, and Jason, show up, along with the Frosts. Ever since our trip to Hawaii over two years ago, I've made it a point to drop by and visit with them, or drop off some goodies when the mood would strike. I really loved their company. A few other relatives and family friends come by as well, slowly filling up the house.

Thirty minutes into the party, catching Ava's eye, I manage to pull her off to the side with Jenifer, leaving their boyfriends to talk to each other. "What's Sean doing here?" I ask her.

"Well, he decided that he missed me and didn't want to spend the holiday apart. So, here he is! He also said he had a big surprise that couldn't wait," she gushes.

"Oh, really? Do you think he will propose tonight?" I ask her, all of a sudden in a happy mood, for the first time all day. Who knew the prospect of someone else's nuptials would turn me around? I look at her expectantly, but she and Jen are looking at me like I've grown another head. I shrug, saying, "What? Marriage talk makes me happy, I guess. Can't I be happy for my friend?"

Shaking her head at me, Ava just smiles and Jen rolls her eyes. "Come on—let's get my mom to bring out the birthday cake. I could go for some serious chocolate right now." I say as I lead the way to find my mom.

They follow me to the dining room where we track her down where she's topping the cake with multicolored candles. "Well, if that wasn't perfect timing," she says.

"Of course, if there's chocolate in this house, this nose—" I say, twitching my nose at her, "will always track it down. Now, shake a leg woman and get a move on. This girl needs sustenance in the form of chocolate." My mom looks at me strangely, wondering if I'm okay, no doubt, then looks to my best friends, who both just shrug, putting on a happy smile. *Well, there you go, I have them all fooled—now, if I can only just fool myself, I'll be fine.*

Why can't I be a better pretender? Why can't I find a way to finally move on? *I don't want to, that's why.* I can't, is more like it. I still have this hope burning in me, and I don't want to lose it. Everyone thinks it's time to let him go, but what do they know? *Nothing.* That's what. It's me that this is happening to, and no one else can understand how it feels.

I need to calm down, as I'm starting to get riled up, internally. I take in a deep breath and let it out, calming my nerves as best as I can, plastering on another fantastic, *everything is peachy* smile.

My mom signals my dad so he can quiet down the house as he gets everyone's attention. "I wanted to thank everyone for coming out tonight. You all mean a great deal to us, and we are truly grateful that you're a part of our family. Thank you for coming out tonight and helping us celebrate Hollie's twenty-second birthday. Now, let's sing happy birthday to her."

I maintain my plastic smile for the gathering crowd and endure a chorus of the birthday song, which ends with a lot of hooting and cheering.

While my mom serves up the cake, I look around the room at the partygoers; my friends and my family, and it really hits home how truly lonely I'm feeling in a sea of all those who love me most. I thought Ava's possible good news could really cheer me up, but I was deluding myself. I scan the room, watching couples share intimate moments with each other, holding hands, talking happily with others, and all of a sudden, my almost good mood has walked out the front door, which is exactly what I want to do right now.

I thought I could keep it together until everyone went home, but honestly, I can't do it. I want to be just as happy as everyone else is with their significant others. And I can't help it; I miss Layne even more now. My heart hurts, and my eyes start to water. *I need to escape before anyone catches me.* As much as I love everyone for coming and making such a big production for me, I really need to be alone with my thoughts, and apparently now my tears.

Grateful that Sean and Jason are here to distract my closest friends, who are off to who knows where, and after making sure my parents are busy themselves, I quietly walk over to the back door into the kitchen. I grab my heavy coat off of the hook on the wall, along with my purse. Thanking my lucky stars that I have my knit hat and scarf in my bag, I twist the knob to the door as I hear guests coming my way.

It's now or never, and I pick *now*. I quickly open the door and slip out, pulling the door as quietly as I can behind me. I think I've just made the narrowest of escapes of all time as I hurry down the porch steps, without falling in my heels, and swing around the side of the house to the fence gate. It's not so terribly late that I can't walk myself back to my apartment off of Holly Lane.

Once I get to the gate, I put on my warm outerwear and let myself out of the backyard. I'm really not sure how I'm going to hold it together as I walk home. I know my family is going to be frantic as well when they realize that they can't find me, which reminds me to put my phone on silent. I don't doubt that someone will see me walking home alone and let my parents know when they put out an alert to the neighborhood watch. I don't know if we really have that here, but I don't doubt it.

I don't live very far from my childhood home. It's probably about ten blocks from Holly Lane. There are a lot of shops on the main street, but there is also a set of row homes and nice apartments at the less busy end of the lane. It seems like the lane just gets longer and longer with everything that is built on the edges of it.

Walking a few blocks up toward Holly Lane, I know I need to distract myself with thoughts of anything else. Like, say, the fact that I'm pretty sure that cryptic present was just a ruse to get me to my parents' house for the party. Or maybe it was the fact that Miller showed up. Maybe my parents thought that having him there would be helpful on this day? *I don't know.* I truly believe they would have said anything to get me to their place to celebrate with everyone.

I know they want me to be happy and to get out there again. Honestly though, you can't blame a broken hearted girl for being sad. In real life, fairytales don't come true, and I suppose it might be time to face the facts. *I'll always have the greatest love story of my life to remember, but it won't have the happy ending that I wished for.* That sad and depressing thought launches me on a trip down memory lane.

Great. Why couldn't I have picked something else to think about? I round the corner of the last block that puts me on the street I so desperately need to be on, but I also need to get off of at the same time, as there are too many eyes around here who could see me and my open emotional wounds.

Finally, I make it to the main road and start on a quick pace back to my place. It's cold, but I don't care as more thoughts of Layne start to flood my mind, causing tears to slide down my face. The wetness doesn't feel great, but I can't stop them even if I wanted to, so I keep on with my pace as I think back to where Layne could be now, and how in the world did things go so wrong when everything was once so right and we were happy.

The last thing I remember Layne saying to me was that he had to deploy for a mission and he couldn't tell me anything about this one. But he promised he would get word to me as soon as he could. Yet, I haven't heard a word from him since his sporadic emails in 2015. Not a single word.

Some time ago, I asked Sean if he had heard anything, as surely he would have. He's Layne's best friend, for crying out loud. It turns out that he hadn't heard anything in awhile, either. He knew that Layne had left the country, the details of his location and mission were extremely classified, and also that he didn't know when Layne would be back. He didn't think much of it, since deployment wasn't new for either one of them. But he did hear from Layne right before we lost all contact.

I didn't know Layne's family. We hadn't gotten a chance for him to introduce me to them yet. Surely they knew about me, but we had never been in contact. Layne and I had spent the majority of our two and a half years together apart, and I felt weird about calling them, so I pleaded with Sean to ask Layne's family for an update. *They had to know something, right?*

But to be quite frank, I don't think Layne ever gave them much information about me to begin with. They knew my first name, but from the sounds of it, Layne would always refer to me as his wife to his mom. She wasn't one to pry too much into her sons' lives, so he never felt the need to give my personal information to her. *Men.* They're definitely the worst at communication.

So, what could have happened to him that he couldn't get word to me? I could only guess the worst: he was either missing in action, or even worse, dead. But no—no, I refused to believe that last part. I feel like I would know if he wasn't alive anymore.

I still feel like I would know the truth in my bones, like when I knew that we had this crazy connection when we first met, but I was too young to really get it then. I just knew we had something special. But Layne knew, immediately.

Sean eventually called me back, telling me that Layne's parents had received word that he was fine. That was about four months ago. *Why didn't he call me?* Why wasn't *I* notified that he was fine? That was the point when I realized he must have just decided to forget about me.

I just want a second chance. A birthday wish to finally come true, or even the perfect Christmas present to arrive for me. Though, seems like I would need a miracle for Layne to show up, or even call, at this point. If Miller hasn't heard from him in all of this time, then something obviously went wrong on his mission, and I'm an idiot to believe that he just up and left me. Though, believing that, it doesn't help matters any further, and it still doesn't change the fact that my heart is broken and I don't even know what happened.

Walking down the sidewalk, I pass the shops all lit up and full of Christmas cheer, and of course notice the Christmas tree down at the other end of town, shining bright for all to see. It's such a pretty sight, and I should be feeling nothing but happiness on this holiday eve, enjoying my time with my family, yet I feel nothing but sadness.

I know that my happiness in life shouldn't hinge on one guy. There are other great men out there, and I'll find love again someday. But what happens when you've lost *the one?* I'm a firm believer in that kind of fate.

It's starting to lightly snow now. My face is cold, nearly frozen with tears, and I'm emotionally exhausted as I finally make it to the front of the apartment complex. I really need to be inside where it's warm. I can curl up in my bed and end this night with sleep. I hear something behind me, causing me to pick up my pace further, yet I can't help but look over my shoulder as I hurry along.

"Miss?" I hear the stranger call out. "Miss! I just need to ask you a question!"

Seeing the man coming towards me, I freak out and hit the pavement running. But as dumb luck would have it for this klutzy girl, I slip on the pavement and start to fall to the ground, flailing my arms as I try to regain my balance. Why, I have no clue. It's not like it's going to help me. However, I never actually hit the ground, as I feel two arms wrap around me, stopping my fall.

"Whoa," he says. "Are you all right there, Miss?" he asks as he puts me in an upright position. *Something seems familiar about this man.*

"I'm sorry I gave you a fright. I was looking for someone, and I had hoped you could help me," he says apologetically while he takes a few steps away, his hands up in the *I surrender* pose. "See, no harm meant. I'm just a bit lost, and I'm trying to find someone. I don't suppose if I give you a name, you could help an old soldier out?"

My head whips up to stare into the face of this supposed stranger, but maybe not such a stranger after all. I brush the hair from my face as his eyes look at the ground, and then all around, but never at me. He seems slightly embarrassed, but I don't know why he would be.

I feel like my heart has stopped, along with the Earth's rotation and time.

"See," he says as he stares off into the distance, where you can still see the tree from this end of Holly Lane, "I'm looking for my girlfriend, but I can't remember exactly where to find her. I know, it sounds really stupid as I say that out loud." He says in a low, sad voice. "But I really need to find her," he woodenly tells me as my heart breaks but wants to jump for joy, too.

My eyes start welling up even more as the fresh batch of tears stream down my face. I can't even say anything. It's like my voice went on vacation and left my body standing here in front of this beautiful man. *It can't be true,* is all I keep thinking to myself, as I continue to stare at him with frozen legs and lost voice. Eventually, I'm able to swallow the hard lump in my throat as he slowly turns back to look at me.

He just continues to stand there as he finally starts to really take in the girl in front of him. He tilts his head to the side as his brow furrows between his eyes. It's as if he thinks he might know me, yet he's not totally sure.

Thanks to this snow, I'm bundle up pretty good, and half of my face is covered with my scarf. To remedy this, I pull it loose then let it fall down to hit my chest.

I open my mouth a few times but nothing comes out before I finally find my voice.

"She's right here."

Chapter Thirteen

"HOLLIE?" HIS VOICE cracks. As if he needs to be sure, he asks again, "Hollie Reed?"

I barely manage a nod to confirm it's really me who is hiding under all of this winter gear.

I watch in wonder as tears trickle down his cheeks while his lips slowly form a smile.

"You have a thing for running into strangers, don't you?" he lightly laughs while he takes me all in with his hazel eyes. I watch him too, looking for the man I've loved for so long in that lost and sad face. He seems to have aged, and his hair has gotten a little longer, growing out of his standard military crew cut.

"Sunshine, what are you waiting for?" he tries to tease me while his emotions get the best of him.

I raise a shaky hand to my heart as it restarts and beats fast against my ribcage. My breath hitches in my throat a few times while the force of it all hits me. I want to go to him so badly, but I'm rooted to my spot. I feel like I'm in another universe, some magical place where wishes come true. It's almost as if I can't fathom that this whole moment is real.

There's no way I'm standing in Holly Grove, on Holly Lane, on my birthday, no less, looking at the man who I would give anything to be with at this moment in time. He stands there with tears in his eyes as well, his arms open wide, beckoning to me. He cocks an eyebrow at my hesitation. "What are you waiting for, sweetheart?" he asks.

I tell myself to get it together and to quit being an idiot. Layne is really here, and my eyes aren't deceiving me when I hear him start to whistle the tune to First Call.

My body starts to relax slightly, but I still can't believe that I'm standing here with him, and for the first time in what feels like ages, I actually get to see the words coming from his lips as he says, "Happy birthday, sunshine." He smiles at me now, as he continues to hold his arms out.

"My gift to you this year, sunshine, is me. I'm the forever kind, sweetheart. There will never be an end with me for as long as I walk and breathe on this Earth. I didn't want to leave you, believe me, but life throws some wicked curve balls sometimes, and they knocked me out of the game for awhile."

He slowly starts walking towards me as he keeps his eyes trained on mine. "So know this, Hollie Reed. You own my heart and soul, and you have always been with me, even when I didn't know it. You will always be my sunshine. You will always be my strength and you *are* my rock. I love you, Holls. That has never changed."

He comes to a standstill in front of me. Then he opens his arms one more time, as I finally find my feet and push myself into his out-stretched arms. He wraps those beautifully sculpted arms around me as tightly as he can, while lifting me off of the ground. My whole body starts shaking as I let it all go and sob into his neck. He stays rooted to the same spot, holding me and trying to soothe me at the same time.

Right here in this moment, I don't ever want to let go, and I pray he never leaves me, ever again.

"I'm so sorry, Hollie. I'm so sorry, sunshine—" he tells me over and over again as he runs one of his hands soothingly down my back.

"I missed you so much, Layne," I choke out.

"*Shhhh,*" he soothes on a whisper in my ear. "I know, sweetheart. I know." The agony in his voice is crystal clear. "Never again, I promise you, never again." He states this mantra like a vow. Then he abruptly stops and I pull my head out of the crook of his neck, only to realize that we have an audience of people who are awkwardly standing there while we have this sob-fest of a reunion.

I'm confused. *When did my family and friends all show up?*

"What are you all doing here?" I ask with a frown.

"Well, sweetie, you weren't answering your phone, and you *did* ditch your own party. We had to make sure you made it home all right." My mom sweetly smiles at me, tears of her own shining in her eyes.

"I'm so sorry," I apologize to the group as a whole. "I wasn't in as much of a partying mood as I thought. And I'm sorry I worried you." *Now I feel like a heel.* I should have told somebody I was leaving.

"Plus, we had to know if your present ever made it to you," my dad winks at me.

"My present?" *Now I'm really baffled.*

"It appears *he* has arrived, safe and sound." Miller beams at us, but his own eyes are also wet with unshed tears. "It's great to see you home, man." He slightly chokes on his words.

My father clears his throat, and it sounds like he was maybe a little emotional as well, as I realize that everyone seems to be.

"Is Layne the big present you were hinting at earlier?"

"He is. Except you snuck out of the party, and we had to call to send him on a search and rescue mission." My dad says as a burst of laughter escapes my lips.

"What?" he innocently asks. I just smile at my dad as I shake my head.

I'm still standing in the arms of the man I love while my family and friends look on at us, joy evident on their faces.

"Thank you," I tell them. "I love my present."

"Do you know how hard of a secret this was to keep?" Mom shares with us. "I didn't think we would ever get her out of bed, or to the party." She shakes her head in dismay.

"Well, it all worked out just the way it was supposed to." My dad tells her. Then he looks at me, "Hollie. Happy birthday, sweetheart. Wishes *do* come true."

All I can do is just nod my head and give my dad a wobbly smile as I lean my head against Layne. A part of me is still afraid that this is all just a pleasant dream, and he'll disappear again when I wake up. That is, until I feel Layne's hand rubbing my back, as I hear my mom sharing the story of how this secret present came to be.

Our friends, including Jason, make their way into our little bubble and give Layne hugs and slaps on the back while welcoming him home. Everyone wants to know where he's been and what happened to him, but I need some answers first, before he shares the story with everybody else.

"Don't worry, buddy. I get it. You just spend time with your girl, and we can catch up later," I hear Miller tell Layne.

"Thanks, man. I need some time to work things out with Hollie first. But I'll be in town for a while, so we can catch up soon," he promises.

"Be gentle with him, Bruiser." Miller gently tugs a strand of my hair. "There's a good reason for everything Layne does." He bends his head closer to my ear and says for me alone, "You'll be able to mend the pieces of your heart, and his, after you hear him out. I promise you." He kisses my temple then reaches out for Ava's hand, as she slightly smiles at me.

"All right, folks, let's move this party back to the house." I hear my father semi-shout.

"I have a feeling we won't be seeing these two again for the rest of the night. Be good and stay out of trouble." Jen teases me as I roll my eyes at her, while shaking my head.

"Do you need a chaperone?" Ava teases me too, causing Layne and I both to laugh with our friends.

"I think we had enough chaperones back in Hawaii a few years ago. I'm definitely good on my own, but nice try."

"Come on, Ava. You'll get plenty of time to spend with them tomorrow." Miller assures her as he gently tugs her down the sidewalk.

Once everyone leaves, I find that I'm still standing in Layne's arms. I start to peel myself away from him, but he doesn't let me get too far.

"Where do you think you're going, Hollie? I just got you back. I'm not letting you out of my sight for a long time to come."

I would love to say 'yes, yes, you have me back.' *But what makes him so sure it's going to be that easy?* Oh, fine, who am I kidding? *It probably will be, but where the heck has he been?*

"Sunshine, settle down." He exhales on a breath.

"How do you know I need to do that?"

"I can read you like a book. Remember my job? Anyway, your body started to go rigid. You're tense. I promise there's a very valid explanation, for everything." He tugs on my chin until I'm staring into his colorful eyes.

"I would never in a million years just walk out on you like that, Hollie. I swear." He's so intense in his words, and his emotions are running rampant across his face.

"I think we need to go inside and get you warmed up, pretty girl." There's a hopeful and yet scared look on his face now, as if he's afraid I'll say no.

I slowly nod my head while he drops his hand from my face, but finds his purchase again with my left hand.

There we are, Hollie and Layne, hand and hand after so much time lost, walking to my apartment together. I never thought that this would happen.

We make it inside, out of the cold, and I drop his hand as I lock the door before heading to the heater and cranking it up.

"Would you like some hot cocoa?"

"Sure." He eyes me warily.

"Why don't you leave your boots by the front door, and your jacket? If you're cold, you can start the fireplace and grab the blanket that's on the back of the couch, to warm up."

I'm doing everything I can to steady my hands and keep busy as thoughts whirl around my head. I can't imagine what he has to say, but it doesn't sound good, and it doesn't sound like he wanted it. *Not that I would think that, but still.* Okay, my thoughts are starting to ramble, as I'm feeling overwhelmed with all of these questions and feelings and emotions.

Two arms go around my waist, as Layne rests his head on the top of mine.

"It's okay, Hollie. Take a deep breath, in and out. Can you do that for me, sunshine? Do you need Dr. Peters?" he worries.

"What?"

"Your dad thought you might have a panic attack when you saw me again. He told me about the good old doc."

"No, no, that's fine. I'm fine. We're all fine. You're here. You *are* here, right? I'm not dreaming you up? I haven't lost my marbles, finally, after all this time?"

"I'm here, Hollie, and I'm not leaving."

"Okay, this is good, right? So, let's get some cocoa, and you can fill me in. Yes, that would be good."

"Hollie, the longer you drag this out, the longer it will be before I can kiss you."

"What's going on, Layne?" I whisper.

I feel crazy, and so lost and mixed up. *Why am I feeling so out of sorts? I know who this man is. I know I want him back, so why am I holding back?*

"It's okay to be scared, Hollie, but it's me. You know me. But I see that I need to earn your trust back. I won't ever leave you again. If I can help it."

He releases me then walks me over to the couch, sits me down, and bends down in front me. He slowly takes off my stupid heels, which I was dumb enough to wear in this weather, then places them on the ground beside the couch. He reaches behind me and pulls the blanket down before he wraps it around me. Eventually, he joins me on the couch, where he promptly places my feet in his lap.

He begins to massage my feet as I lie there just staring at him, willing him to say something, but to also be silent at the same time. I don't want to ruin this calm before the storm hits. I'm not sure if my heart can take it.

"You know, I used to think about doing this." He points to my feet. "Back when I was deployed, before it came crashing in on all of our heads. Literally, I would daydream during my off time about what we would do together. I liked to picture us having nice, quiet nights in, with the fire going, me massaging your toes, and just enjoying the peace, away from the loud world."

"Sounds nice."

"Now I know what it's like, and so far, it *is* nice."

"Tell me something else you used to think about."

"I used to think about how much I missed you, your face in your daily photos." He smiles to himself as he stares off into the fire now. "When morale was down, I would conjure up my only source of sunshine, and daydream away. The guys would harass me, but they never got it. What it truly feels like, to have someone you've waited for, to be waiting for you at the end of the long road home." He inhales and exhales deeply, slowly letting go of any tension. I feel the tension in my own body loosen up while he works over my feet, one at a time, in even intervals.

"I tried to write you emails whenever I could. And every month, I would find a scrap of paper just so I could write you, trying to hold true to my promise. Did you ever get any of those? I tried to find the letters," he frowns, with a tinge of sorrow on his face, "but I don't know what happened to them."

That sparks the memory of a package I got a long time ago, but never wanted to open, afraid of what would be inside. It took me months before I finally viewed the contents, and cried my eyes out when I finally did.

"I did receive your emails, but for some reason, my responses were always bounced back when I tried to reply."

"Well, at least that puzzle is finally solved. I would go crazy with thoughts of what you must be thinking and feeling. It puts my mind at ease, at least a little."

I know the harder questions and answers are to come, but if this is the way he wants to play it, then I can do that. I also decide that he should know that I received his letters.

I hesitate at first, not wanting to bring up something very painful and heartbreaking, but I know it's the right thing to do. "I received your letters, too." I quietly tell him.

His face finally relaxes once he hears the news of his letters. It's like a weight has been lifted off his chest as he takes a deep breath in. "Can you please tell me how you received them? I don't remember how they got to you." He quietly asks as he watches me with a painful look in his glassy eyes.

Mentally preparing myself, I take a moment before I can fully explain it.

"One day, back in January sometime, a package came to my parents' house. They called me, telling me that I had mail, that it looked important, and would I please make sure to stop by that evening, offering me a place at their table for dinner, too." I inhale a deep breath. "I couldn't think of who would send me a package at this point, knowing you were still deployed. Also, I hadn't heard any news from you, or Miller, about when you would return. So imagine my surprise when I finally encounter this package, and eventually the contents inside," I shake my head sadly.

"I was both happy and sad. I was happy to see something in your own writing, something that was a piece of you, but sad because it didn't give me any further information." My gaze meets his, and I quietly state, "*Or you.*"

My eyes start to well up with unshed tears as I continue to look into his agony-filled eyes.

"The only clue about anything important was you stating that you were coming home. However, I didn't know when or how to reach you. I instantly reached out to Miller, and had him check in with your base. He didn't get anywhere with the guys, except that you hadn't made it back yet, and they didn't have any more details. I even asked him to call your parents, who said you were well and still overseas."

"Hollie, sweetheart, I can't really remember everything that happened while I was gone, or from this whole year. I have holes in my memory." He hoarsely states as he looks down at his hands that are fiddling with my toes, smoothing his finger over the black nail polish.

"Holes?" I can't help but ask him. I'm confused, and don't understand what he's trying to say. "What does that mean, Layne?"

"Can you first tell me who sent you the letters?" he looks back up at me.

"There was a note inside the package. Apparently, the letters were sent to me by one of the men in your unit. The letters were found by a soldier you served with when you were deployed. He had given them to your roommate back on base, who in turn found my address in your address book and thought I would want them. They figured you had left them behind without realizing it, and neither one had a clue about how to reach you, so they sent them on to me."

"Hollie, I would never leave something so precious to me that was meant for you behind." He closes his eyes, inhaling again as he leans his head against the back of the couch. Now his hands are idle, but still resting on my feet like he can't bear to let go, even for a moment.

"Is this the part of the story where things are going to be hard for us?" I quietly ask him.

"I wish I could tell you differently," He sighs. "Do you still have the letters?"

"Yes."

"Do you think I could see them in a bit? Not right now, I need time to talk to you first." He says as he rolls his head against the couch to look at me.

"I can do that." I give him a weak smile.

That's really the last thing I want to do, smile at him. What I really want to do is jump off this couch and climb into his lap, but something is holding me back, and the expression on his face is so completely heartbreaking. I'm afraid to go to him completely. I feel like I need to hear him out before I can cross that bridge.

Reaching over me, he takes my hand in his, interlacing our fingers as he runs his finger over the ring I've never taken off. Actually, I wear both of his rings. The one he gave me in Hawaii, and the one he gave me on his first visit here, when he asked me for a promise. I could never find it in my heart to take them off, and thankfully, no one ever says anything to me about them.

"I can only tell you some things, the parts I was told but don't remember, from when I left my final mission, and some parts that I do remember. I'll do my best to give you the important facts," he begins.

Frowning at him, I wonder why he said his *final mission,* and I shake my head to clear my thoughts as I quietly ponder this new information.

"We had received word that we had one week left before we were to return stateside. We were just a couple of days out from going home when we were tasked with a night patrol. I remember everything being up to par as we cleared our sector. We were just about done when something went terribly wrong. There were several explosions, lots of gunfire, and men yelling all around me. I don't remember anything else from that night, except that the last thoughts I had—" he closes his eyes, and I see a line of tears trickle down his face. He clears his throat before he continues. "Were of you, Hollie. You were the last thing I saw in my mind before the world went black."

I can't handle the agony in his voice, the pain and hurt he's feeling, coupled with my own painful emotions as I lie here. I know there's no way I can take this lying down. I draw my legs away from his lap and slowly sit up so I can rest on my knees, letting the blanket fall off of me as I wipe the tears away from his tired-looking face.

He opens his eyes to give me a small, sad smile. I lean in, searching his face for approval. I don't know why, as it's been there the entire time. He doesn't make a move. He lets me move at my own pace as I lower my lips to give him a small kiss, then pull back long enough to sit next to him, placing my hand in his and my head on his shoulder.

"That was the hardest time of my life, Hollie. I can't remember what happened, and only know what was told to me. But for the next year, my life would be hell." He continues with his story as he places his head on top of mine.

"My understanding of what happened that night was that I had been hit by a blast from one of the explosions. Apparently, I was pretty close, and the force of it threw my body back against a building. My helmet came off, and I slammed my head into a hard, cement wall.

"I fell into a coma for a couple of months as I had sustained a traumatic brain injury. When my unit found me, I was already out cold, and at first, they thought I was dead. As they were checking me over, they found a faint pulse. They called for backup as some of the guys kept me covered from incoming gunfire before the other team arrived. Eventually, the team was able to catch our ride home, with the exception of myself. I ended up in Germany, at one of the base hospitals, for medical treatment. That's where I stayed until I was stabilized and out of the coma. The military reached my parents, and they came out to stay with me while I was hospitalized."

I don't think my heart can take anymore of this. I bury my face into his chest and wrap my arm around his middle as my body slightly shakes.

He runs his free hand down my arm as we both sit there in complete silence, lost in our own thoughts. The realization of what we both could have lost is hitting me hard. I would rather have him lose his memory forever, knowing he was alive, than to the grave.

He places a kiss to the top of my head before he goes on with more details that I need to hear, but don't want to know.

"Once I was cleared to fly, they sent me home, as in here, to Oregon. I wish so badly, Hollie that I had told my parents more information about you. You have to know that when I woke up from my coma, I didn't know anything. I didn't remember the explosion, why I was in the hospital, what day it was, or who my own parents were. I woke up with Post Traumatic Amnesia, but I was still alive, and they tell me I was lucky that I came out of the explosion with my skull fully intact."

I put my finger to his lips, silencing him. I don't want him to continue. I feel like I've heard enough. He kisses my finger, and then pulls my hand to his lap.

"Hollie, I know this is hard, and it kills me to relive it for you. But, you have to know what kept me from you. All of it.

"I spent a while in Germany in a coma and then once I was awake, I had to stay for assessments and rehabilitation before eventually coming back to Oregon. During the time I was home, I slowly started remembering things, though the day I was injured is still lost to me. I'm not sure that will ever come back. I also lost parts of memory where other things were concerned, and Hollie, this is painful to say, but I couldn't remember you. I had no idea." His voice is full of so much emotion and sorrow.

"I could remember a lot, but yet, I couldn't. It took a while for my memory to fill in on its own. I continued with rehabilitation, therapy, and assessment appointments. My parents were afraid of sharing parts of my past with me. They didn't want to overwhelm me, or agitate me more than I already was. My memory was riddled with holes, and my concentration was shot. At one time, too much information and noises were my undoing and I felt overloaded, so they let me figure things out as they came to me. It took me a long time to remember Miller and some of our time served together in the military, but even he was warned not to bring certain subjects up. And Hollie," he pauses.

"Don't be mad at him. He wanted you to know everything once he finally found out, but he was sworn to secrecy. What if I never remembered you? What good would that do for you, *or* me? He didn't want to continue to break you further apart than you already were. He tells me you've been in a fragile state ever since I went missing."

Okay, now part of me wants to scream and hit something, and part of me wants to break down and sob. I'm mad, yet I do understand what he's telling me. I don't want to. No, I really want to be mad at his parents, and Miller. But, I know that I can't, or at the very least, shouldn't be.

Layne reaches up and wipes the tears that I didn't realize were still trailing down my cheeks.

"I tried to find you, too," I tell Layne. "I begged Miller not too long ago to call your parents again and ask what happened to you. He told me that basically you were fine, and I was so mad that you had checked in with your family and not me. *Why not me?* I wondered. I didn't know, and I couldn't understand what had gone so wrong. I remember trying to find you by calling your roommate, too. I think he must have been given the same information, because he would never tell me anything, and eventually I couldn't get ahold of him anymore. At one point, I braved calling your parents, though I never got anywhere with them, either."

"I'm so sorry, sunshine."

We sit in silence for awhile. I feel like I'm on information overload, and I need to sit in a dark room, blocking everything and everyone out until I can wrap my mind around what he has just told me. Though, I have a feeling, he's far from done.

Eventually, he picks up his story. "Once I thought I had my memories back, I took off for a while to travel. I needed time and space away to figure out my life. I knew I couldn't continue in my chosen career, and I hit rock bottom. I was lonely, but I didn't understand why. I was depressed. I was mad at the world, at my head for leaving me with missing pieces, and I was so angry about my fate with my career. I didn't want my parents to live through those hard times with me. So, I took off to parts unknown, looking up old Army buddies to stay with for a couple of months while I gathered my thoughts. It wasn't until I came home again to get my belongings, so I could move out of my parents' house to live with a friend in California, that I saw something that was kept hidden from me."

My breath catches. "What would your family keep hidden from you?"

"Do you remember what you made for me, the Christmas I came to see you?"

Slowly, I nod my head *yes*. I remember perfectly, as if it were that very Christmas day.

"I found the book you made, with all of our photos and communications in it. I was so floored that I had this big chunk of my life missing, and that something so important was being kept from me. I felt betrayed, Hollie. I was so angry." He still sounds hurt by this, too.

"I thought I had gotten over the anger for the most part, but then this, *this* happened, and it hurt me. Why would they do that to me? I didn't understand. My parents found me in my room later that day, and we had an all-out shouting match. Then they cried with me as they tried to explain it. They didn't *want* to keep you from me, but they didn't know how to give me that part of my life back. They didn't want to force the memories, and most importantly, they didn't want you to be hurt any further, not knowing what I would do if I had found out the information.

"Honestly, how could they think I would do anything that would go against you or our relationship? I don't know, and I still don't understand it. It's not like I was unpredictable back then. Though, I do understand that they were trying to protect you and myself as well, even if it meant hurting and betraying me. Or, that's how I see it, anyway. Because Hollie, I would never remove myself from your life on purpose, unless you kicked me out." He tries to lighten the mood, and I believe he is also trying to calm himself down.

"What did you do, after you found out?" I'm pretty sure I know, but I need to hear him say it.

"I stayed with my parents for a while, taking the time to comb the book over as thoroughly as possible. I went through all of my stuff again, trying to find any more evidence to clue me in. But really, I didn't need to be clued in, because deep down, I knew it was true in my heart. I could feel you in the depths of my soul. Eventually, the pieces slowly came back to me as well. At first, even though I felt this was true, I knew I couldn't just show up on your doorstep with no true memory of you. Eventually, my parents, and yes, even Miller, started to tell me stories about us. I had to relearn them and let them come back to me so I could come get my girl back with true memories. I needed to be more of the man you knew when I left you, not this broken down, angry, depressed, washed up, has-been of a soldier."

"Stop right there." I shake my head as my lips tremble. "Just stop," I hoarsely plead. "I would never look at you that way. Never." I vow to him.

I'm done sitting at his side and decide to climb into his lap so I can snuggle into him. I've missed his touch, his smell, his warmth, his love. Everything about this man, I've missed. Why I felt so guarded before seems so ridiculous to me now. Now, I just want to curl into him and stay rooted to this spot for the rest of my life.

"I don't care about those things. If I could have been by your side to help you recover, I would have, Layne. Every heartbreaking moment, I would have been there."

"I know that now, and appreciate that you would have done that. But I didn't want you to see me that way, sweetheart."

"Stubborn old fool."

"I didn't realize that twenty-six was the magical age for being old. I guess you better put me out to pasture and upgrade," he teases me.

"It looks like you didn't come with a warranty, and now it's too late to return you. It's been over 30 days. I guess I'm stuck with you forever." I lean in and kiss his cheek.

He squeezes me with his arms. "Do you *want* to be stuck with me?"

He's not joking anymore.

"Are we going to be okay?" I ask him nervously. *I know what he wants from me, and I know what I would like. Still, how will we recover from this?*

"Hollie, we can only be as okay as we allow ourselves to be, taking this at a speed that we can both handle. I know that the first time, we went full steam ahead. But this time around, I'll let you set the pace."

I don't say anything to that as we sit here in silence. I gather my thoughts and recompose myself after everything he has told me up to this point.

Layne has other ideas, though, as he lowers his lips and kisses my temple, then leans his head against mine. "I've missed you so much, Hollie, and I've waited too long to hold you in my arms again. To feel you, kiss you, and inhale the intoxicating smell of your perfume."

He's not going to make this easy, that's for sure. I'm pretty sure that there is no slow pace for us, and there never will be. It's either all or nothing, it would appear.

"I want to say we will be okay, Layne. But I'm scared. What if something bad happens the next time you're deployed?"

"Sunshine, there won't be a next time. And just so you know, I've had a good track record up until this last mission." He slightly brags, but he's very serious, too.

"Layne, I remember you telling me about the things you've been through, when we first met in Hawaii. That was cause enough to scare me, and now you've survived an explosion? I don't know how much more my poor heart can take."

"Hollie, maybe I'm not the only one with holes in my memory," he taunts me.

"No, I remember distinctly what you told me, and you flat out told me that—"

But I don't get the rest of the sentence out before Layne's lips cover mine, purposefully silencing me. He wraps me up in his arms as he thoroughly kisses me into submission. It takes some time, because honestly, I just got the man back. I wasn't going to end this kissing session any time soon, if I didn't have to.

Eventually, we both come back up for air, and Layne has the biggest, smug grin on his face.

"I see I still have a great effect on you, my dear." He laughs, and I can't do a thing about it but smile back at him with the biggest, happiest smile I've got.

"Yeah, I know, sweetheart. It was that good," he winks.

It's good to see some of the familiar parts of Layne working their way back to me.

"I have to tell you, Hollie, I haven't been this happy since I came home. I always knew I was missing something, but I obviously didn't know what it was. Now I do know. It was the other half of my heart and soul." He kisses me again.

Later in the night, as we snuggle up on my couch with the fire going and the blanket over us, I realize something that Layne had stated earlier, and I know I need to follow up on. The kissing got us a bit sidetrack, and we never did go back to our serious conversation. I'm sure neither one of us really wants to continue on with that line of questioning. But now, I need a few more answers.

"Layne, I know we're going to be okay, as much as it scares me about the next time you leave. But, I need to know something." I say, as I turn on my side so that we're face to face.

"What is it, sweetheart?" he asks, stroking the hair out of my face.

"What did you mean when you said that was your last mission?"

"Oh, now she clues in," he teases with a small grin. "That's exactly what I meant. That was my last and final mission. No more deployments for this oldie but goodie." He tries to tease me, but I'm still confused.

"You can't know that for sure, soldier."

"Actually, I can. I'm no longer in the Army. I was medically and honorably discharged from the military this year."

I'm stunned and I don't know what to say, so I stare at him, not really believing what he has just said.

"If you keep leaving your mouth open, I'll have to find a way to close it."

"Layne?" I search his face for the truth of the answer. "What will you do now?"

"Well, I was hoping that this hot chick I know would take me back, keep me forever, and let me hang with her in Holly Grove, on Holly Lane. Do you think she will say yes? Or should I take my one-man act on the road and headline some USO tours? If I recall, her dad thought I was a comedian. Do you think I have a shot?"

"I don't see why she would turn down a hunk, such as yourself. If I were her, I would hogtie you up and keep you forever. If she says no, let me know." I wink at him. "Unless you steal the covers, snore, walk around in your underwear, and neglect the toilet seat, dishes or trash. Then, we'll have to part ways," I laugh.

"Lean in a little closer, then. I want to kiss that smart mouth of yours."

I do as he requests, and I'm rewarded with the most tender kiss of the night.

"Does that mean you'll keep me?"

"The best birthday present ever," I reply.

"What's that, sunshine?"

"You. Here in Holly Grove. So, yes, I plan to keep you."

"Good. I wasn't going to leave you alone, anyway."

"Oh? And was your new job title, stalker?" I giggle.

"Only when it comes to the prettiest girl in the whole world, until she gave in. Though, my form of stalking would have been sweet, flowery, and filled with love letters. I probably would have thrown in some selfies along the way too, so you could fill up another book."

"You can still stalk me any day, but only as my partner in life." I kiss his nose. "What do you think our friends and my family are up to right now?"

"Oh, Jen's probably betting them when they'll see our faces next." He laughs. I laugh too, because I'm sure he's right.

"I think tomorrow we should leave this love nest and have breakfast with everyone. So, who gets the honors of sharing this news? Me or you?"

"Oh no! I'm not doing it. I think we should just stay in silent communication and then surprise them for Christmas morning. I'll let you take the lead on this mission."

"Speaking of missions, I seem to recall one that I gave you years ago. And it was fortunate for me that you kept a book to help me remember it." He raises his left eyebrow at me.

My mouth begins to curl into a smile, but I pull it back in between my teeth.

"I see someone else recalls this mission, too. I think I would like to explore this task. What do you say, Hollie? Are you ready to close this mission out with me?"

"Hang on—I need to go get something first." I tell him, as I peel myself away, hopping off the couch, but in the process, I end up tripping over my feet, causing myself to crash and burn.

Layne flops back on the couch as his body is wracked with laughter.

I get up on my knees and smack him in the gut. "Thanks a lot. What kind of gentleman are you?" I huff, but I'm not really mad. So I get up and go into my room so I can pull out something that no one else knows I've been keeping this whole time.

I find the box I'm looking for, hidden on the shelf in my closet, then go back to the living room and set it on the end table, next to Layne.

"Sunshine, that box looks dangerous. I think you need an expert to help you." He tells me as he pulls me into his lap. Then reaches over and pulls the box onto the couch.

I watch as he opens it and pulls the first jar out.

He eyes me, as a sheepish smile crosses my lips. I can't help it, but a giggle escapes my lips.

"Hollie. I don't know if we can put this mission to rest in one night's time. I'm amazed that you kept this up." He says, shaking his head with a small smile.

"Well, I say you have your work cut out for you. And I know you don't have any holes when it comes to kissing, so soldier, man up and get to work. These lips aren't going to kiss themselves!" I wink at him.

Laughing, he pulls out the first Hershey's Kiss from the jar, unwraps it and pops it in his mouth.

"I think it's safe to say that we won't be eating these." He coughs and makes a nasty face. "This is some really old chocolate, sweetheart."

I fall back against the arm of the couch in hysterics.

"Oh, you think that's funny do you? I think it's time to stop horsing around and get to work." He says, right before he kisses me.

We never did end up eating the rest of the candy. I wasn't sure which jars were the new ones anymore. I had kept them hidden from prying eyes, whenever I had people over. At one point we gave up keeping count, and agreed that this was a mission that would never be complete, as Layne promised to see to that. He had plans to carry this mission out until he was too old, and his lips caved in when his teeth fell out. I wasn't too sure about that part, but whatever. I just wanted to keep kissing this man forever.

Chapter Fourteen

December 25, 2016

THE NEXT MORNING, I wake up to the sun shining, even though it's still cold outside with plenty of snow falling, and my face stuck to Layne's shirt.

We fell asleep late into the night, curled up on the large couch as we kept warm by the fire. *Thank heavens for that.* I wouldn't appreciate waking up to my body hitting the floor if it had been on a smaller couch.

I know it's Christmas, and I know our family and friends will be counting on seeing us, but who wants to leave this warm, comfy spot? *Not me. That's who.*

"Rise and shine, sunshine." Layne kisses my head.

"Trust me, I'm already awake," I grumble.

"Good. I've been up for a while now, just watching you drool and hearing you snore like a lumberjack."

I'm really not a morning person, and apparently, Layne thinks it's funny.

"I'm not even going to dignify that with a response. I'm in a happy state, because one, my man is back, and two, I'm cozying up to him, and three, I'm not moving from this spot. So, say what you want, old man."

"I thought you weren't going to make a comment?" he laughs. "Besides, we can't stay here all day. You know we have some busy-bodies that are beside themselves in wanting to see us. They're probably chomping at the bit."

"Soldier, I just woke up. I'm a hot, grumpy mess. I'm not going anywhere until I feel like it," I grouch at him.

"Well, it's a good thing I kept the Grinch here last night so she couldn't steal all of the boys' and girls' Christmas gifts. I bet Noelle is glad too, so you couldn't snag the giving tree gifts, either."

I sit up halfway, so I can lean on an elbow, peer into his smug-looking face, and decide, it's Christmas, so I'll just kiss the smile off of his rugged face. I lean in and plant a long, lingering kiss on his firm lips.

"Wow. That was *some* good morning kiss, sweetheart. Now I know that you give good morning kisses like that, you'll never get rid of me. In fact, that's going to be one of my top demands when we get married."

"Well, I guess you might as well start planning the wedding. We never do anything at a snail's pace, so it's warp speed ahead for us. But just so you know, that's not me saying yes. I still expect you to get down on one knee, if your old joints can handle it." I laugh as I fall onto his chest.

He gives me a tight bear hug before he ruffles my hair, making it look worse than it already does. "You're so lucky I'm in good spirits this morning. I hate to see what would happen if you tried that on a non-holiday."

"I'm not really worried, so I'll take my chances in the future." He winks before he rolls me off the couch and dumps us on the floor. Then he stands up, towering over me, as he looks down with a gleam in his eye.

"Look at that lazy bag of bones on the floor. Who's going to clean up this mess?" He looks around then back down at me. "Well, seeing as how I'm the only man for the job, I guess I'd better get to it."

He bends down and picks me up, tossing me over his shoulder like a sack of potatoes. I'm too busy laughing to stop him when he smacks me on the butt.

"Tell me where you keep the towels, and I'll let you go."

"Right, like you'll really do that. And what do you plan on wearing? I don't think my clothes would look cute on you."

"Well, that's a darn good question. I had my military duffle bag with me. I hope no one is in the business of stealing around Holly Grove. What do you think sunshine? Is it still outside where I left it?"

"I see someone really does have a holey memory," I tease him.

"I'm so glad to know that you love my holes. I'll try to forget things more often, just to test you. Let's hope you never wake up to use the bathroom in the middle of the night, in the dark, and fall in," he laughs.

"I have enough confidence in myself to check the lid first." I scrunch my nose at him, but realize it's wasted as he can't see me.

"Now, be a good girl and tell me where the towels are. We have to hustle double time now."

"There's a cabinet in my bathroom where you'll find all the shower goods. But don't use my razor! And you're in luck, I have two extra toothbrushes. You can have the pink one or the teal one. But, if I were you, I would prove my masculinity with the pink one." I crack up, and he whacks my bottom one more time then marches us down the hall, where he dumps me on my bed before he leaves for the shower.

I hear him turn it on before he heads outside to find his bag. *I hope it's still there.* Before I think too much on it, he's back in a flash.

I listen as he comes back down the hall. "I was in luck—someone had placed it outside of your door. It might have helped that I have *Property of Hollie Reed* written on the outside," he smiles at me shyly.

"Were you afraid you would lose that, too?" I shake my head at him, but it does make me chuckle.

"You never know, these days. I couldn't take my chances. Anyway, I'm off to shower. Find something beautiful to wear for today." He winks at me, and then leaves me to myself, shutting the door behind him.

I search my closest while I wait for my turn and find something a bit dressy to put on, which is perfect for the one item I really want to wear today. Something Layne got me a while back.

It's finally my turn to get ready, so I leave my room and head towards the bathroom. Layne is stepping out into the hall as I catch a whiff of his cologne.

"You smell really good today, soldier." I step up to him and kiss his cheek when something catches my eye.

"What do you have around your neck?" I wonder out loud.

He looks down at his chest for a few extra moments before he pulls the silver chain out. It's then that I recognize it's his dog tags.

"I may not be in the military anymore, but I will never go anywhere without these. Plus, I've added something to them. Would you like a closer inspection?" he casually asks.

I lean in closer as he shows me a third tag that looks new. I grip it between my fingers so I can read what it says.

"*Your heart belongs to me. I will always carry it with me.*" I read out loud, then I notice a fourth tag, and it's a picture of me. My eyes start to water as I look up into his handsome, rejuvenated face.

"How long have you had these?" I had no idea they even existed. He never told me. *Is it new? Or has he always had it?*

"I had it made right before I went on my last deployment. I slept with it against my heart every night, and during the day, it was under my pillow. I didn't want to chance wearing something so personal. But I needed a piece of you while I was away, and it helped when I needed to see your face. It was in my personal belongings that were sent home, and my parents had put away for safe keeping, until I could come to my own conclusion that I had this amazing woman waiting for her soldier to return, safe and sound, and whole." He kisses me on the forehead. "Now, that's enough sad memories, woman. Go get dressed, or we'll be late."

He doesn't know it, because I didn't have the chance to do it last night, but every night I sleep with his dog tags, the ones he made for me, as well.

I hurry up the process of getting dressed, but still it puts us behind, which Layne taunts me about the whole way to my parents' house. Layne pulls the car up into the driveway, as he insisted that the man should always drive.

He gets out and makes his way to my door to open it, then takes my hand and helps me out. As he is assisting me, he stops and stares at my wrist for a good minute.

"Hollie," he breathes, "you kept it?"

"Of course, you silly man. I would never give anything you gave me away, even if we weren't together." I say, as I twist the turtle bracelet around my wrist once. "I would never get rid of your memories.

Those are the best days of my life."

"Thank you." He kisses my hand, and continues to help me the rest of the way out of the car.

"I hope that we don't get mauled at the door by the salivating pack of wolves in there," he semi-jokes as he points to the front window. I look over and see for myself too many heads to count, knowing that they're going to bombard us the moment we walk in the door.

"Great. Can we pretend we didn't see them and leave? I bet Noelle has the diner open again this year. We could make a run for it now."

Layne scoops me up into his arms, carrying me as a groom would carry his bride. "We wouldn't want you to embarrass yourself if you face-planted in these high heels you insist on wearing. Not that I'm complaining, they do great things for your legs," he winks.

"As if this isn't an embarrassing moment. No, not at all."

We make it to the front door without any injuries before it flies open and outpours all of our loved ones. Even Layne's family appears at the back of the group. *What in the world?* I look at Layne, be he just shrugs his shoulders, then sets me on my own two feet."Merry Christmas, you two! We were beginning to wonder if you would make it at all. Jen was placing bets right before you showed up." My mom laughs, as she hugs us both tightly.

"Can't. Breathe." I manage to get out.

"Oh, and look!" she exclaims. "Layne's parents are here. Sean decided to invite them to Holly Grove so they could be here with their son. Isn't that great?" She claps her hands.

"That's wonderful, Mom. Thank you, Sean."

"I would do anything for a brother." Sean tips his head to Layne.

"Now everyone is here, finally. Let's get this show on the road. My food's getting cold. I knew we shouldn't have let her sleep in. She's the slowest slow poke I know." My dad grumbles to my mom, as he points a finger at me. I duck my head into Layne's chest and try to stifle my giggles. Layne wraps his arm around my shoulders as we all trek back into the house.

It's so weird having such a large production in my childhood home on a Christmas morning. But this year, I wouldn't have it any other way. After Layne and I peel off the layers of our warm clothing, we head to the dining room and situate ourselves for the feast on the table.

"Wow, Mom. You've out done yourself this year."

"That would be thanks to Mrs. McKay, Tilley, and Judy." My mom beams at us from across the table.

"You can call me, Sandy, Carol. No need for formalities." Layne's mom politely tells mine.

"I'm so glad you could make it out here." Layne tells his parents as he looks over at his siblings, "And I can't believe they managed to drag you two away with them."

"It wasn't a hardship. A road trip and free food? Who turns that down," Levi, Layne's brother jokes. The whole table laughs and falls into easy conversation now that the ice has been broken.

A while later, after breakfast is done, and we're not so full, we decide that it's time to open gifts, as everyone gathers around the tree. I feel bad because I didn't know that Layne's family would be here, and I don't have anything for them. But I see mom wink at me, letting me know not to fret because she worked her Christmas magic like she always does, somehow. It's one of the things that I admire about her. She's good under pressure. I give her a grateful smile as I lean into Layne.

I have a gift for Layne under the tree, as I've had every year. These last two Christmas's, I've put them there in hopes that we will find our way back to each other again. So, he will have two presents from me this year.

When it's finally his turn to open them, he's quite surprised and he looks uncomfortable and embarrassed. "Hollie, I don't know what to say." He ducks his head a little.

I pat his knee. "It's okay, soldier. I put a present under the tree every year for you, in hopes that a Christmas miracle will happen. Please, don't worry, and just make me happy by opening the gifts."

He hesitates for a moment but decides to finally get into the spirit of gift opening. After unwrapping the first one, he pulls the lid off and just stares at the gift before a big grin spreads across his radiant face.

"You made me another book. I can't wait to read what you made me this time. Thank you, sweetheart." He leans in and plants a big smack of a kiss on my cheek.

"It's of 2015, and has the few letters that were sent to me from that year. I couldn't make a full book for each year, so I improvised."

I choke up a little and duck my head to hide my eyes, not wanting to see anything in Layne's face. I can only imagine the pain he must be feeling, too.

He pulls me to his chest for a few moments while I try to compose myself and put on a bright smile. I think he did it to calm himself a bit, too. He whispers in my ear, "*It's perfect. Thank you,*" then kisses the top of my head before pulling slightly away so he can wipe the few tears from my eyes that lingered.

I hear a few sniffles in the background that make me want to bawl all over again, but I manage to pull it together and hand Layne his second gift. Opening it, he pulls out a box that reads, *Open When You Miss Me.* He looks up at me with a question in his eyes. I nod my head for him to open it. Pulling off the lid, he puts his hand into the box and takes out a letter.

"Since I came back from my last visit to you in Hawaii, I decided I would write you every week, like you used to do for me. I've never stopped. Whenever you feel sad, lonely, or like you missed something, I want you to pull a letter out and read it. I wanted you to know that I never gave up, or stopped loving you. I wanted you to know that somewhere in this world, your sun was still trying to shine down on you." I suck my lips into my mouth because honestly, I can't hold back the tears anymore, and neither can Layne, because his are now flowing down his face. Once again, he pulls me to him as we sit on the couch, crying in each other's arms.

"I've missed you so much, Hollie. I've always loved you, no matter what, even when I couldn't remember. My love runs deeper than my mind, sweetheart. I love you."

"I love you, Layne."

"Will you do me a favor?" he asks after a short while. "Will you put these letters into one of your special books so I can always have them? And one day, our kids can see these books and know what a special love we have for each other. Thank you so much for the gifts. They're perfect." He kisses me softly then hugs me tight for a few more moments.

We get our bearings back under control, and once we have it together, we realize that we have an audience, whose eyes are bright and shiny, too. I know they feel it just as deep as we do, so we make no apologies for our heartfelt moment.

Clearing her throat, my mom brightly says, "What do you all think about an early evening of caroling, later?"

I eye her, wondering what she's up to. This isn't something that's usually up her alley.

"Oh, stop that, Hollie. You act like I'm a Grinch with that look you're giving me."

"Nope, Hollie has you beat there. She's definitely a Grinch in the mornings. I'm just glad that everyone's presents were safe this year. I can't help what happens next year, so you should all best be on guard." Layne gets everyone laughing, causing them all to give me their own teasing insults. I elbow him in the ribs for that one.

It appears that the crowd is on board with the singing idea, even Dad, which is hilarious.

"What, old man, no boycotting and hiding in the man cave?" I tease my dad.

"Oh, and miss the reactions of everyone in town when they see how well I can sing? Are you mad, girl?"

"Uh-huh. Right. Well, everyone better bring along their ear plugs. Just saying!" I laugh at my dad, along with everyone else.

We have a great afternoon spending time with our families and friends, enjoying a low-key lunch before it's time to bundle up and venture out into the cold. My mom tells us all that we're going caroling on the blocks between our house and Holly Lane. Then we'll grab some hot cocoa at *Noelle's Café,* before ending up at the Christmas tree at the end of the lane. My mom is such a nut. She thinks everyone should see the amazing Christmas tree in all of its glory.

So, here we are, freezing our faces off, caroling with the most out of sync people in Holly Grove to our neighbors as we walk the blocks to the main road. I'm surprised that the cats haven't started making noises at us, and the dogs didn't chase us away, howling. Maybe we aren't that bad, but I know we aren't that good.

I look at Layne, and we smile at each other before I shake my head and he rolls his eyes, then winks at me, giving me a nudge with this elbow. He's having a good time being with everyone on Christmas. I'm glad his family came up here; he really needed them, too. I can see the old Layne shining through the more he relaxes, and that's honestly thanks to everyone we're surrounded by tonight.

As we sang from door to door, we started gathering a collection of our neighbors. They follow us out by the dozens as we make our way to Holly Lane. Eventually, we get to *Noelle's Café* for hot chocolate, before my mom insists that practically the whole town should come with us to see the lights. I think mom might be losing it a little this year. I may need to have a talk with Dad, or tell her to lay off the nasty eggnog.

After a lot of fun chitchat and a nice, hot drink to warm our bones, we slowly make our way to the tree in time for the event coordinator for Holly Grove to light it up for the night. It truly is a spectacular sight to see, and Mom is right—everyone should see this event at least once, when they come to visit our town during the Christmas season.

We're all standing around, enjoying the lights, when I hear the event coordinator make an announcement over the microphone.

"We would like to get everyone to quiet down for a moment, please." She tells the crowd. "We have an important moment that someone would like to share with the rest of us. So, without further ado, would Layne McKay come forward, please?"

"What's going on?" I ask Layne. "How in the world does she know your name? You don't even live here yet." I laugh nervously at him. He gives me a wink and cuts a path through the middle of the crowd to the front where the tree is.

"Ladies and gentlemen, would you please help me this evening? I need Hollie Reed, front and center." The crowd cheers, and I don't know what he's playing at, but that sounded like an Army command to me.

"Last time I looked, I wasn't dressed for the Army." I yell to him, and the crowd laughs.

"Woman, when your man calls, you come running," he jokes.

I look all around me then ask, "Oh, did you mean *me?* Sorry, I don't believe I answer to those kinds of demands."

"Hollie, sweetheart, would you please stop goofing off and get your gorgeous *tush* up here? Is that better? I remember how much you loved that word. Tush, or was it tushy? I can't remember. Maybe you'd better get up here and set me straight."

"Oh my gosh. Stop talking!" I embarrassingly laugh as I make my way, now double time, to the Christmas tree, where Layne is standing.

"Oh folks, now she listens. Gentlemen, take note. That's how you get it done." He winks into the crowd, causing the men to laugh and some whistles fly through the air.

I smack him in the chest once I make it up to him, causing him to laugh even more than he already was.

"Someone's enjoying himself up here." I try to whisper, but not doing a very good job at it. "I hope you don't plan on singing me a love song. You heard how bad we were at caroling." I joke, trying to get the spotlight off of us and make Layne put the microphone down.

"Now why would I embarrass myself and you by singing?" He gives me one of his signature grins.

"Like this isn't embarrassing enough?" I give him a look like he's got to be kidding.

"Hollie," he takes my hand in his, as he continues to use the microphone to speak.

He sets all the joking to the side now and puts on his serious face.

"Layne?" I search his face. I don't know if he's having a memory lapse, or if something else is wrong. I'm about to ask him, but he starts to speak first.

"As fate would have it, we've been brought together now to make sure that we would spend this Christmas together. It's beyond a miracle, really. Do you believe in miracles or fate?"

Shaking my head yes, "I do now, thanks to you."

"Do you remember when we met in Hawaii? I asked you for a couple of things the first day we met?"

"Yes, I remember." *Where is he going with this?*

"Hollie, I know I've just come back into your life, but remember, you said we never do anything at a slow pace. It's all or nothing for us. And right now, I'm banking on the fact that it's at the *all* stage again."

My eyes widen. I'm pretty sure I know what's coming next, and I can't believe this is happening. Like, right now, in front of the whole town. *What the—?*

"What?" I echo my thoughts.

"First, I have a few presents for you, which I want you to open right now."

Miller walks up to us now, with Ava, Jason, and Jen in tow. Ava has a gift box in her hands, as does Jason, and Jen is carrying something really big, but wrapped with a beautiful red bow.

"Where did you all get these gifts?" I eye them all suspiciously.

"It doesn't matter, just open them." Ava says before handing me the gift.

I tear it open to find a big letter 'H' that's decorated like a map.

Then Jason hands me the next one and it's the letter 'L,' also decorated in a map print.

"The 'H' is a map of Oregon. The 'L' is a map of Hawaii. It represents us and where we were living when we first met." Layne clears up my confusion.

"Now, open the last gift."

Upon opening it, I see a frame of three maps, all shaped like hearts in their own formatted areas of the frame.

The first map, I can tell, is of Hawaii. Under it says, *Where we first met and fell in love.* The second map is of Oregon, and under it, the words read, *Where we met again and fell in love for the second time.* The third heart is a world map, and I'm not sure what Layne is trying to tell me where this one is concerned. Under this map it says, *No limits.* I look over to him for some guidance, but instead of standing where he was, he's now down on one knee in the snow, smiling up at me. I look around at the crowd, who are all eating this up, and back to my friends, who are smiling at me and shining their own sunny faces on me.

I look back to Layne as he takes my hand and draws me to stand right in front of him, as close as possible. Even through his smile, he's communicating all of his love for me from his eyes and the expression on his face. I can feel it as I watch him.

"Hollie Reed, I have loved you since the moment I saw you. You were my girl then, and you're my girl now as I fall in love with you all over again. My day doesn't truly start until I see your face, and it shines so brightly on my world. Do you remember when I asked you to be my fake wife in Hawaii?"

I nod my head *yes.*

"This time, sunshine, I'm asking you to be my *real* wife. So, what do you say, Hollie? Will you be Mrs. Layne McKay, for the rest of our lives?"

I close my eyes briefly and take it all in. *This moment. Our family, friends, and the town. The presents. The words he's just said.* Then I open my eyes again as tears freely flow, and smile at my man, because I know that this is the one and only guy I will ever love.

But first, I have to know where that third map leads us to.

"Where does that third map lead to, soldier? I thought you gave up that life?"

"Well, sweetheart, do you remember once upon a time, when I told you that the sky is the limit?" He asks, as he slides both of the rings off of my ring finger on my left hand, before replacing the promise ring again.

"Yes." I reply as I watch him place my not so fake wedding band on the ring finger of my right hand.

"This time, I'm telling you that there is no limit on where we'll go next. You pick a spot, and that's where we will live, even if we end up right back here, in Holly Grove. So, what do you say, Hollie? You sure do know how to make a guy, who has Swiss cheese for a memory, sweat bullets out here. And I thought the Army was tough." The crowd laughs in the background.

"Come on, Bruiser. What's it going to be?" Miller shouts from the side.

"He always has something to say, doesn't he?" I chuckle before turning my full attention back to Layne.

And just because I can, and I know he loves it when I say this, I answer him with a, "Sir. Yes, sir." As I give him the biggest, watery grin a girl can give her soldier who has finally returned home.

He throws his head back and laughs, just as I had intended for him to do.

"*Woman.*" He says, shaking his head with his smug grin, causing me to laugh now, too.

Then he takes my left hand and slides a beautiful ring into place that matches the promise ring he placed on this very finger a few years back.

And because I can't contain myself anymore, I tackle him, causing him to fall over, with me landing halfway on top of him as I kiss the heck out of him. He eventually rolls us over and then gets up before he pulls me to my feet, where he kisses me again and tightly hugs me.

I look into his eyes and see how glossy they are, and I give him another big smile. I'm so happy and excited, and I can't contain my joy, nor do I want to.

We hear the crowd going crazy with hoots and hollers and some whistles, plus a lot of laughter. I forgot about them for a split, crazy second, and bury my face in Layne's chest, feeling like a big idiot.

"Don't worry, sunshine, I'm sure I can get a retraction for the picture and story that will headline tomorrow's paper." Layne laughs in my ear, causing me to blush a deep shade of red and hide myself further into his chest. *I can't believe I did that. How embarrassing.*

But then again, I wouldn't have it any other way. I'm glad our friends and family were here to experience such an important event in our lives. It's one that no one will ever forget, or let me live down.

"When's the wedding?" someone shouts out from the crowd.

"December 24, 2017, and you're all invited." Layne decides for us, as he shouts it back to the crowd.

I really give him a crazy look, and he just winks at me.

"Don't worry, you'll love it, and you'll thank me for it later."

"I'm not so sure about that. I think we need to talk about this."

"Do you really want to make the guy who has a disabled memory have to remember too many important dates? When he just has to deal with one day that holds two special and important meanings to him?"

"You're really going to milk this whole 'I have a holey memory' thing, aren't you?"

"Is it working?" he laughs.

"Fine, you can have it your way. Just don't be too frugal when it comes to each occasion. They both 1get their own, special moment." It's my turn to give him a smug smile now.

"Oh, don't worry. I have many plans for that day for the rest of your life." He wags his eyebrows at me. "Besides, that goes for you, too. See, perfect solution."

"Convince me first, and then I'll let you know."

Before he can flirt back or make any other suggestions, our audience converges on us, wrapping us up in one giant group hug and taking their turns welcoming us to their respective families.

The long journey home was bittersweet, but fate has made sure to realign the lives of two lovers, so the soldier could be reunited with his one true love.

Christmas miracles really do come true.

230

Epilogue

Wedding Day

December 24, 2017

Layne

IT'S EXACTLY A year later, from the day I showed up on Holly Lane to get my girl back. Which means, we will share Hollie's birthday from now on with our wedding anniversary, and the day before Christmas.

I still wonder why I talked her into doing such a crazy thing, but I'll never regret it for as long as I live.

I'm standing here at the altar, inside of a local church in Holly Grove, waiting for the wedding to start. I'm looking forward to seeing Hollie in her dress, walking down the aisle to meet me.

Miller's my best man, as no one else would do, along with my brother, Levi. Ava and Jenifer are both Hollie's maids of honor. I'm sure we're breaking some cardinal wedding rule here, but I couldn't care less. *Really, there was no way out of that one.* When the subject came up, I told both of the girls that they would share the title, so they

231

wouldn't stress my girl out. She had enough on her plate, and she didn't need to deal with the drama over something as trivial as that decision.

Everyone are in their places now, ready for the ceremony to begin, and I'm standing here in my monkey suit, ready to get the show on the road. I only care about one thing, after seeing Hollie that is, and that's to get the heck out of here as soon as is humanly possible. I can't wait to have Hollie all to myself, with no distractions or interruptions. I didn't even tell our families which hotel by the airport we would be heading to later.

I don't really think they would bug us, but stranger things have happened, and I'm taking all necessary precautions. This day has been in the making for far too long, and no one's going to sabotage us on my watch.

Just as I try to loosen the collar around my neck for the fifth time, I hear the wedding march start to play. My eyes dart to the doors of the chapel, willing Hollie to walk through them at any minute now.

I don't see her yet, so I let my eyes scan the crowd, noticing that practically the whole town has shown up to support Hollie. *Or maybe it's just to gossip about her dress and how the decorations look and how the cake will taste.* In reality, I know it's because they really do care for their hometown girl, even if they are a nosy bunch. I'm still not quite used to that yet.

I continue to scan the crowd when I look over to my family sitting on the front pew to my left. My mom smiles up at me, and I see she looks teary already. My dad slips his arm around her shoulders and gives her a light squeeze, causing her to gift him with one of her warm smiles.

My parents deserve happiness after what happened when I had my brain injury, even though I'll always have issues about what they kept from me. Otherwise, I'm healthy, happy, and I'm surrounded by love, which is evident by the turnout of people in this room. Living on Holly Lane, while Hollie finished school, gave me the perfect opportunity to really get to know the town and why she loved it so much. It also gave me a chance to bond with her dad out in his man cave. *Holly just loved that, I know.* The thought makes me want to laugh, but I can't do that now, standing up here for the whole world to see.

Finally, the organist starts to pick up speed as the doors begin to open and the presiding officiator of the church asks everyone to stand.

Miller walks through the door first with Ava on his arm, causing me to choke up a little. I still can't believe this day is happening, and I get to share it with my best man, Miller. Ava and her large, but beautiful, belly come waddling down the aisle, and I'm overwhelmed with emotion for all that they've been through just to achieve the unthinkable, the gift of life. They had a hard road to get here, but finally made it.

Next to walk down the aisle are Levi and Jenifer, followed by Jason and my sister.

Once everyone is in their places, the doors open one final time. I'm waiting with bated breath to see the visage of the one who has captivated me from the very moment I laid eyes on her.

She walks through the doors of the church, on her father's arm, and all I can see is this stunning princess, floating down the aisle on a white cloud of happiness. She's my living dream, and she's making her way towards me with a small smile on her face while I stand here, soaking her all in.

I can't stand the suspense any longer and decide that I'm going to get my girl, who's taking her sweet time getting down this long aisle, causing the chapel full of people to laugh at my audacity to capture my bride.

She shakes her head at me, but I can tell she's trying to hold in her laughter. *Good.* I wanted to give her something to calm her nerves, and probably mine, too.

"Did you plan to marry her or give her away to your best man?" the officiator jokes.

"I plan to give her away to me *and* marry her, does that work?" I joke back. "Plus, I don't think the best man's very pregnant wife would appreciate that." I wink at Ava. She rubs her belly and gives me the sweetest smile in return.

"I'm sure that we can find someone to marry this beautiful bride, any takers?" he looks out into the audience. "None? Well, that's a relief. I guess she's all yours, young man. Now, take each other by the right hand," the officiator instructs, beginning the ceremony. I pray he makes the ceremony go quickly so we can get to the reception, and then hightail it out of here.

"*Someone's antsy,*" Hollie whispers for my ears alone.

"I'm just glad someone didn't trip down the aisle in those monstrous shoes," I wink at her.

"*I'm not that clumsy.*" She continues to whisper back.

"Okay, Bruiser. It's your day, and if you want to believe that, I'll let you be right for a day. That's my wedding gift to you." I chuckle as she rolls her eyes.

"*Someone's sleeping on the sofa tonight.*"

"We'll see." I say as I turn my attention back to the officiator, trying to mentally will him to finish up already. He turns to me, letting me know that it's time to say my vows.

I turn back to Hollie, taking both of her hands in mine, as I take a moment to really look at her. I try to project all of my feelings from my eyes into those hazy blues that I love so much.

"Bruiser," I begin. The audience laughs, as they know this is my nickname for Hollie every time she injures me or herself, or is dangerously close to causing some kind of general bodily harm.

"From the moment you literally crashed into my life, I knew it was fated that we would one day end up here. Though," I start to choke up and her eyes begin to water, "there was a time when we didn't know what would become of us. But I'm glad that I finally found my way back to you, my sunshine. You are my strength, my support, and my rock. Hollie, you fill in all of the missing pieces, and I couldn't love you more than I already do. I promise to be your firm foundation, as you are mine, and to love, protect, and cherish you for all of my days. There are no limits when it comes to you, sweetheart."

I take a moment to gaze at my new bride to be as she composes herself. She's beyond any other beauty, and I'm lucky to call her my very own. I watch as her chest rises then falls, as she steadies her nerves before she makes her vows to me.

"Soldier," she winks at me, and calls me by the name I love to hear her say. "You were definitely hard to shake, though I didn't try that hard. As fate would have it, there was no shaking you off. I will love and cherish you for all of my days. I promise not to hold it against you when your memory fails when it comes to dishes, trash, or any other things in life. I also promise to fill the Kisses Jar every day." As she says this, she takes a hidden chocolate kiss out of her bouquet and places it in my hand.

"And I promise to fulfill those kisses at the end of every day, and of course, eat the chocolate kisses, too." I grin at Hollie, before I pop the unwrapped kiss into my mouth. Leaning in, I kiss her cheek, just about giving the whole church a heart attack. That just makes me chuckle.

Grinning at me, Hollie continues. "I promise to always be the sun that shines brightly in your life."

"I promise to catch every last ray," I semi-whisper.

"And finally, I promise to never go to bed angry at you, just as I promise to wake you up each morning with a kiss before you leave. I also promise to never take for granted our second chance at love, and the life we will make together." I watch her as she swallows the lump in her throat. "I'm grateful for each new memory we've been able to make together, and I will always care for you, watch out for you, and protect you in the best ways that I know how. I love you with all that I am, Layne. Every last piece of me." Her eyes shimmer with her unshed tears.

Placing her hands in mine again, I stare deeply into her eyes and add my last promises to her. "Hollie, I too promise to never go to bed angry at you. I promise to cherish every new memory we create, and I promise to care for you in sickness and in health. And lastly, for the sake of the time, as I'm sure the officiator would like us to hurry this along," I tease her, trying to help her tears stay at bay, "I promise to let you kiss me every morning, though we both know I'll be the one kissing you awake first. And Hollie, I love you, with every piece of me."

I pour as much of my love as I can into my facial expression and my eyes, so she knows that I'm in this with her one hundred and fifty percent.

The rest of the ceremony flies by, and I don't remember a thing about it, except for the beautiful woman standing beside me, and of course the moment when the officiator instructed me to kiss the bride.

And boy, do I kiss her. I kiss her for all she's worth. Eventually, the officiator had to break it up, but when I pulled away, Hollie was smiling from ear to ear in her dazed state.

Last year, the photo of our post-engagement kiss and subsequent tackle was featured inside the newspaper, but maybe this year our wedding kiss will get us on the cover. *Hey, you can't blame a man for trying to cause a stir two years in a row, can you?* I'm sure on our first anniversary, I'll think of a new and crazy way to land us on the cover of the *Holly Grove Times.*

The kiss had to be the second part of the night that I loved the most, only bested by calling Hollie my wife for real and gifting her with her new last name. That would always take the figurative cake.

We had a great reception, though Hollie will probably tell you something gushing, like how amazingly beautiful it all turned out. I barely survived the dinner, cake, dancing, and toasts. By the time we finally got out of there, I was beyond ready to leave. My impatience to have Hollie to myself only served as fodder for our family and friends to fling back at me. They were relentless with their taunting and laughter at my eagerness.

And poor Hollie, she was beyond embarrassed, which actually served to fuel my purpose in leaving as fast as possible. So in the end, I can't be irritated as they all played into my plans, without even knowing it.

Of course, I'll never let Hollie in on that tidbit. Though, I'm sure she knows. She always knows. *How do women do that?*

Luckily, we only had a short drive ahead of us to get to the hotel, which was right across from the airport. Hollie has no clue where we're going for our honeymoon, but she knows that we're getting on a plane in the morning, and I can't wait for her to find out. However, I'm cool under pressure, so she won't be getting any details from me until right before we leave. I have it all planned out, down to the last possible minute.

We pull into the parking lot, and as luck would have it, find a spot right in front of the hotel's entrance.

I hop out of the truck, which by the way, is done up to the hilt in all kinds of decorations, thanks to our family and friends. I remind myself, as I go to get Hollie's door, that there's a little bit of payback coming for them in the near future. I foresee Hollie getting in on this plan, as well.

I open her door and lift her out of the truck, so she doesn't tear her dress. I set her down on her feet before unloading our luggage from the bed of the truck.

I lug it all up to the front desk so we can check in for our one-night stay.

A bellhop comes over immediately and loads all of our things onto a cart. *Thank heavens, now I'm free to hold my new wife's hand.*

I smile to myself.

"What's that smile for, soldier?" Hollie wants to know.

"I'm thinking about holding my wife's hand as we walk to our room. It's exciting stuff. Don't you agree?"

"You're so cheesy sometimes, but I still love you. And yes, it *is* exciting stuff," she hip checks me as we connect.

"I'm glad your shoes didn't throw you to the ground with that hip check, sweetheart. We don't have time for a doctor's appointment in our foreseeable future."

"Where are we going, by the way?"

"Nice try. No matter what forms of torture you try on me, or how much you ask me, I'll never give up the intel." I lean over and kiss her soundly on the lips, trying to shut her up. *And hey, who wouldn't want to kiss his new wife as much as he could?*

"Fine," she huffs with a little pout. "I'll give in *this* time, but in the future, I'll find ways to get what I want out of you. Know that."

"You can try, and I'll enjoy every moment of it." I wink at her, then turn back to the front desk clerk and check us in.

He gives us room number eighteen and tells us congratulations, and to have a good night. I don't really think that was necessary—it *is* our wedding night. *How could it possibly be bad?*

I reach down, taking Hollie's hand in mine, and draw it to my mouth for a lingering kiss. She rests her other hand on the crook of my elbow as we follow the bellhop to our room.

I unlock the door and hold it open so he can unload our luggage, while I make Hollie wait in the hall. Once the bellman is done, I tip him and send him on his way. *Now it's finally Hollie and Layne time.*

"Well, Mrs. McKay, what do you say to a little old fashioned, husbandly charm?"

"Why, what do you have in mind?" she says curiously, while eying me suspiciously.

"Nothing mischievous, my dear." I say before I sweep her off of her feet and into my arms so I can carry her over the threshold of our hotel room.

I let the door slam firmly shut before making sure to lock the top latch and deadbolt. Then I carry my bride over to the bed and place her down in the center.

I slowly take off her shoes before I ditch mine and loosen my tie.

I lean over the bed as far as I can, as I scan my wife in her princess gown of a wedding dress, then slowly I lower my head, as I hold her eyes steady with mine, right before I kiss her. She grabs ahold of my shirt and pulls me into her until we're both lying on the bed.

But that's as far as I'll share, as a gentleman never kisses and tells.

Honeymoon

Rolling over onto my side, I watch my beautiful wife's face, as she sleeps peacefully. Her fiery, long hair fans out around her on the pillow, as her delectable lips are inviting my thoughts to pluck a kiss from her. Her fair skin is soft to the touch as I run the back of my fingers over her rosy cheeks, causing her to stir, but not strongly enough to wake her, not just yet.

I want to look at her for a few more minutes and savor this moment.

Today is the first day of the rest of our lives together, and I can't believe I thought this moment would never happen. There was a time, years ago, when there was a very real possibility that she was lost to me forever.

During those dark moments, I would dream that I could wake up to find this beautiful ray of sunshine laying next to me. Her presence in my soul was truly what got me through those rough months, before I couldn't remember her at all. She brightened my days then as she only continues to brighten them now.

With the radiant smile that always reaches her eyes and lights up every space in my mind, I can't wait much longer until I see her face when I tell her where we're headed for our honeymoon.

Leaning over her, I place a kiss on her forehead, then her nose, and finally on her soft, plump lips.

She starts to wake from her deep slumber, and I'm fascinated by her beauty as I watch her slowly open her eyes. She blinks a few times, then graces me with her infectious smile, causing me to smile right back at her.

"Good morning, sunshine." I lean in one more time and kiss her nose.

"*Hi,*" she says, in a deep, soft whisper. *I have to say, I love her morning voice.*

"What time is it?" she asks, as she gazes up at me.

"It's a little after eight." I smile at her as I await her ribbing about me always waking up way too early. She appears to be a night owl, while I prefer to not waste the day away by sleeping. I guess waking up early will always be ingrained in me from my military days.

"I'm not sure how long this marriage is going to last if you continue on this path of waking me up so early," she says, as she pinches me on my chest, then tries to push me away.

"I don't think so, Bruiser." I tell her as I gather her up into my arms before rolling onto my back, pulling her down to my chest.

"I'm already thinking we need separate rooms, and I definitely need a Layne-proof lock on my door," she teases me.

I'm pretty confident when I tell her, "You'll get used to it. Trust me."

"I'll be the judge of that, when the time comes." She nuzzles her head against my chest, getting more comfortable. "So, what's on the agenda today, soldier?"

That's one thing that hasn't gotten old, or ever changed between us. I may not be in the military anymore, but she still calls me soldier. It's the term of endearment that she started using when we first met in Hawaii all of those years ago. It's also a habit that she will never break, and one I'll never let her stop.

A soldier will always be who I am, whether I'm still enlisted or not.

"Today, I plan to reveal to you our honeymoon destination."

She pops her head up to look at me. I watch her lips as a slow smile forms there. Looking back up into her eyes, they appear shiny, and her face is full of curiosity mixed with excitement.

"When do I get my surprise?" she waggles her brows, then bounces a little on the bed, like a kid with no patience.

"In a few hours, to be precise."

Pushing out her lower lip out, she pouts a little, but I know she won't push me further. I'm not a pushover when it comes to this part of our relationship, and she knows she won't get any more information from me until it's time.

Time to change the subject, with my favorite tactical maneuver.

"I think you've forgotten a very important wifely duty," I grin at her.

"Oh? What would that be? Are you already demanding breakfast in bed?"

"Well, now that you mention it, I wouldn't turn down the offer." She smacks me on the chest. "Of course, I wouldn't expect it during the week. Only the weekends," I laugh.

"You'll be lucky if I don't burn boiling water."

Good thing I know she's playing around, because this little woman can definitely cook, as well as bake up a storm.

"Nice try, sweetheart. Pick a new tactic." I smile at her.

"What did your new wife neglect this morning?" she eyes me.

"I think it's best if I show you, rather than tell you." I say as I go in for a kiss.

She falls back onto the bed, wrapping her arms around my neck, pulling me to her. I deepen the kiss for a few more minutes before pulling back to look at her.

"That's what you forgot, wife. Your husband needs a good morning kiss to really kick-start his day."

"Well, if that's all your list of demands includes, I can handle that, any day."

"I'm sure I can find other items to add to that list." I say, as I nuzzle her neck.

"*Mm-hmm.* I'm sure you can." She says before kissing me some more.

"I see you're finally learning your place in this marriage." I tell her as she tries to knee me, but I swiftly block her and render her legs useless as I tangle mine around them.

"I don't think I will ever win against you in any kind of physical matchup," she huffs.

"Did you only *just* learn that?" I start laughing. "Holls, when will you get it in your head? You can't take down the master, baby."

"One day, you'll see. Maybe when we have kids, I'll have some boys and they'll teach me, since their father clearly won't do it."

"Then we'd better hope for daughters," I laugh some more.

"Oh, so you want to deal with all of their girl drama and boy troubles? I'll be sure to make them daddy's favorites." She laughs in my face.

"I know what boys are like. I can handle anyone who thinks he's brave enough to take my daughters out. You might be forgetting that I have a few rifles in my closet." She raises his brows at me.

"Why do you always have to win the battle, soldier? Don't you want your pretty, hot wife to have a moment of joy, just once?"

"Nope. It brings me joy to see you getting all pouty. It makes me want to kiss that pout right off of your pretty face." I lean in and kiss her soundly on her lips.

"What's our ETA for getting to the airport?" she asks as she pulls slightly back.

"We have an hour. What do you say we make the best of it the short time we have this morning?"

Grinning coyly, "I like the sounds of that," she flirts.

"Hurry up, sunshine! We can't be late." I holler through the door.

"I need my suitcase." She yells back.

"You have everything you need in your carry-on, I promise. Just trust me. Put on what's in that bag, and you'll thank me later."

Opening the door, she peeks her head out.

"Why can't I get into my suitcase? And by the way, who packed it? Mom, or Jen and Ava?"

"The girls did, and seriously, trust me. Everything you need is in there. And by everything, I mean *everything*. I don't even want to go into details. If I do, we will really be off schedule. Now, get your sexy self back in the bathroom and finish getting ready."

"Pushy!" she teases.

"It's a good thing one of us is the planner and scheduler in this relationship." She must recognize that one of us has to be, or we would never make it anywhere on time. I think she runs on her own mental timeframe, and that's nowhere close to being on schedule.

"How did you ever manage to keep your job at your folks' business?"

"How do you think I became this way?" she cracks up.

"Well, how about you get a move on so we don't miss our flight," I urge her.

I hear her giggle as she shuts the door behind her.

Since I'm ready, I gather up all of our belongings and check to reconfirm all of our reservations one more time as I wait on Hollie to finish up.

About 40 minutes later, she's ready to leave, and we go down to the lobby to check out and pay our bill. Then we order a shuttle to pick us up and drop us off at the airport. Miller and Ava will swing by the hotel later to pick up the truck. Okay, so I had to trust someone to know where we were so they could pick up our vehicle.

The shuttle parks in front of the curbside check-in, and the driver helps us with our luggage.

"Hey, sweetheart," I get Hollie's attention, "why don't you go inside and warm up while I check our luggage in real quick?"

"Okay, thanks." She says as she leans in on her tip-toes and places a kiss on my cheek, then heads for the airport's entrance. She still hasn't a clue as to where we're going, and I don't want her to know just yet. *If I can help it.*

I get our bags checked, then set off to find my wife.

I find her sitting just inside the doors, off to the right on a bench, waiting by the window. I walk over to her and reach down to take her hand, pulling her to her feet.

"Okay, sweetheart, are you ready to go through security?"

"Yep." She says, as she lightly bounces on her feet.

"Don't worry, Holls, we're getting closer to your surprise." I raise her hand to my lips, placing a kiss there before lacing my fingers with hers as I move us along towards the short line of people waiting to get to their boarding gates.

"A little anxious, are we?" I can't help but tease her.

"A little. I wish you would tell me where we were going already. But, I know that won't happen. So, I'm just being good and biding my time."

"Well, I will concede that you are being semi-patient. This may well be a record for you." I laugh as she scrunches her nose at me. "You're cute, and you know it. But you'll just have to wait until we get to the gate to find out."

Finally, we make our way to the front of the security line, go through the tedious process of being scanned, and then get resituated with our belongings.

It takes us another ten minutes to walk to the area where we will board in another 50 minutes.

Right as we get to our designated spot, I quickly pull her closer to me, so I can spin us around. I don't want her to see the sign behind the counter. It's a dead giveaway.

"What's going on?" she frowns up at me.

Reaching up, I trace her frown line with a finger, urging her to relax. I lean forward, placing a kiss to her forehead before slightly pulling away. We're still really close, so I gently rest my forehead against hers.

"Are you ready for the big reveal?" I ask, as I stare into her eyes.

She simply nods her head in reply.

"Good. But first, I have something for you."

Unfortunately, I have to pull my head away from her for a moment to do this next part.

I reach into my lightweight jacket's pocket and pull out a bright yellow flower. I had the flower shop in the hotel deliver it to the room while she was getting ready.

She looks at the flower and then back to me, and I can see a bit of confusion cloud her pretty face.

I take the flower and place it in her hair, just over her right ear, before wrapping my arms around her back and gently resting my head against hers again.

"Hollie, I love you." I say, as I stroke her back. "You're the sunshine that brightens up my life."

"I love you too, Layne." she leans in and places a soft kiss on my lips.

Carrying on with the rest of my thoughts, so I can see her face when she finds out where we're going, I tell her, "I could only think of one place that would be perfect for our honeymoon."

I watch as her eyes light up. I think she is starting to clue in.

"Back to Hawaii," I pause, waiting for what I've just told her to fully register.

She slowly starts to smile and her eyes begin to water. She looks so happy in this moment, so I decide to finish my little speech.

"Where it all began, and where this hot mess of a girl walked right into me and changed my life forever."

Tears of happiness slide down her face as she gazes up at me with so much emotion, and a face full of love.

"Thank you. You're right. It's perfect. *You're* perfect. Thank you for coming back to me."

She leans in and kisses me, and this time, I hold on to her a little tighter, kissing her for a very long time. I don't even care that we're in the middle of the airport, stuck like glue. I'm going to savor this moment, and every other moment I can, while we can.

I don't plan to ever let her slip out of my reach again.

The End

Thank You

Lindsay—Thanks for all the late night chats, emails, suggestions, photo designs, PA work, and making me laugh and over all, your moral support, your friendship and especially for your time.

S.R. Grey- for your support as an author, friend, and for all of your help with the right tools I needed to get this book off the ground.

Amy- for beta reading, letting me bounce ideas and cover/teaser designs off of you, and your awesome feedback and patience with me. Most of all, thanks for your friendship, time, encouragement, and support.

Bethany, Jennifer, Anna- for putting up with my text messages and giving your opinions on the cover/teaser ideas, and any other things I threw your way. Thanks for your friendships, feedback, and moral support.

To my kids and husband for dealing with me as I went through a new process in life and tried my hand at something new. Anything is possible, all you have to do is believe and make it happen.

My mom and sister-in-law—for your support, positive words, checking on me and encouragement. I love you both.

My brother, you know who you are. Thank you for your help in research information and your personal feelings as well regarding the info you provided. I love you.

Hope—one of my dear childhood friends for taking the time to help me with research information. By the way, I miss your face.

A big thank you to all who had a hand in helping me put the finishing touches on this story so it would be ready for publishing.

Thank you to those who don't know, and will probably never know, that you were the inspiration for this story.

A big thank you to all of you I've mentioned as you were there from the beginning, you helped me push through this project, dealt with my texts, and emails about anything and everything to do with this book, and over all were my biggest group of moral support. Thanks for holding my hand as I achieved something new.

About the Author

J.B. Morgan resides in Oregon where she's a wife and a stay-at-home-mother of two. When she's not writing she can be found carting her kids everywhere, volunteering at their school, busy with her church, or reading. She loves the NY Yankees, traveling, her family and chocolate.

J.B. likes to write Clean New Adult & Contemporary Romance stories. Her up-coming books are mostly suitable for older teen- YA readers, as well as those in the New Adult/Contempt genre.

She definitely knows how to write a swoon worthy leading male, or so she's been told.

When J.B. was younger, she would make up hero-rescuing stories in her head, revolving

around boys she had crushes on at school.

She's definitely in love with the idea of love.

J.B. Morgan's Website:
http://jbmorgan-author.blogspot.com

www.ingramcontent.com/pod-product-compliance
Lightning Source LLC
Chambersburg PA
CBHW060131130626
46556CB00006B/2308